MY TRUE LOVE LIES

MY TRUE LOVE LIES

LIES

Lenore Glen Offord

FELONY & MAYHEM PRESS • NEW YORK

All the characters and events portrayed in this work are fictitious.

MY TRUE LOVE LIES

A Felony & Mayhem mystery

PRINTING HISTORY
First edition (Duell Sloan and Pearce): 1947
Felony & Mayhem edition: 2017

ISBN: 978-1-63194-096-5

Manufactured in the United States of America

Library of Congress Cataloging-in-Publication Data

Names: Offord, Lenore Glen, 1905-1991 author.
Title: My true love lies / Lenore Glen Offord.
Description: Felony & Mayhem edition. | New York : Felony & Mayhem Press,
2017.
Identifiers: LCCN 2016030236 | ISBN 9781631940965
Subjects: | GSAFD: Mystery fiction.
Classification: LCC PS3529.F42 M9 2017 | DDC 813/.54--dc23
LC record available at https://lccn.loc.gov/2016030236

To Marie

The icon above says you're holding a copy of a book in the Felony & Mayhem "Vintage" category. These books were originally published prior to about 1965, and feature the kind of twisty, ingenious puzzles beloved by fans of Agatha Christie and John Dickson Carr. If you enjoy this book, you may well like other "Vintage" titles from Felony & Mayhem Press.

———◆———

For more about these books, and other Felony & Mayhem titles, or to place an order, please visit our website at:

www.FelonyAndMayhem.com

Other "Vintage" titles from

FEL♀NY&MAYHEM

ANTHONY BERKELEY
The Poisoned Chocolates Case

ELIZABETH DALY
Unexpected Night
Deadly Nightshade
Murders in Volume 2
The House without the Door
Evidence of Things Seen
Nothing Can Rescue Me
Arrow Pointing Nowhere
The Book of the Dead
Any Shape or Form
Somewhere in the House
The Wrong Way Down
Night Walk
The Book of the Lion
And Dangerous to Know
Death and Letters
The Book of the Crime

NGAIO MARSH
A Man Lay Dead
Enter a Murderer
The Nursing Home Murders
Death in Ecstasy
Vintage Murder
Artists in Crime
Death in a White Tie
Overture to Death
Death at the Bar
Surfeit of Lampreys
Death and the Dancing Footman

NGAIO MARSH (continued)
Colour Scheme
Died in the Wool
Final Curtain
Swing Brother, Swing
Night at the Vulcan
Spinsters in Jeopardy
Scales of Justice
Death of a Fool
Singing in the Shrouds
False Scent
Hand in Glove
Dead Water
Killer Dolphin
A Clutch of Constables
When in Rome
Tied Up in Tinsel
Black as He's Painted
Last Ditch
A Grave Mistake
Photo Finish
Light Thickens

LENORE GLEN OFFORD
Skeleton Key
The Glass Mask
The Smiling Tiger

PHILIP YOUNGMAN CARTER
Mr Campion's Farthing
Mr Campion's Falcon

MY TRUE LOVE LIES

CHAPTER ONE

THIS WAS THE TWELFTH OF SEPTEMBER, six-thirty of a mild, overcast evening. On clear days about this time, San Francisco's tall buildings would reflect the level sunlight in a dazzle of windows, but tonight they rose into an atmosphere of veiled softness. A few blocks away the traffic of Market Street sent up a muted clatter and roar. The sidewalks around the Civic Center were alive with people hurrying home.

From where Noel Bruce sat at the wheel of a parked sedan, most of what met the eye was Navy: sailor collars, stone-gray summer uniforms and dress blues concentrated in front of the Twelfth Naval District building. It was the more remarkable, therefore, that at a distance of fifty feet Noel should be able to recognize one particular officer, whom she had met only once before.

She was a paid driver for the Navy. Since noon on this September day she had been transporting naval personnel about the city, returning after each call to the Twelfth Naval

District. At the end of her working day she still looked trim and her uniform was becoming, a fact brought home to her by the side glances of three ensigns standing and talking at the curb.

Noel put on what she hoped was an official look. She was not, however, thinking about the ensigns, but figuring that in about an hour she'd be through. It wouldn't leave her too much time to dress for the party at the Sherwin Art School, but she'd make it. She was going off into vague musings about what to wear when the man appeared in the doorway and stood glancing up and down the line of parked sedans and station wagons.

He came toward her car, with that long free stride and indefinable look of race that had caught her eye among all the other blue uniforms. There was a terrific snapping of salutes as he neared the ensigns on the sidewalk, and the three younger men melted away, for some reason looking abashed and startled. Lieutenant Miles Coree met Noel's eyes and gave her an odd, shy grin that belied his air of complete assurance.

"So it *is* you," he said, and folded his long frame into the seat beside her. "Luck's with me, for once! I asked for your ticket on the off chance you'd be free."

"Why, thank you," said Noel in a tone of sweet reserve. She glanced at the ticket and reached for the ignition.

"Wait a minute," the man said. "Will you let me tell you something? The other night, at the Servicemen's Art Center, I didn't have a chance to say goodbye to you. I've been regretting it ever since."

"And you want to say it now?" Noel inquired helpfully.

Lieutenant Coree made a sound between a groan and laughter. "Nothing of the sort. Do let me tell you, Miss Bruce. I thought I saw someone I knew looking in the doorway, and then turning to leave without coming in. I thought I'd catch my friend in the courtyard; no. Then I really put on steam, and got clear down Grant Avenue before I saw I was chasing the wrong person."

"Annoying."

"You do agree?" said the lieutenant with relief. "Thank heaven for that, first sign of relenting. It seemed I couldn't go back. I was just too damned embarrassed, because I'd walked out on you, and I'm embarrassed now. But I've been trying to catch up with you ever since, and that makes two women I couldn't find. Could we wash out my bad manners and start again?"

She said, "Don't be embarrassed. I didn't mind a bit, I was just surprised."

Lieutenant Coree clicked his tongue and gave her a reproachful look. "And I thought of you languishing there with a broken heart. Well, well, I might have spared my conscience, but it's a blow to a man's vanity." He met her eye and grinned again, so ruefully and disarmingly that she dissolved in friendly laughter.

"And now," said Noel Bruce, "maybe we'd better get started on the Navy's business?"

Listening to his pleasant, easy conversation while she threaded the northbound traffic of Larkin Street, she thought: How queer that two of us should have been mistaken, last Friday night, about the person we saw in the studio doorway; I'd have sworn it was Tannehill, with her hand in a sling, but she told me she hadn't been there that evening. Double hallucination—does that make us soul mates, or something?

She was disproportionately pleased to see Miles Coree again and to learn that he'd been looking for her.

An hour later, while she was waiting for him outside the Army docks at Fort Mason, she took stock of her feelings once more and found that a new element had crept in. It was as if that pin-prick of curiosity and annoyance from last Friday night had disappeared under a counter-irritant. For now, with no tangible reason, she was uneasy. It had nothing to do with Lieutenant Coree, surely? It was only that each time she met him, something remotely puzzling occurred.

There was no reason why they shouldn't have made that brief side trip to the Plaster Works on their way to the docks, and it was natural enough that he should have suggested it after she'd been telling him about Sherwin and her special friends who were sculptors. Nothing had actually happened there to disquiet her, unless you counted that unintelligible muttering from the crazy old watchman beyond the fence.

Noel turned to look behind her, but nothing untoward appeared in the grayly lighted street that flanked the docks. She noted with approval and some relief the presence of a stalwart pair of guards at the entrance. The illusion that someone was following her wasn't her style at all, and she turned back with determination to the official eyes-front position.

Lieutenant Coree, it seemed, was a radar technician. He was inspecting equipment on a ship which was due to sail in the morning. The inspection shouldn't take too long, he had told her, being considerate and anxious about her working over-time. At the moment that aspect seemed unimportant to Noel. She was quite frankly wondering if she would ever see Miles Coree again after this evening. His leave, he had said, would begin on Friday, the day after tomorrow. He was going back to St. Louis to see his parents.

"If I never do see him again," Noel told herself with a sudden chuckle, "I have a fine souvenir of the evening." She slid a small drawing pad from her uniform pocket and flipped over the half-dozen sketches on its first pages.

One of her term assignments at the Sherwin School was the production of forty "character portraits," which meant pencil drawings in a more or less finished form, taken from life. There were several other pads at her apartment, filled with quick notes which she had made while she sat waiting in this very Navy sedan: cheerful young faces under white-topped caps, more weathered and responsible ones under the same caps heavy with gold braid; figures on the sidewalk; her own friends. This pad was scarcely begun.

The Graphic Arts instructor would accept most of these sketches once they were worked up, she thought. Her chief talent was the catching of a quick likeness. There was the one of Chester Verney, Anna Tannehill's recently acquired husband, the heavy good looks of his Roman-emperor face felicitously echoed in the dusty plaster cast which she had sketched behind his head. There were the two or three others she had done at that same party. And here were the two which she had flung down in twenty lines apiece, half an hour ago: the white-overalled legs of a man, sprawling in an irresistibly comic attitude from behind a cement mixer that hid the rest of his body, and a more elaborate one. The latter had started out as an atmosphere sketch in the Doré manner—shafts of light falling from a high window across eerily shrouded forms—and had changed with the introduction of a figure, that of Lieutenant Coree standing on one leg, clasping the other shin in both hands, and looking agonized. Noel Bruce laughed aloud looking at this souvenir. The lieutenant had been swearing under his breath, and you could almost see his lips move.

She gave a little start and closed the pad. Lieutenant Coree himself was standing beside the car. Noel's dark glance turned to him, her artist's eyes once more taking in every detail of his face. It was a long face, good-looking, tanned, hazel-eyed, with two heavy black bars of eyebrow that lent a humorous emphasis to his direct gaze. There was nothing ingenuous about it. Lieutenant Coree had seen all kinds and could handle them, and had enough good humor left over to look like that.

His first remark was unexpected. "What are you doing now," he inquired, glancing at the sketch pad, "'booking a delicious bit composed of a stone, a stump, and one mushroom?'"

Noel looked amazed and then grinned. "You're continually surprising me, Lieutenant Coree. How come you can quote *Little Women*, of all things?"

He gave her a sidelong and confidential look. "My sister and I had measles at the same time. I used to pretend to sneer when Mother read it aloud…However—" He became suddenly businesslike, gesturing toward the dock. "I got myself into a jam, in there. That ship lacks a radar part that has to be installed tonight—and the only one we can get hold of is out at Point Montara, which they tell me is a good way off."

"Not so bad," she said. "About thirty miles, down the Skyline Boulevard. It's a slow ride, but otherwise—"

"Here's the thing. You're working overtime already, aren't you? I'd better call the Twelfth Naval District and ask for another driver who's just come on."

"What is this," said Noel, "a dishonorable discharge? Your ticket said I was to take you wherever you wanted to go."

"Naturally I'd rather have you." He smiled at her. "And it would save time. Look, you must be hungry. Why don't we find a place—No? You mean you'll eat with nobody under the rank of commander?"

"Rear Admiral," Noel corrected him. "But I'd like to get your job done first."

"Nobly spoken," said the lieutenant approvingly. "And then—might we have dinner afterward? The Navy would owe you a bang-up meal by that time."

"I'd like that," she told him. The party she was supposed to be attending had vanished from her mind.

The drive to Point Montara took well over an hour, and long before they had reached the fork in the road which led to it, Noel was conscious that she had made a mistake in declining the chance to eat before she started. At least it must be that which was affecting her disposition, for to her surprise and shame she found herself trying to squabble with her passenger. He'd made some remark about having asked for the introduction to her at the Servicemen's Art Center. Since numerous other men had maneuvered for a meeting with her, she couldn't exactly be blamed for taking this as a personal compliment, but she felt foolishly annoyed when his next words gave it a different meaning: he had wanted to meet someone who knew the art school crowd, who could tell him about the places they frequented both for work and relaxation. Well, why not? She bit her lip in vexation at herself and changed the subject to the scenery, which should have been safe, and five minutes later flared into a regular temper over some opinion he expressed. Miles Coree only looked amused and kind, and that made her crosser than ever. Something was certainly wrong with her, and she preferred to blame it on hunger.

She sat fuming outside the supply warehouse at the Point, and when he returned she had the car's rear door open. "Won't you ride in style this trip?" she invited. "I might snap your head off again if you were in the front seat."

He accepted this also with entire good humor, saying that if she didn't feel like talking he might try to sleep. He stretched his long frame slantwise across the rear seat and looked utterly relaxed. Noel started the car with a jerk.

The night was warm and mild, but an autumn fog muffled the western side of the peninsula. She drove steadily but cautiously, although on such a night the traffic on the Skyline was thin. The headlights of a car some distance behind kept illuminating the fog and then disappearing as her sedan rounded curve after curve. The rhythm was almost hypnotic: a straight stretch, and the fog milkily shining; a curve, and the return of darkness cut only by her own lights.

She became aware that the illumination behind her was steadier, that the car behind must have lessened the distance between them. She supposed it would be passing her, and she pulled to the side of the road.

It was not passing her. It was slowing as it came abreast of her car, edging over, pushing her deliberately toward the ditch. She fought to drop back, but there was no room. Her left hand gripped the wheel, her right automatically groped behind the seat for a wrench. She opened her lips, but the choked sound of warning and appeal was lost in a terrifying roar from the back seat.

Her passenger, bellowing imprecations, had flung open the rear door and was out on the road almost as soon as the car had stopped. He was heading for the other car; but its driver, after one quick look around, tramped on the gas pedal. The tail-light shot ahead, rounded a corner, disappeared.

"Get over!" Miles Coree grated, shoving Noel bodily from behind the wheel and flinging himself in. The engine was still going. It seemed as if he lifted the car out of the ditch by main strength, sending it flying forward in pursuit. "Trying to hold you up, were they?" he said in a grimly conversational tone. "We'll catch up with those gentlemen and point out their error."

The car swung right and left, throwing her against the side. She managed to gasp, "No, please don't try. You don't know the road. It's no use!" They wheeled around another curve and he fought the steering gear, cursing under his breath. "Look," she cried, "the fog's thinner here—it's straight for half a mile and we can't see a tail-light. They got away."

"I'm afraid you're right," said Lieutenant Coree, still grimly. The car slackened speed. "And what's more, I'm afraid this axle's bent."

"When I went into the ditch," she agreed, taking a shuddering breath.

He put on the brake at once, turning toward her. "That scared you, didn't it? I don't wonder. If you feel like crying, don't mind me."

"Thank you, but I don't. Not my style," said Noel, fighting to keep her voice level. She felt the man move close to her and link his arm firmly with hers, clasping her hand. His other hand settled over hers.

For several minutes neither of them spoke. She found her heartbeats settling to normal, her prickling skin smoothing out; and dimly she was aware that in the past quarter-hour she and the man beside her had passed from the beginning stage of friendship into a new sphere in which anything could happen. She turned her head and looked at him, nodding swiftly.

He released her hand and said, "All right now? You made a quick job of it. That's good going."

"The reaction got me for a minute," said Noel competently. "You won't mind if I take the wheel again? Then I'll be really over my scare."

A moment later, starting the car, she began to laugh. "If I was scared, it can't have been anything to the way those men must have felt! They thought I was alone, of course—and then to have you rise from the back seat with that quarter-deck bellow—!"

"Rather like old-style Chinese warfare, wasn't it?" said Coree cheerfully. "Make hideous faces and yell and try to frighten your enemy without firing a shot. Just the same, I'd like to get my hands on those characters."

"I wonder," said Noel, "if those ensigns on the sidewalk—you remember, when you came up with my ticket?—if they could have been talking about you. They were referring to somebody who could 'go off like a block-buster when so inclined.' Does this happen often, may I ask?"

"Certainly. The whole Fleet trembles when Coree merely steps aboard ship. And when it comes to active duty—well, you noticed that the war had stopped? But I don't much like that term 'block-buster.' Obsolete," said Miles Coree with a rueful shake of the head. "Don't you think, Miss Bruce, that—oh, the hell with this formality. Should you mind if I called you Noel?"

"Considering that you saved me from worse than death, or something, how could I mind?" She swung the car into Geary Boulevard.

"Worse than death. I suppose so, yes." Coree looked straight ahead, the street lights illuminating his dark face, which just now wore a puzzled expression. "There was something queer about that attempt at a hold-up. Did you catch a glimpse of the men in the car?"

"I didn't have a chance, what with trying to avoid a smash. Did you?"

"Not what you'd call a good look. There were two of them, one smallish, with his collar well up around his face, and the other—the driver—a bigger man. His collar was turned up, too, but I could see he had a heavy neck—looked as if he hadn't a neck at all, it was so thick…The license plate of the car had been carefully smeared with mud, did you notice?"

"I see what you mean about its being queer," said Noel slowly, "because I had the feeling that they'd followed us all the way out from town and waited at that fork in the road near Montara, and then followed us back, choosing a place and time—as if it were this special car they were after, instead of any lone woman's. I don't know—is that a very secret radar part, Lieutenant Coree?"

"Make it Miles, will you?—The radar part doesn't signify. Those men, if you remember, didn't know I was in the car."

"Well, it's over. I suppose we'll never know." Noel was silent for a long time, until she drew up once more at the Fort Mason docks. Miles Coree also seemed to put the inexplicable adventure behind him; he completed his errand, returned to her, and was openly cheerful about the prospect of drinks and a late dinner. "I suppose you've got to turn in some sort of explanation with your car?" he inquired. "I'll do a signed statement as witness, got to preserve your reputation as a driver. Full speed ahead, sailor!"

San Francisco's curfew laws being what they are, there were only two hours left of the evening, but those two hours were plenty.

Noel knew pretty well what was happening to her, from their sudden mood of gaiety over dinner, from the way it felt to dance with Miles Coree, and the confidences that slipped out to the surprise of each. "I've never told that to anyone else," they kept saying, looking amazed. She kept reminding herself to go easy, that she didn't know anything about this long-faced man with the laughter in his eyes.

And yet, actually, by the end of the evening she did know a good deal about him. She knew that he'd studied at M.I.T.

and meant to go back into communications work after the Navy released him. Its reluctance to do so, he said, was flattering but inconvenient. There was an uncle whom he described vaguely as having something to do with radio, who'd give him a job. He talked about his parents, with an affectionate softening of his face that made her realize, even more than his words, how close was his tie to them. He produced pictures; Noel's eyebrows went up at the unstudied glimpses of background, and the stamp of aristocracy on the faces of his father and mother. "Isn't she lovely?" she breathed over the last photograph. "Like a duchess. Was it taken after you went to sea? She looks so sad—"

"I'm afraid she was," Coree said, "but not over me. Here—I haven't shown you this one. That's my sister…" He bent his head, considering, and added, "rather a tragedy there."

His voice stayed low and unemotional, but came intimately to her ears; the music and the deafening babble in the Cirque Room went far away as she sat close beside him at their small table. He said that there were only the most formal relations between his sister and the elder Corees; she had cut herself off by marrying someone who'd been involved in a rousing scandal. The sister believed he was innocent, and he may have been, but her parents' hearts were nearly broken by the marriage. If he'd been proved innocent—if the situation had meant only a quiet divorce—if he had been socially unsuitable but thoroughly respectable—in any of these circumstances they could have accepted it. As it was, she was lost to them. "My brothers and I see Kitty, of course," he added, "but Mother's feelings won't change."

Noel looked at him, her eyes dark with sympathy. He met the look and held it. "A nice girl, aren't you?" he said softly. His tone was light, but she'd never liked a compliment better.

A little after midnight he dismissed the cab at the mouth of the narrow street in which she lived. They stood in darkness at the foot of the steps that rose to the gray door of her gray lodging-house. He said, "You're fun to take out, Noel. This evening did something for my state of mind."

"Including the Chinese warfare?"

"That added a new flavor, though I shan't expect it on our next date." He put a finger under her chin and gently tilted up her face. "Do you ever?" he asked elliptically.

"Now and then, for an unusually nice man," she said, and laughed, and lifted her mouth to his.

It was the last carefree moment she was to know for a long, long time.

When they finally drew apart they gazed at each other in an almost comic consternation. "Did that really happen?" Miles Coree murmured, and tried it again. Whatever it was, it had really happened. Noel stood there in the half darkness and gazed mutely up at him, shaken and dazzled.

He said in a rather unsteady voice, "This—this calls for some thought. No, my lovely girl, don't move away. Stay here a minute. Damn it, I can't think, I'm dizzy—everything's changed."

She said faintly, "I knew it was coming, but I didn't know it would be like this."

He laid his cheek against her dark hair, rocking her gently to and fro. "Bless you, you darling," he said. "Here, can't we sit down on the steps and talk this over? What a place for discovering you've fallen in love. I should have kept that cab and bribed the driver to go away."

"Miles, I can't stay long. There's tomorrow—"

"Tomorrow! Hell, I can't even see you in the morning, I'm on duty! There are a few things I'd like to get straight. In the first place, are you spoken for, or anything?" She shook her head. "It'd be a bit ironic if I tried to move in on another fellow's territory. You see—I'd better tell you why I'm free as the air myself. My fiancée lived here in town, and it seems that while I was away she married somebody else."

A dozen remembered phrases rushed together and fused in Noel's mind. She turned in his encircling arm and gazed at him. "Miles, you don't by any chance mean Tannehill—Anna Tannehill?"

"Yes."

"But—she couldn't have done that to you."

"Seems she could."

"Not Anna! She's the loveliest—the kindest—Miles, I never knew that she was engaged to you, to anyone."

"No? Well, it's all over now. She is lovely, and kind. I've thought that perhaps it wasn't her fault. She had to wait a long time, though she seemed to think it was all right that I put off applying for discharge when I found my specialty was needed. The—man in the case may have taken advantage of that kindness of hers, knowing well enough that he was poaching. Not a nice trick," said Miles Coree softly.

Noel gave an involuntary gasp, and his grip on her shoulder slackened. She said in a whisper, "Miles, I—I have to—"

Down the narrow street footsteps sounded, wearily approaching the rooming house. She got to her feet swiftly. "That's Miss Ibsen, she lives on my floor. Oh, I must say good night. There will be time later, we have all the time there is, now."

"But not right away, worse luck!" He stood looking down at her, frowning. "Tomorrow there's some unfinished business I've got to do, and Friday morning I've got to take up my reservations or I'll miss seeing my family. I'll be back by the twenty-seventh at the latest, but—"

She said nervously, "We can talk then. We can write letters. I'll be right here, Miles."

The woman of the tired footsteps was nearly upon them. He said, "Good night, dear." Noel turned and almost ran up the steps, waiting at the top for her fellow lodger. She did not look back.

In silence the middle-aged woman and the young one mounted the inner flight of stairs. At the top, Miss Ibsen said testily, "That draft! Somebody's left the door to the back staircase open." She clumped down the hall to shut it, and then unlocked her own door and disappeared.

Noel went to her window and looked cautiously down. Miles Coree was still on the sidewalk below; he tilted his head up toward her lighted window and touched his officer's cap. She drew back and sat down, shivering. That's a nice beginning, she thought; I was too much of a coward to tell him that I was the one who introduced Chester Verney to Tannehill, that I fairly threw them at each other. Well, all right. I'll put it in a letter. Maybe it won't mean anything to him, and maybe it will. Might be I never will see him again, after all.

She felt absently in her pocket for that souvenir of the early evening, the sketch pad topped with the portrait of Chester Verney. It wasn't in her uniform pocket and it hadn't been on the seat of the car when she turned it in at the Twelfth Naval District. Funny…Miles had noticed that drawing, and had asked who was its subject. He didn't know Chester Verney by sight, then.

Well, he would after he looked at that picture. She'd never done better at catching a likeness. Where on earth had that sketch pad gone?

She thought, Just forget it. Forget everything until he comes back, on the twenty-seventh…She took off her coat and blouse and her brows drew together as she inspected the bruise on her shoulder where Miles Coree's hand had gripped it unconsciously. "Not a nice trick."

Forget it until the twenty-seventh.

On the afternoon of the twenty-first of September, Noel saw the screaming headlines.

CHAPTER TWO

THE NEWSPAPERS, OF COURSE, played up the Bohemian angle of the case for all it was worth, and maybe more. Given as fantastic a crime as San Francisco had seen in years, they were not content. They saw fit to imply a background of attic studios lit by guttering candles; characters in velvet jackets and flowing ties; parties straight out of *Trilby* and Rudolph-and-Mimi relationships which outdid opera.

Like many journalistic implications, these were partly true and mostly a long way from accuracy. A few of the persons involved were cheerfully amoral, to be sure, but not one of them would have been caught dead in a flowing tie—witness Papa Gene Fenmer, whose full-dress elegance at the Sherwin Art School soirées fairly dazzled the beholders. It was a far cry from a candlelit attic to Anna Tannehill's apartment on Post Street, though it was called a studio and housed some of her smaller works of sculpture. There was Rita Steffany, of course, and there was Will Rome. Those two lived up to some of the tradition. On the other hand, consider Daisy Watkins (sculpture), who never went any place unless escorted by her cousin Paul Watkins (ceramics); consider Noel Bruce (line drawing), who earned her living and tuition fees and did hours of class work besides, leaving no time at all for orgies.

Also, scarcely any of the action took place either at the School or in the studios. This was a nasty blow for the reporters, who had to compensate by stressing the drama of contrast. You know the sort of thing. Utilitarian background, no more colorful than a factory—artists working so hard and seriously that you could hardly distinguish them from the laborers casting cement fixtures in the next room—and then, in the midst of all this, the grisly discovery, the sudden intrusion of a corpse from high life into the Plaster Works. There was drama, indeed, but what wouldn't they have given for a few fishnet draperies in the old Bohemian style!

There are several Plaster Works in San Francisco, and at more than one of them sculptors have taken over a portion of floor space for work on their larger models and sculptures in stone. This one was near North Beach, not far from the Sherwin School, and so placed between two obscure cross-streets that it occupied nearly a solid chunk in the middle of a block. It was a great warehouse of a place, the exterior weather-beaten and ramshackle, with a gray wooden fence enclosing a small paved courtyard; the interior divided into two unequal portions by a dingy wooden partition six or seven feet high with a second-hand door hung crazily in its single opening. One entered the building by a broad entrance where trucks could drive in, by a smaller door from an alley at the opposite end, or by a door from the courtyard.

In the larger space there were high windows. Their glass was none too clean, and their warped frames let in thin streams of air. The whole place had the chill and drafty feeling of an old barn, and added to it was the dank smell of cement, damp plaster, wet clay. White dust had been ground and grimed into the floor for years, and under the long tables with their marble slabs for casting were corners which held hardened deposits of dirt. Besides these tables, the chief article of furniture was a cement mixer. The decor consisted of an unending frieze, just below the windows, of plaster casts furred with the dust of twenty years.

Behind the wooden partition, in the smaller portion of the Works, were the same high windows—here somewhat cleaner— and the same frieze of casts. Here, however, the foot trod upon heavy clay that smeared thin, dried, and powdered into countless footprints. There were sacks of it propped against the walls and some wooden boxes lined with metal that held still more. Tools, pipe, great folded squares of dingy cloth were placed and stacked in a purposeful confusion. Dominant, catching the eye as a figure or nearly human shape will do in any composition, were the three large statues in progress of work. When these were swathed in their protective cerements of wet cloth, the scene was far from glamorous to uninitiated eyes.

Naturally the sculptors and their friends saw something different: their place of work, comfortless but alive with creation. The hideous long-bodied stove could be coaxed to a cheering heat for thawing numbed fingers and making coffee on cold days, and the fact that its counterpart in the mold-making section was used for cooking up countless batches of malodorous glue had ceased to bother anyone. As for the masses of clay in work, no matter how formless a stage they might be in, the sculptors saw life in them.

On September 21st, at half-past one in the afternoon, Eugene Fenmer paid his regular visit of instruction to his students at the Plaster Works. He left his car outside the wooden fence and marched through the courtyard with a dignity nowise impaired by the voluminous white overall suit he was wearing. His was the complexion of Santa Claus and the expression of G. B. Shaw, with some length and shagginess subtracted from the white beard and mustache. Papa Gene's elegance was as much a part of him as his overwhelming vigor, a combination that made his reputation with young women easy to understand.

"Afternoon, Rome!" he bellowed cheerfully to the man working in the courtyard, and as he went by cast a swift appraising glance at the shape emerging from Rome's block of stone. Will Rome was an independent sculptor, not one of the Sherwin students, and old Fenmer's eyes expressed the respect of one artist for another.

Rome only looked up and nodded in acknowledgment of the greeting, but after Fenmer had disappeared inside the building, he laid down his hammer in order to light a cigarette. He stood smoking it in quick deep drags; once he looked as if idly at the open windows of the sculptor's section. This season was high summer in San Francisco, and Rome wiped sweat from his forehead, with the same gesture pushing back a shock of unkempt dark hair. His full mouth moved slightly as if he were talking to himself; he flung down the cigarette, took a deep breath of the sun-heated air, and once more bent his melancholy eyes upon his work.

Inside the building, Eugene Fenmer had completed his march through the plaster-casting section and his affable words and nods to the workmen, had gone through the door in the wooden partition and had made his ceremonious entry into his students' workroom. His dark gaze traveled swiftly about the space, noting the two uncovered clay models and the third one still swathed in wet rags with an additional covering of oilcloth. Then his white eyebrows flew up and he sniffed mightily.

"God, what a stink!" Papa Gene shouted. "Who's been here, the Art Critics' Association?"

There was appreciative laughter from the three students in the room, echoed by subdued snickers from the plaster casters outside.

"It's that damned glue, Papa Gene," Rita Steffany said in an annoyed drawl, low-pitched. "They've had it on to cook every day this week, and I'll swear they've forgotten it at night and let it boil dry."

"So? It must be a new brand. Haven't you complained?"

Steffany shrugged. "Necessary evil, we figured." She was an arresting young woman, white of skin and shining black of hair, with a sensuous curled mouth lipsticked a deep crimson. Her long black eyes slid sideward at the instructor as she spoke, as if she could not even discuss boiling glue without a suggestion of sex.

Fenmer nodded, dismissing the subject. "Let's get to work," he said, and turned to one of the uncovered clay models.

It represented a young flyer striding forward—presumably toward his airplane—with uplifted face and a dedicated expression. To the lay eye it appeared conventional in conception and somewhat hesitant in execution. How it looked to Fenmer was apparent more in his omissions than in his words.

He remarked kindly enough, "Well, Watkins, you're getting along with it," and went on to point out some technical faults; few enough, one would think, but when he had finished and turned away, Daisy Watkins' face was red and she bit her lip as if to keep back tears. She stood beside her statue with her angular body drooping in relaxation after this weekly ordeal, but her gray eyes were disappointed. Each week it seemed as if she hoped, against all the honest dictates of her training, that genius had magically visited her; each week Papa Gene praised with faint damns, and visibly she acknowledged his justice.

She threw a quick glance at the young man who sat in a corner, well out of the sculptors' way, in a position where he could rest his head against an angle of the wall. This was her cousin, Paul Watkins, a Sherwin student but not one of the sculptors. His presence here in the afternoons had become habitual. He sat watching, saying little or nothing, hardly moving except for his fingers which absently kneaded a heavy ball of clay. He was not looking at Daisy now. He gazed straight before him, his head and neck stiffly held.

Fenmer said nothing for a moment while he scrutinized Rita Steffany's model of a soldier crouching to talk to a small child which leaned against his knee. Steffany braced herself, but wore a look of confidence; when Papa Gene really criticized one took it as an honor, at the same time wishing he did not have to bellow in competition with the cement mixer beyond the partition. He was outdoing himself today. He raved, called on all three members of the Trinity, and thought up some surprising ways to describe her modeling of the baby's cheek and the soldier's thigh. Then he came to a dead stop, took an immaculate handkerchief from his overalls pocket, and wiped his heated brow. Then he beamed suddenly at the students.

"Well," he said, "quick enough work with only two of you to take apart. Not enough to keep the old man busy."

"It's hardly our fault, Papa Gene," Daisy Watkins said in her pleasant voice, "Tannehill walking out on us the way she did. You could have spent a full hour with her!"

"Ah, Tannehill!" Fenmer heaved a mock sigh. "That gorgeous wench! Still honeymooning, I suppose?"

"Nobody's heard any different," Steffany drawled.

Papa Gene turned to the shrouded statue, lifted the oilcloth cover and tested the dampness of the covering rags. "Better wet her down," he said, and began deftly to lift off the cloths. "Our bride ought to be back some day soon, when her hand heals up. If she lets that Verney character she married keep her away from this piece of work, I'll strangle her personally. Him too."

"You think she has a good chance in the memorial competition?" Watkins asked.

"How do I know what those idiots of judges are going to think?" Fenmer roared. "She's done a damn good job, though, and I'd be a fool myself if I didn't recognize it." He went on working, whistling softly, and the two women sat down on boxes and lit cigarettes. Summer air drifted through the high windows, wafting to and fro the disagreeable odor which Steffany had diagnosed as glue. The cement mixer clanked and ground, clanked more slowly, and stopped so that in the comparative silence the sound of hammer and chisel came loud and rapid from the courtyard.

Fenmer's whistled tune trailed off into incoherence; he paused in his task, looking puzzled. "I thought Tannehill had got farther than this?" he said in a tone of unusual mildness.

The torso of the third statue was uncovered. Its clay seemed to be roughly streaked and lumpy; Fenmer began to lift off the cloths which covered the rest of the figure.

The students had been murmuring to each other, paying little attention to the unveiling. They had seen this piece of work from its inception, and had frankly admired and envied it so that it was as familiar to them as their own models. It was called "Woman at the Grave"—sentimental enough, as Anna Tannehill herself admitted, but lifted far above banality by its power and certainty. The figure of the Woman was sprawled prone in the terrible awkwardness of unself-conscious grief, the head lifted slightly to rest on a low mound.

Yet now, as they looked at the model with sudden attention, there was something odd about it: as if the artist, dissatisfied with the surface modeling, had torn down most of her work and begun again.

"But that's not—" Steffany said, startled into vagueness. "That doesn't look like—she hasn't worked on it for about two weeks, but it couldn't have dried in that time?"

"It isn't dry," said Eugene Fenmer. There was electricity in his voice now. "There's been some mischief." He turned an awe-inspiring glare on the three students. "Did anyone—no, I can't believe that one of you would have touched or uncovered another's model?"

"Certainly not!" Steffany got up, her black brows knitted, and moved for a closer look at the clay torso. Daisy Watkins was doing an extremely slow take, sitting still with her mouth slightly open.

No longer working with delicacy, Fenmer took the cloths from the statue's head. "Good God," he said, "what's this supposed to be, collage? There's hair—"

Watkins, finally aroused, stood up and craned. "It's got—*shoes* on!" she said in a loud unnatural voice, and drew in her breath with the effect of a shriek.

For an instant nobody moved; there was no sound in the room, for outside in the courtyard the chipping noises had abruptly ceased. Then Eugene Fenmer stepped back hurriedly, swung toward the partition, and in a voice that seemed to rattle the plaster casts on the wall, shouted "Beef!" It was the traditional cry for help in moving heavy objects.

A husky workman enveloped in grimy white overalls came through the door. "Whatcha want done, Mr. Fenmer?" he said casually. "Can the two of us do it, or d'ya want Mike too?"

Fenmer looked down at his hands, as if surprised to find them shaking. "Yes, yes—get Mike. And bring a lever."

"A lever?" the workman began, when the door opened abruptly and Will Rome walked in, wiping stone-dust from his hot face with a sleeve. "Something up?" his deep voice asked casually; his eyes, sad-shaped like a hound's, moved from one to another of the students. "What's got shoes on, Watkins?"

"Don't know," Fenmer answered for her. "It may be a practical joke, or vandalism, but I—here, Rome, you'll do to help." He moistened dry lips and jerked his head toward the stolid workman, returning with the lever. "I—I want to look under Tannehill's statue."

"Under it?" Rome said uncomprehendingly; but he bent his big frame to assist. Fenmer squatted on his heels and peered under the shell of clay.

"Let it down," he said in a stifled voice, rising hastily. "There's a—a dead body there."

Again, for the space of seconds, nobody moved. Rome stayed where he was, gazing up over his shoulder at Fenmer, his heavy face slack and pale with horror. The workman named Mike, standing idly by, let out his breath as if he had been struck in the stomach.

Then Paul Watkins slid carefully from his stool. "Daisy and Rita," he said crisply, "get out of here!"

His cousin glared wildly around at him, clapped a hand to her mouth and bolted for the courtyard. Rita Steffany followed her, pale and wide-eyed, but alert. In the silence the men could hear her feet outside. She began to run purposefully as soon as the door closed behind her.

Paul said, "Mike, shut the partition door, will you?" The faces of the plaster workmen staring through were abruptly pushed back, and the dingy panels cut them off from sight but not from hearing. "Papa Gene," the young man went on in a low voice, "there's no doubt, I suppose?"

Fenmer's neat white head moved from side to side.

Paul went with his odd stiff-necked gait toward the grisly exhibit and bent over it. "We thought it was the glue," he said, with a wry smile that sat oddly on his young face. While the others watched him dully, he pulled aside the oilcloth which Fenmer had dropped over the head of the statue.

Upon the low mound on which the Woman's head rested a thin layer of clay had been smoothed, and faintly scratched on it as if on a flat gravestone were four words and two dates. There was a sound of harsh breathing as the men leaned forward; one of the workmen said, "What the hell—" in a muffled voice. Will Rome cleared his throat and read aloud slowly, "Claude Pruitt, 1903-1943."

He shook his untidy head as if he were dizzy. "But if this is—if somebody called Claude Pruitt's been stuck into Anna's model, God knows why—it can't be, Fenmer! This is 1946!"

One of the craziest things about the whole set-up, Red Hobart later pointed out to his colleagues on the San Francisco *Eagle*, was the way this Paul Watkins took command and the others let him get away with it—that queer fish with his immature-looking face, like a college sophomore before the war; with his old-maidish concern about his own health and that uncanny habit of sitting still and letting his eyes follow you around.

Sure, he'd had a commission in the Army, but he hadn't been a lieutenant for more than a few months before he was thrown out of that jeep at Camp Edwards and brought in for dead with a broken neck...Maybe he was just too dumb to take in the horror.

Red, in his capacity as reporter, had arrived at the Plaster Works a good five minutes before the police. It was Rita Steffany who'd tipped him off—gone straight across the courtyard to the little office and telephoned. Nothing like a girl friend on the scene of the crime! She had managed to slip him a few extra details before the cops arrived and threw everybody out of the sculptors' workroom. Some beat, hey boys?

Thus Red in the *Eagle*'s city room, on his return from the scene of the crime: a blond young-old man, his eyeballs veined with tiny red threads, his voice rough from smoking but indomitably cocky, his face as knobbily round and his manner as brash as those of the comedian Red Skelton to which resemblance he owed his nickname. "What a yarn, what a yarn!" Red exclaimed, casting himself down at his typewriter desk. "And what'll you bet those so-and-sos in the office pull me off it? They've got a down on me—"

He proved a true prophet. When the corpse turns out to be somebody against whom a reporter has violent prejudices, the editors generally choose someone with a more open mind to cover the story.

Paul Watkins had called the Homicide Division from the small glass-enclosed office at the far side of the courtyard. He had also, after a minute's thought, put in another call during which he spoke low and soothingly. It was not a long conversation, but he had scarcely finished it and returned to the awed and unsteady group in the mold-making section when the police came. The tall, grizzled man with the mournful Irish face, Inspector Geraghty, went through the preliminary routine with a speed which attested to his long experience on the force. Then there was a wait, while muffled voices and sounds and flashes of light came from behind the board partition; a long, nerve-racking twenty minutes or so. The sculptors sat without a word and consumed cigarettes; Daisy Watkins kept gulping nervously; Eugene Fenmer's Santa Claus cheeks had faded to a mottled mauve.

When the tall man came through the partition he was looking grim and more elderly than when he had gone in. He said, "Any of you know Chester Verney personally?"

His eye happened to catch that of the plaster-works foreman. The man coughed; he said nervously, "Jeez, Inspector, you mean the big-time mouthpiece?" The remark, however, was drowned out by a horrified babble from the artists.

Geraghty waited until it died down. "You all did?" he said thoughtfully. "It was this group he went around with, then? H'm."

"Inspector," said Fenmer in a shadow of his usual great voice, "that isn't—that body in there—" His white head trembled.

"The body has not been identified. It will take some identifying," he added without inflection.

"But—your question, Inspector."

"I think I may tell you," said Geraghty, "that under the body there was a wallet which seems to be Chester Verney's property. Had his identification cards in it, and a wad of money."

"Under the body," Rita Steffany repeated faintly.

"Also, the corpse was—" Geraghty cleared his throat. "Was wearing a belt with an initialed buckle."

"Wearing a—"

"A belt. Nothing else except shoes." He went on, impervious to the looks of sick horror on the faces of artists and workmen, "We've been in touch with Mr. Verney's office and we find he hasn't been in town for a couple of weeks, not since his marriage was announced. If this body isn't his, it's something of a coincidence that his wallet should be—hidden with it, and that the initials on the buckle are the same as his. I don't think we'll be wasting time if I ask you a few questions about your connection with Verney. You first, please, Mr. Fenmer."

"Wait, please, Inspector," Papa Gene said. "This is almost a community proceeding. Not for our friends the plaster casters, naturally, but for the rest of us. If you're going to ask us all when we last saw him—I believe that's one of the stock questions?—I can almost answer for my students here, and Mr. Rome. We were all together in the workroom here"—he gestured toward the partition—"along with one or two other guests, Hobart from the *Eagle* and a young girl named Noel Bruce, another Sherwin student. I can tell you the date: Saturday, September the eighth. It was," said Papa Gene, rising and moving toward the detective with his hands thrust into his overall pockets, "on the occasion when Verney's marriage was announced. His bride arranged the party—Anna Tannehill, one of my students."

"Oh my God," Daisy Watkins said as if talking to herself, "Tannehill's statue. No, that's too horrible! Not Verney, not her own—"

"Cut it, Watkins," Will Rome broke in. His voice sounded surly. "Everyone's thought of that."

"Maybe you'd enlighten me, Mr. Rome," said Geraghty dryly.

Rome had not taken his eyes from the inspector's face since the questions had begun. "Anna Tannehill was working on that clay model up to about four days before that party Fenmer mentioned." He spoke rapidly, sounding hoarse. "She hasn't been here since, except to the party. Somebody—if that's Verney, somebody tore down her work and—"

"I see." The inspector's head turned toward the partition for a long look. None of these revelations seemed to startle him. "His own wife's statue, h'm?" He turned back briskly. "Now I think I've got the general idea. There'll be a few questions, as I said, and we—"

The door to the courtyard opened and hastily shut after admitting a plainclothes officer. For the moment when it stood open, the crowd of reporters waiting outside surged forward, straining for a look at the silent group within. As the officer finished his low-toned remarks to Geraghty, a woman's voice was clearly audible in the yard. "But I belong in there!" it said. "Please, won't you take me to the person in charge?"

"That's Tannehill," Will Rome said sharply.

Geraghty glanced at him. "Somebody must have let her know what happened," he said mildly. "You, Mr. Rome?"

"I did," Paul Watkins said, clearing his throat. "I—of course I couldn't know who—I called her up. You see, I knew where she was, and it—well, Inspector, it was her clay model that—"

"I see, Mr. Watkins. That's enough." Paul fell silent, dropping his eyes to the ball of clay he was still mechanically kneading. The inspector added, "Saves time, maybe. Just the same, I'd rather not have had her come here. Okay, Kotock, I guess you can let her in."

The plainclothes man opened the door again. From the murmuring voices of the newsmen Hobart's cocky tones rang out: "Good girl, Tannehill! But how's about an exclusive for me?"

"Exclusive? Don't be silly, Hobart," the woman entering the Plaster Works called over her shoulder. "If I have to give an interview, it's for all of you."

She faced about, blinking at the westering sun which shone through the dingy windows, nursing a bandaged left hand against the breast of a thin dark coat. Her gray-blue eyes, widely set under a serene forehead, went from the silent and uneasy group of workmen to the haggard faces of her friends. Then, with a turn of the head that brought out the beautiful modeling of her chin and throat, she looked at Geraghty. "You're the police captain?" she said in a gentle voice.

"Inspector. Geraghty's my name. You're Mrs. Chester Verney?"

Anna Verney inclined her head, the expression of puzzled awe still in her eyes. Her smooth blonde hair, upswept, seemed to catch and hold the light as she stood poised for another moment against the dull background; then she moved forward with effortless grace. The inspector looked at her gravely, as if weighing what he should say to her.

"I heard that there had been a—a dreadfully tragic discovery. Is it true, Inspector?" she said.

"Yes, it's true, Mrs. Verney."

"A man, dead, in my clay model?" Geraghty nodded, his shrewd look still taking her measure. Anna Verney smiled at him uncertainly. "I suppose you know," she said, "that I haven't touched it for nearly three weeks. I burned my hand"—she gestured toward the thick bandages—"and then I went away for a few days, so I—of course I know nothing about it. But I felt I must come."

"Where were you staying, Mrs. Verney? Mr. Watkins said he 'knew where to find you.'"

"I wasn't at home, that is, in my own studio. I was at my aunt's home in St. Francis Wood."

"With your aunt?"

"No. The housekeeper is there, no one else."

"Your husband wasn't with you, then."

"No. He's not in town."

"Oh? How long ago did he leave?"

The golden girl took her eyes from his face momentarily, and glanced at the motionless group of sculptors. She smiled at them, an alluring flash of vermilion and white. "About ten days ago. My friends there will tease the life out of me, Inspector, because we were supposed to be on a honeymoon! But—you were wrong after all, Papa Gene." She glanced at Fenmer, whose dark eyes came up to meet hers with a spark of something like warning. "Both Chet and I had our own way! We're civilized, after all."

Daisy Watkins had been sitting close to her cousin, gazing pallidly at Anna Verney and the inspector. Now, as if galvanized into involuntary speech, she said loudly, "Chet's in your statue! It's Ch—" and broke off with a strangled gasp as the police guard sprang forward and Geraghty swung round toward her.

Anna Verney had understood. Her face flushed a deep sudden crimson and as suddenly went white. She recoiled a step, looking piteously at the inspector.

"I'm sorry, Mrs. Verney," said Geraghty in a swift low voice. "Sit down over here, will you please? I couldn't foresee—" He turned back to the group, palpably controlling himself. "The rest of you," he said, "had better go down to headquarters and wait there, till I can talk to you. We can bring you back if it's necessary—Yes, just as you are, Miss Steffany, nobody minds if you're in working clothes—Got statements from the plaster casters, Kotock? Okay. They can go home. We'll keep in touch with them."

He waited until the two groups had dissolved, until the sound of their feet had died away through the courtyard gate. The voices of the reporters sounded like an embodied stage direction: "Mob mutters offstage." They were getting out of hand, waiting in the hot courtyard, seeing the witnesses rushed past them to the police cars.

Geraghty watched through one of the high windows—he was tall enough to see over the sill—until they had quieted down again. He looked twice at a round-faced young man who was leaning against the fence and chewing gum in a slow comfortable rhythm. "Lockett, by all that's holy," he told himself, silently chuckling. "Standing outside like a good little boy."

He turned back to the barnlike room, empty now except for the woman sitting with bowed head on the rickety stool in a corner. He spoke with the sympathetic courtesy that was one of his greatest assets.

"This has been a shock for you, Mrs. Verney, and perhaps an unnecessary one. We haven't made any positive identification. But—if you feel strong enough to talk to me a few minutes...?"

"Yes, I'm strong enough," said Anna Verney quietly.

CHAPTER THREE

THE SHADOW OF THE PLASTER WORKS crept eastward across the courtyard and the half-formed shape in stone which was Rome's statue was engulfed in shade. The newspaper men got as close to it as they could, loosening collars in the heat and waiting with enforced patience, their talk from time to time lapsing into dulled silence. It was about half an hour between the time when the sculptors had gone, in a body, and the moment when Inspector Geraghty opened the door to the courtyard. His long face wore a peculiar expression, compounded of dubiety and admiration. He said in his deep, dispassionate voice, "I may have something for you, boys. I don't want to keep Mrs. Verney any longer than I have to, though, and she says she's promised you an interview. Now, wait!" He held up a hand as the group surged forward. "You got to make it snappy, and cut it short if she gets to looking strained, and don't try for any exclusives. She'll tell the story to the whole crowd of you at once."

The newspaper men looked quickly at each other. Something behind this, the look said. The round-faced young man caught Geraghty's eye and pointed hopefully at himself; the inspector gave him a brief nod in answer.

"You can come in," Geraghty said, and opened the door.

Anna Tannehill Verney was still sitting on the unsteady stool in the corner. She met the barrage of eyes with a dignity that ignored the traces of tears on her face; she was pale, but the blue-gray eyes under her serene brow were level; only, from time to time, she caught and held a deep breath as if it were hard to get enough air into her lungs.

"Thank you, Mr. Geraghty," she said. "I heard what you told them. You see, gentlemen, I'm—I haven't had time fully to realize what all of this means, and—I'd like to talk now, while I can. Chester always played fair with the press. You reminded me of that, Red. And I promised you this interview before I— knew, so I'm keeping the promise."

Somewhere in the group sounded a low whistle of astonishment, abruptly cut off. Someone else started to speak, but Geraghty raised his hand. "No questions yet," he said.

"Shall I tell them just what I told you, Inspector? Well, you gentlemen all know that Chester Verney and I were married last June, in Las Vegas, and that we kept the marriage a secret for professional reasons until about two weeks ago. I kept my studio and he his bachelor quarters. Then we decided to announce it. Chester wanted to get away for a—a real honeymoon, and I'd hurt my hand and couldn't work, and it seemed a good time."

She paused and moistened her lips, from which the lipstick was all but gone. It gave her an appealingly vulnerable look. She went on, "That was the eighth of this month, as you know. All your papers carried the story. And on that night Chester entertained some of my friends, here and at a restaurant, at a sort of belated wedding party. You were here, Red," Mrs. Verney said, looking at Hobart, "for part of the time, anyway. If the others want to know about it, perhaps you could tell them? You remember, probably, that Chet and I couldn't agree about where we were to go afterward. He wanted to drive down to his cabin in the Santa Cruz mountains, where he used to go for complete seclusion. I—well, I'm a town sparrow at best, and my hand was very painful—the burn got infected somehow, and I didn't want to be so far from a doctor, and I thought we could be just as secluded at my aunt's home in St. Francis Wood. There's only a housekeeper there, and I told Chet we needn't even see her. We didn't discuss all this at the party, of course. It was just that—I didn't want to go to the cabin, and there was a lot of teasing about my always having my own way. And it's true, of course, people have always spoiled me—Chet, too."

She stopped again, and for a moment her lashes dropped in utter weariness. The skin seemed taut over her cheekbones, with the hint of the Slavic in their beautiful modeling. The looks the reporters exchanged were now heartily puzzled, but no one spoke.

"We went out to St. Francis Wood that night," she said with a visible effort at composure, "and the next night—Sunday—we came down here for a few minutes, to wet the wrappings on my statue. Chet didn't want to be seen in town; when he said 'seclusion' that was what he meant, and that's why we chose Sunday. I—Mr. Geraghty, you asked if Chet had any enemies—"

"Yes, go on, Mrs. Verney," Geraghty said. He was standing by watchfully, his eyes fixed on her face. "You may tell them anything you told me."

"Well—you know that a lawyer who's previously been an assistant district attorney is bound to have—antagonized some people," said Anna Verney, her voice momentarily faltering. "I've been trying to think if there could really have been someone following us that night. It was only an impression, and after all, nothing happened—we went home, and stayed by ourselves in my aunt's guest suite, and—everything was—it couldn't have been happier.

"And then about Tuesday Chester began to feel restless. I couldn't blame him, he needed the outdoors. And so we—we came to an amicable arrangement! He would go down to the cabin by himself, and I'd stay in town, and each of us would have what he wanted." She raised suddenly wet eyes to the group of men. "We made a joke out of it, we composed headlines, 'Bride Deserted on Honeymoon'—only, of course, I wasn't a real bride, and there was no reason for anyone to know except the housekeeper. Chet slipped out on Wednesday morning to take the train down there and leave me the big car. I was just able to drive if I had to"—she touched her bandaged hand—"and he—it was like him to want me to have it." She scrubbed the good hand across her cheeks in a youthful gesture. "And he—telephoned me that night, Wednesday. He—he said he was in Los Gatos and was planning to get the jalopy he kept there and drive up to the cabin and he'd mail me a letter the next time he was in town. That was on the twelfth. I—I didn't hear from him, but I thought he—"

"What—the—hell!" said a muffled voice in the group. There was a curious electric stir among the listening men.

"He was coming back on Sunday, day after tomorrow," said Anna Verney in a voice that had grown almost inaudible. "We were going to—to start our real life together—"

Her teeth began to chatter, all at once, and her slender body sagged on the uncomfortable seat. Geraghty held the reporters silent with one of his flinty looks. He beckoned with his head to a man standing by. "That's all," he said. "You drive her home, Marshall. I've talked to the housekeeper. There'll be a doctor out there. Now, boys! Hold it half a minute. There has been no positive identification as yet of the body found in Mrs. Verney's clay model. Got that? We are trying to get hold of Mr. Verney through the Los Gatos authorities. He may be safe and sound at his cabin. But if he is, he'll want to know, himself, what his belt and wallet are doing under that body...No, nobody in that other room yet. I'll give you a look through the door and that's all. Okay, ten minutes for questions. I only hope I can answer some of 'em!"

One of the men glanced at Anna Verney as she disappeared through the doorway. "There goes a thoroughbred," he said audibly. She gave no sign of having heard. She went swiftly, her head bowed, through a barrage of clicking cameras.

The young man called Lockett found himself being herded out with the reporters. He looked back wistfully as the door closed; he hung about, still wistfully, as the reporters jostled for the telephone in a small shack across the yard that served as an office. He was still there when the last of them departed and Geraghty himself came out and passed him without a word or a glance.

He wandered about the courtyard for a few minutes, working on his gum, his round blue eyes seemingly fixed on vacancy. Then he shrugged, sighed and ambled through the gate. There were still a few members of the curious crowd standing there with an air of being stuck to the spot through sheer inertia. "Show's over, folks," Lockett remarked to nobody in particular as he moved through the group. His words seemed to carry conviction, for these remnants also melted away.

Few pedestrians used this narrow street of warehouses, but one figure was shambling toward the gate in the wooden fence. It was that of a shabby and elderly man, seeming just on the edge of disintegration; yet there was a tinge of purpose in his gait.

As Lockett came abreast of him the man stopped, peering at the entrance to the Plaster Works. "Hey, bud," he said hoarsely, "what's the coppers doin' there?"

"Been a murder," Lockett said. "They found a corpse this afternoon."

"A murder? 'Round the Works?" There was a sudden brightness in the rheumy eyes. "When'd that happen?"

"A while ago. Your guess is as good as mine."

"Say, c'n ya tell me about it, bud?"

"Nope. Don't know from nothin' myself. Here," Lockett produced a dime, "buy a paper when they come out."

"Okay, okay, I get it." A grimy hand grabbed the dime. "You a dick?"

"No." Worse luck, Lockett added to himself. Not yet, worse luck.

The old man gave a mighty sniff, seemed to dismiss him with a nod, and moved past him toward the gate. Lockett strolled on in the direction of Columbus Avenue. After a moment he looked idly over his shoulder. The man had changed his mind, it seemed, for he had turned and was now shuffling along half a block behind. He was looking at the ground and the unshaven flabbiness of his face was lifted by a broad grin.

He looked up and met Lockett's eyes and the grin abruptly vanished.

While San Francisco was greedily absorbing the first newspaper accounts of Crime in the Art World, Mr. Geraghty was plowing patiently through the next stage of his investigation.

"Make yourself as comfortable as you can, Miss Watkins. I'm sorry to have kept you waiting so long down here. Now, you and all the others say you don't know anything about this crime, so you can take these as just routine questions. You hardly knew Chester Verney, you told me. Okay. Now, as to your own observations—"

"I didn't notice a thing, Inspector, not a thing! We all worked at the Plaster Works, four or five days a week—yes, we've been there since Tannehill left, every day. Well, not weekends. Maybe some of us would work Saturdays and Sundays if the time was getting short, but the clay models for this competition don't have to be finished until December... No, it was just the same as always, except that Tannehill wasn't there...What? Oh, we'd come about one, after morning classes at Sherwin, and work until five-thirty or six, the light's been good, you know. And then sometimes we'd sit around until seven or so, talking and maybe having a beer, and our friends would come in and we'd go to dinner—and it'll never be the same again, that place is all wrong now—"

"Yes, I know, Miss Watkins. It's been a bad shock to all of you...Yes? Well, we always say no idea is too crazy for us to consider."

"It's—it's just a feeling, of course, but the person who did that wasn't responsible, he couldn't have been, it's the act of a crazy man. He must have been crazy! That—that headstone— Paul, my cousin, told me about it—the name of a stranger that died three years ago—"

"Then you've never heard of Claude Pruitt?"

"No, never. Never. I never heard the name. It was a crazy man who did that..."

Daisy Watkins, released from questioning, was shown out of the Hall of Justice by a rear door. She went on foot, swiftly, to her oddly neat studio in a cheap district at the foot of Telegraph Hill; went slipping through the gathering darkness, once or twice looking over her shoulder as if she hoped rather than feared that someone might be following her.

She sat down on her carefully made-up couch and waited. There was more than one knock at her door, but she ignored the sounds. Those were only artist neighbors, and the particular knock she was expecting did not come. Once she got up as if on impulse and uncovered a clay model of a head and looked at it for a long time. She said, aloud in the quiet room, "Tannehill. She even sat for me and coached me. So damned generous!"

The special knock didn't come.

"What made you think of telephoning to Hobart, Miss Steffany?"

"Well, really, Inspector! He's the boy-friend, you know—the present one, anyway—and I couldn't let him miss a story like that!"

"Seems you keep your head in a tight place."

"Well, Inspector, you might say that. It was something to do, anyway. Something to take my mind off that ghastly business inside. Now, Inspector, you give Red the breaks, won't you?"

"I'm afraid the Department can't play favorites, Miss Steffany. Now, if you'll tell me where you first met Chester Verney?"

"Oh, only through Tannehill! I never saw him before he began coming to her apartment, and we'd all be there—he was almost a stranger to me. I never really knew him well at *all*. Oh, you know, we'd talk and kid around, but that was all. Really, it was."

"Yes, I see. You noticed no evidence of—any dislike toward him, in your group?"

"Oh, no, certainly not. He was a grand fellow, he had everything. I thought Tannehill was—in luck. Listen, Inspector, was it really him? Do you know it for sure?"

"Verney? Yes, Miss Steffany, he's been identified...You noticed no evidence of dislike on Hobart's part?"

"Oh, that. That was just—professional. Red kind of likes to needle people, especially higher-ups like Chet."

"Nothing personal?"

"Oh, certainly not. Nothing of the kind. Honestly."

Rita Steffany renewed her lipstick and ran a meticulous comb through the shining black of her hair. She looked a bit taken aback when she was ushered out the rear door of the Hall of Justice, where there were no reporters, but she rallied quickly. There was still the Art School; no reason to suppose that classes would be called off. After all, the other students had to attend life class, and it wasn't as if the corpse had been found at Sherwin.

Her eyes were brighter than ever, and her curled red mouth more sensuous as she walked into the building on

Buchanan Street and stood poised, waiting for the avalanche of questions. It came, most satisfactorily. In the midst of her ready answers she stood on tiptoe, peering above clustered heads. "Hey, Bruce!" she called out. "Meet me at the Tavern after class? I want to talk to you!"

❋ ❋ ❋

"How's this going to affect you, Gene?"

"By God, Butch, I don't know. Either it'll ruin the school or double the enrollment. Personally, it doesn't mean a thing. Or do I have to tell you that?"

"You mean really not a thing?"

"Ah, you're catching me up, you old fox. Yes, I mind for Tannehill. There's a queen of a woman, Butch. You didn't miss her special quality, I hope?"

"Very handsome young woman. Plenty of courage and poise."

"More than that. That girl has something that sets her apart, in her professional life as well as her private one. She's gone up as steadily as—as the sun rises. Never a step that didn't get her nearer the goal she'd chosen. And it's enough to make you retch, let me tell you, to see that piece of work she started—'Woman at the Grave'—wrecked. Ruined, just when it was shaping up. Whoever did that—"

"Here, hold on, Gene. Is that why you feel sorry for her? How about losing a husband?"

"Husbands are nothing but a liability for an artist. Maybe she could have done the social stuff, wife of the prominent criminal lawyer, and gone on working in her odd moments. I doubt it. And why are you looking like that? You think I removed Verney because he might have hampered the career of one of my students? Ho, ho, *ho!* Art doesn't mean quite that much to me!"

Eugene Fenmer went majestically out the rear door, found a taxi, ignored the curious glances of driver and passers-by at his voluminous white overalls, and went home. He summarily dismissed a young woman who was curled appealingly in a corner of his huge and comfortable couch, waiting for him. He poured himself a thumping drink and dropped heavily into a chair, all his robust vitality drained away. He sat there for a long time, looking steadily at a cold fireplace.

❀ ❀ ❀

"This is only a routine proceeding, Mr. Rome. You'll help us most if you'll just relax and not allow yourself to be antagonized."

"What d'you expect me to do, after this afternoon? Behave as if this was a bottle party?"

"H'm. Perhaps it's because you're more mature than the others, both as a man and an artist, that I'd hoped for some valuable comment from you."

"Mature? Fenmer's mature enough. Old billygoat."

"Very well, we'll leave out Fenmer. The rest of them are young and inclined to be hysterical. You've been around, Rome. You were in the Army in the First World War, isn't that right? And worked at some rough trades afterward, until you discovered your talent for sculpture?"

"What of it?"

"Just that I'd expect you to take a rugged experience, like today's, more in your stride."

"Do *you* ever get used to violent death? Don't you find it haunting you? Christ, perhaps it's because I do know something about it, know what it means."

"Yes, you've got a point there. Well, you scarcely knew Verney, you say?"

"Enough to pass the time of day with him, not much more. I didn't go to most of their fool parties, only once in a while when Tannehill made a point of it."

"That's easy to understand. She's a charming woman."

"You don't know what that girl's like, I'm telling you. She'd do things for you that nobody else would think of. Maybe they told you, last winter when I was sick in that stinking little hole I live in, Tannehill came round herself and nursed me? Nobody else cared if I lived or died. There was nothing between her and me, no reason for her to care, but she got me through pneumonia. Didn't give a damn what anybody said. That girl—"

"In love with her, Rome?"

"Love. Ah, hell, how can you name it? It's more than that, and less. She's not for me. I know it. Just the same, there's something special."

"How'd you feel about her marriage to Verney?"

"Verney? Well, she married him, and anybody she picked out, who was decent to her, it'd be jake with me. None of my business, was it?"

"Smoke, Rome?"

"If I want one I'll smoke my own. How long has this got to go on, for God's sake? I've told you I don't know anything about—the way he died. It was just my lousy luck to walk in there when Fenmer wanted that model lifted, or I wouldn't even be a witness. And I'd like to get out of here and get a drink!"

Will Rome stopped at the first bar near the Hall of Justice and had two quick ones. He stopped at the next bar he came to, and the next. It was still early in the evening and there was little attraction in the room which he had so aptly described as a stinking hole. He went on out Columbus Avenue, toward Fishermen's Wharf, turned into a small bistro sometimes frequented by the Sherwin students, and sat in an obscure corner for a while. When he left he was still cold sober. From some minds no amount of watered bourbon will erase the thought of death.

❀ ❀ ❀

"Sit down, Mr. Watkins. These chairs aren't as bad as they look. I understand you were a training-camp casualty? Your spine still bothers you?"

"Some, thank you. They tell me I'm well, but—no use talking about it. I hope there's some way I can help you, Inspector."

"Thank *you*, Mr. Watkins. I'd like to check on a few points besides your official statement. First—were you the only one to know where Mr. and Mrs. Verney were staying in town?"

"I think so."

"How'd they come to tell you?"

"Tannehill wanted a small errand done at her—at the Art School. I seemed the obvious person to ask, I suppose. She telephoned me."

"Why were you obvious?"

"People think I have plenty of time on my hands, Inspector. I'm not actually idle, perhaps, but—well, you know; a grown man with none too much talent, playing around with ceramics—seems like no more than occupational therapy."

"Wouldn't make it much easier if people used you as an errand boy."

"Don't mistake me, Inspector. I was glad to do it."

"What was the errand?"

"I don't—well, it was just some papers. Drawings or something, I suppose. Naturally I didn't look at them. She wanted me to—to mail them to her."

"Uh-huh. Now, about this Claude Pruitt. That name mean anything to you?"

"Nothing at all, Inspector."

"Haven't struck anyone yet who'd heard of Claude Pruitt, or would admit to it. It did seem to me that your cousin Daisy was a bit upset when I asked her."

"That needn't mean much, Inspector. Daisy's kind of intense, and she'd take anything you asked her pretty hard."

"Uh-huh. She's also the one person who has any kind of theory about who killed Verney."

"She does? Daisy?"

"She thinks it's someone who's mentally unbalanced."

"That's—interesting. But it sounds intense, too."

"Mr. Watkins, you kept your head admirably this afternoon. Did you happen to observe any reactions on the part of the other people who were there?"

"Well, good Lord, Inspector Geraghty! They were shocked and horrified and nauseated—what would you expect? But that sounds as if you thought we—one of them, one of us—"

"Why not, Mr. Watkins? Almost anybody could be a murderer, given sufficient reason, and—let's say, emotional spur. And there's the way that body was concealed. Isn't it likely that whoever killed Verney had to know about sculpture, and the Plaster Works, and the fact that that statue wouldn't be disturbed for some time?"

"I—yes, I see. But that needn't—Why, good Lord, Inspector! There were half a dozen persons besides the ones who were there today, who knew enough to have done it—if you could imagine them committing a crime like that."

"Okay, Mr. Watkins. Name three."

"Well—any of the plaster workmen, any of the gang who used to join us there, the little Bruce, or Hobart, or—that's absurd, of course. But no—"

"No more absurd than considering any of you. I know. Well, that'll be all, Mr. Watkins. Thank you. You'll be staying in your own place, I suppose?"

"I shan't leave town, Inspector."

Paul Watkins went out with that odd somnambulistic effect caused by his stiffly held neck. He had gone only a block along Kearney when he paused, half wheeled about as if to return to Geraghty's office; and then reconsidered and went on, passing with no more than an upward glance the old building where his cousin roomed. It was only a little after ten o'clock, but he had the air of someone going wearily home, with bed in mind.

Inspector Geraghty, left in his office, turned a bleak look on the notebook in which he had made so few entries during the interviews just finished. His assistant, a silent small man in a derby hat, wandered in from the corridor, pulled out his watch and consulted it pointedly.

"No, I'm not quitting yet, not by a long shot," said Mr. Geraghty irritably. "Got to make something out of what all those characters said, and how they looked and acted. I tell you, Al, most of 'em are lying and every one of 'em is scared."

The assistant, Mr. Kotock, spoke little but always to the point. "*I'd* be," he replied.

"Not of me, that's a cinch," said the inspector, still morose. "I'm getting too damned gentle in my old age."

Mr. Kotock permitted himself a grin.

"Well, it's early in the investigation yet, I'll make that much excuse for myself. You got those reports? Strike oil, any place? I thought not. At that," Mr. Geraghty murmured, swinging round to his desk, "that set-up would kind of give you goose-pimples. Working around for a couple of weeks within two yards of a corpse—and a corpse stark naked except for belt and shoes, and a coat of shellac!"

CHAPTER FOUR

NOEL BRUCE SAT in an uncomfortably small booth at Joe's Tavern, gazing fixedly at Rita Steffany across the table. The air was heavy with smoke, pulsing with the clink of glasses and with voices raised in controversy or song. Noel's only drink of the evening, a glass of beer with about two inches gone, could not very well have produced this effect of fever, of phantasm. The room seemed to swing in slow circles. She kept putting a palm to her forehead.

Steffany noticed it once, during her avid recital of happenings and emotions. "What's the matter with you, Bruce?" she said. "This business doesn't mean anything to you, does it?"

"I don't know. I mean, of course not. It's just—hard to take in."

"If you were right in the middle of it, like we were, you'd take it in fast enough." Steffany's black eyes glittered. She was enjoying it thoroughly, Noel realized, like a small-town gossip retailing a juicy scandal over the back fence. "But just the same, you look kind of broken up. I thought you were through with Verney a long time ago."

"I never had him to be through with," Noel said. "Don't *you* feel any sense of—of loss?" Steffany said, "Huh?" in a startled voice, and Noel bit her lip in compunction. "I'm sorry, probably I wasn't meant to hear—but at the announcement party, you told Paul Watkins that you'd had an affair with Verney before he married Tannehill."

"Oh, God. Did I? I didn't mean—naturally that wasn't said for publication, Bruce. Oh, sure, I know you wouldn't repeat it. It's all water over the dam, long ago, anyway." The black eyes were suddenly evasive; she changed the subject with a jerk. "The worst part, the very worst part of that questioning the detective took me through, was when he asked me about Red and how he felt about Verney. I think I passed it off all right, though it's no secret—but anything they find out won't come from me. A girl's got to stand by her fellow."

"You're right, of course." Noel thought, Of all the situations in which I'd find myself agreeing to the letter with Steffany! Steffany, who was fond of saying haughtily, "I have no principles!" who according to her own story had lived enough for five women in her twenty-something years, and out-Trilbied Trilby in her present life. She always made Noel feel contradictorily older and wiser and calmer than she. There was an untouched core of naïveté within her.

"Good grief, it's after eleven. I've got to run. Look, Rita, how's for coming home again with me tonight?"

"Tonight?" The brilliant eyes widened. "Don't be a sap, Bruce! Everybody in my building'll be crazy to hear what's been going on."

"Would you have room for me?" The question cost Noel an effort.

Steffany, renewing her shining lipstick, gave a sly sidelong glance. "Bed's full tonight."

"I'm sort of nervous about going across town so late."

"Your own fault, baby, for not denning up with the rest of us. She has to get her sleep, she says!" Rita grinned. "What's hit you? You never used to be afraid."

"I have been in the past ten days." Noel also grinned, but faintly. "Wishful thinking, you'll call it, but I've felt as if someone were following me or waiting in the alley. I've been careful not to go home after dark, alone. That's how strong it was."

"Well, nothing happened, did it?"

"Somebody got into my room."

"Really? Crown jewels missing?"

"Laugh away, pal. Nothing was touched that I could see, but the room smelled funny. Sweetish, somehow—not perfume, something queer."

"For the sweet Lord's sake, you have got it bad. When was all this?"

"Last week some time. One of the nights I dropped around at the Plaster Works to join all of you for dinner. Rita, I'd swear that my keys had been in my bag all day, but when I came to go home they weren't there. I got the landlady to let me in, and there they were, on the bureau."

"Go on," Steffany said. She drained her beer and got up. "You did forget them after all. Of course, Bruce; don't be a sap. And did you think one of *us* stole them? Watkins, or Rome, or Red?"

"No, of course not." Noel found herself thinking swiftly, We were together the whole evening, anyway; all of us. "Just the same, I bought a new lock and had it put on. And I'd surely love company."

"Snap out of it," Steffany advised her light-heartedly. There was a gleam of interest, but little sympathy, in her eyes. "I'll see you as far as the streetcar, scaredy-cat."

Some forty minutes later, Noel Bruce swung off the Geary car and walked at a rapid pace down the cross-street to her rooming house. She told herself that Steffany might very well have been right in thinking that her fears were illusory;

she kept her eyes front, refusing to dart apprehensive glances toward the dark nooks between the buildings, yet little waves of cold kept going over her. There was no traffic now, except on the main arterials. That was one thing, she could be fairly sure that no car was following her.

She reached the mouth of her own narrow street and turned in. It was only half a block long, and blind; one of those lanes or alleys that so confuse a newcomer trying to find his way about San Francisco. A dusty streetlamp burned at its entrance, but the lane itself was dull with shadows. The high thin houses, built of wood, their paint weathered to a dingy gray, seemed at once to absorb and to keep out light. Most of their bay-windowed fronts were dark.

At the end of the alley, a little distance past her own rooming house, a car was parked, facing her. This was in defiance of the parking sign, and she wondered at it idly until she came a few steps nearer and could see a pale blob that might have been a face behind the steering wheel. She glanced across the street at the steps of her house.

Her heart went up on a surge of incredulous joy. There was someone waiting there, too; someone who stirred in the shadow of the steps, turning toward her, that disc of white on the man's head looked like a naval officer's cap. She thought, He's come back a whole week early, and of course he didn't know where to find me tonight, and he came to wait here.

Only pride kept her footsteps even and unhurried. No matter how much in love you thought yourself, you couldn't run to meet the man. She walked on, smiling.

A light went on in one of the houses at the end of the row. It barely tempered the darkness, but it was enough. She caught a clear glimpse of the man who sat behind the wheel of the car, and her breathing stopped. She had seen that abnormally thick neck before, nine days ago, on a lonely road overlooking the ocean.

She thought her heart had stopped too, but the message of discipline she had sent to her body was still in effect, and her feet went on at a steady pace. To have pulled up short, or turned to run, would have given her away. If she could pretend to belong in one of those houses opposite her own—dart in at the door and call for help?

And if the door she chose were locked? The man could reach her in thirty seconds, and her throat was so dry that she doubted if a sound would come out.

From the corner of her eye she saw a wooden door that closed off a passage between houses. In the same moment the man who had been waiting by the steps moved forward, half-hesitating. The light was dim, but he was too short to be Miles. The car at the end of the alley began to coast down the slight slope. Noel's hand went out of its own volition and pushed the wooden door. She was in the black darkness of the passage. Her hand touched the rough metal of a trash can and, again acting almost independently of thought, she eased it down on its side against the door. That would delay them for a moment, give her warning.

She couldn't stay here. If there were any luck in the world, this passage would go through to the next street. She went scurrying blindly into its depths like a small animal pursued, her heart beating in painful throbs. Once she looked back. Something was just visible at the alley's end: a head rising above the door she had blocked. There was no sound from the vicinity of the cans.

The alley did not go quite through, a fence marked a lot boundary halfway down. She climbed over the fence without hesitation, as if her terror had propelled her. The second half of the alley was better lighted; no door blocked the light from the through street at its end.

Once more she waited, listening, but heard no sound behind.

She had almost reached the street, slipping along the dank brickwork of the alley like a dark ghost, when a door closed smartly in one of the neighboring porches. Quick feet sounded on a long flight of outside steps and then on pavement. Past the mouth of the alley a woman went briskly, hatless as if she had come out on some brief errand. She wore a short coat, light in color, resembling the one that Noel herself had on; a replica of the coat worn by five thousand women in San Francisco this season. Her steps went quickly on, down the street, audible for a time after she had passed in the quiet of the late night. Halfway down the block she began to run.

Noel waited in the shadows for a long minute, fighting to control the thumping of her pulses. She thought, If I'd had my wits about me I'd have called out to her, asked to join her—but no, it might have scared her away. I'll pull myself together and—

The sounds came so hard upon each other that they seemed like one single, shattering noise. There was a shot; while its first echo was still crashing back from the street, there was the roar of a gunned motor, and a car flashed past the entrance to the alley. Then the screaming began.

The buildings on the through street blazed into sudden light and spilled their occupants onto the sidewalk. Within a few seconds a hundred voices were shouting a hundred versions of the incident.

"Car full o' men, it went that way—"

"There was just one of 'em, I seen it when I pulled up the shade—"

"It's Mary Berg, they've killed her, lookit the blood—"

"—ain't dead, she's groanin'. Call the ambulance!"

Noel Bruce crouched where she had collapsed, invisible in the mouth of the alley. She thought, That girl looked something like me. They believed I'd come out. They—they shot at her! She may be dying right now.

Until five minutes ago her one thought had been to avoid the police. Unless they summoned her, she had meant to say nothing, volunteer nothing at all. Now, they represented all of safety.

The tall elderly man swung a little in his swivel chair beside the desk and encompassed her in a mild and paternal gaze.

They had brought her up to this drab office in the Hall of Justice when she had told them that she might be connected with the Verney case, and this Geraghty had met her with the announcement that she was in luck to find him still working so late. There was something about him, a sympathetic courtesy, a patience of listening that had made her story come spilling out faster, almost, than she could find words; but not all of it, not quite all.

"Okay," he said. "Now we've got the main facts. You rest a minute. Smoke?" He leaned forward with a match, and settled back. It was very quiet in the office. The smallish man taking notes in a corner might have been an automaton.

In the dark glass of the window she could see her reflected image: round-oval face, fine lusterless black hair cut in a soft bang and curling up just above her shoulders, dark eyes, the full-lipped mouth that she always wished were larger. Even in that most flattering of reflections, the fatigue showed clearly also, straining her face.

"Now, Miss Bruce," said the inspector calmly, "let's go back and pick up a few references. You say you knew Chester Verney a couple of years ago?"

"Yes. My mother's lawyer, when he heard I was coming out here to study, gave me a letter to Verney and his wife. I went there to dinner. I naturally had no way of knowing that they were on the verge of a divorce; they seemed on good terms. Then the next time I heard of them, Mrs. Verney was in Reno and Chester was free and happy. He took me out to eat once or twice. It—it was really through me that he took to playing patron of the arts at Sherwin. Well—he was very nice to me for those two or three dates alone, and then I saw it might get to be something I couldn't handle. He was attractive, you know, Inspector, a lot of charm and power, but not really my style. And I—I got Anna Tannehill to help me out. It worked beautifully."

"You made the marriage, in a sense?"

"I'd hardly say that. I believe Chester was known as a marrying man—"

"On his way," said Mr. Geraghty dryly, "to becoming the Tommy Manville of the West Coast."

"But I was as amazed as anyone when I heard that they had been married. I was surprised even though I didn't know—" The pause was infinitesimal. "I mean, I knew he was rather a romantic at heart, and she'd be just the type to appeal to him."

"And you and Verney stayed friendly?"

"We'd hardly got as far as friendship. Pleasant acquaintances, yes. He had every reason to be grateful to me!"

"You're in and out of the Plaster Works a good deal?"

"Yes. I go around with the sculptors; I met them mostly through Anna."

"And you've seen nothing within the past ten days to give you the feeling that—something was wrong?"

"Not there. Not really. That time I told you about, that Wednesday when I was taking the naval officer to the Fort Mason docks—he had to be in there for half an hour or more, and I went to the Plaster Works to see if the gang were there—" It was out, glibly enough, and it was all true in actual fact; she hoped the indirection couldn't be called a lie. "I'd forgotten that they'd all be leaving early to dress for the party at the Sherwin School. When I saw that nobody was there, naturally I didn't stay long. I didn't want to anyway. You don't know how different that place can be when everybody's sitting around and talking. It just happened I'd never seen it empty before— empty except for those clay figures under the wrappings, with a queer cold dusty light slanting on them." An involuntary shiver went over her. "It seemed as if it wasn't a friendly place, then."

"But you noticed nothing special?"

"I can't think of anything. There was—but that was nothing unusual, the old man's probably not quite right in the head. You know that old watchman who's there for part of the evening? He was muttering to himself behind the fence when I went out."

Mr. Geraghty sat up slowly. "Watchman? Nobody's mentioned one to me."

"He's quite unofficial, I think. Rome hired him to come around in the evenings and keep the neighborhood kids from writing dirty words on the stone work in the courtyard. He probably leaves when it gets dark."

"What did he say when he muttered behind the fence?"

"I didn't hear the words. Mi—" She caught herself just in time to keep the name from slipping out. "My engine caught just then."

"Uh-huh. And it was that same night you got chased?"

"Yes. I still don't know what for."

"You don't know what for. You think those same two men have been after you ever since, and really turned on the heat tonight? And that it must, therefore, have some connection with the murder of Verney?"

"Yes; but I don't know what," she said truthfully, and gave him a brief look. "If I'd seen anything that could be important, you'd think I'd realize it; and certainly I'd tell you."

"I hope so, Miss Bruce. I hope so, indeed. Can't you make a guess as to why two thugs should suddenly want you out of the way?"

"In a way, I did have an idea. Is it possible that, without knowing it, I'd be able to prove an alibi for someone—someone whom they're planning to frame for the crime?"

Mr. Geraghty caressed his chin and gazed at her. "That's a thought," he said mildly. "Idea being that they're bumping off the possible witnesses before an arrest is made? I see. But for what time could you prove an alibi for—anyone whom we might suspect?"

"But I don't know, that's just it! When *was* Verney killed?"

"Between us, Miss Bruce, *we* don't know. Might have been a week ago, or not more than two, the coroner tells me. Makes a nice job for us, doesn't it?"

"I suppose you can narrow the time in other ways, though? After all, Chester couldn't very well have been dead on Wednesday night, when he telephoned Anna."

"Presuming that," said the inspector gravely, "we've still got three days and nights to check up on. Well; your two thugs got into your room—we'll say for the sake of argument that you weren't imagining that—and left it again; they shot at somebody who resembled you, tonight, and didn't kill her—just nicked her shoulder and scared the daylights out of her."

"And me. At the last second they may have seen that they were making a mistake."

"And maybe not. You were scared, you say; ever occur to you that there was no more to it than that? That the thugs were trying to scare you out of town?"

"Could be," Noel said with a sigh of utter weariness.

"You going to let 'em?" Mr. Geraghty inquired without emphasis.

She looked up at him slowly. "If you put it that way—no, I'm not. But if I had anywhere to go, perhaps I would. I don't know anyone in these parts, though, except the art-school people, and I—if I went to stay with any of them, I'd be more in the thick of things than I'd care for."

"I see your point," said the inspector deliberately. "Well, what are we going to do with you? I can't very well hold you in jail as a material witness, especially since you haven't witnessed much—according to your story. And you say you're scared to go back to your room."

"I thought," Noel said in a low tone, "there might be some place you'd recommend—but I guess there isn't a vacant room in the whole Bay Region."

"Maybe not. I could ask the flatfoot on the beat to keep an eye on your street, but we're still so short-handed on the Force that we're running in circles." Mr. Geraghty looked morose. "If—"

The small man in the corner spoke, so unexpectedly that Noel suffered a painful start. His one-word utterance sounded like "Jam."

Geraghty looked at him, and made a sound like a grunt, deep in his chest, which might have been a laugh. "Chan. I'd forgotten him, so help me. You might have something there, Kotock; you think he's still around?"

"Yeah," said Mr. Kotock with a wealth of meaning, and departed.

The inspector stood up. There seemed to be a twinkle in his deep-set eyes. "Maybe that's the solution, Miss Bruce. We might be able to provide you with an unofficial bodyguard."

"You don't mean—to go everywhere with me?"

"Not quite everywhere; just to keep an eye on you at crucial moments. You wouldn't want to go anywhere, or do anything, that'd embarrass him?" Geraghty inquired mildly.

"Not that way." Noel found herself chuckling. "But—a strange man obviously keeping an eye—"

"Well, Lockett won't embarrass you, either, not if I have you sized up right. I'll tell you, he was on the Force just before the war, and we'd taken him onto the Squad for a trial, and now he's crazy to get back into harness. Seems he hasn't got his medical discharge from the Army yet, though, and the Force can't give him a job till he's actually separated. In the meantime he's hanging around here like a kid with his nose against a candy store window." The Irishman shook his head pityingly. "Seems as if he doesn't know what a bellyache he may get if he breaks in!"

Noel looked up and grinned at him. She had at last perceived that there was something to this elderly detective besides patience and courtesy. There was a stir in the doorway and Mr. Kotock reappeared, followed by a young-looking man inclining to beef. He had round blue eyes in a round pink face.

"Miss Bruce," said Geraghty gravely, "let me present Mr. Lockett. Chan, how'd you like a job as bodyguard, strictly off the record?"

"Her?" said Lockett. He took a good look at Noel, and blinked. "Say, Chief, you want to get me in bad with Sarah?"

"He's got a girl in the Nurses' Corps," said the inspector, still gravely. "Sarah needn't worry, Chan. This'll be the most platonic job you ever heard of."

"I don't dig you, Chief," said Mr. Lockett.

"Never mind. It'll be strictly on the up-and-up. Means you have to go without sleep of nights, but there'll be times when Miss Bruce will be in safe company and you can take it then."

"That's okay. I'm pretty well caught up now on sack time."

Mr. Lockett was still looking at Noel, wonderingly, completely without offense. She said as the thought struck her, "What about my job with the Navy, Mr. Geraghty?"

"Might better take leave of absence for a week or so. Too many chances of getting caught out in a lonely spot."

"Would you want me to keep on going to Sherwin?"

"Why not? See your friends, do just what you'd ordinarily do. Might confuse those thugs a bit." Geraghty straightened his shoulders with an effort and took a side glance at the clock.

Noel got up, knowing she was dismissed. "But—how should I explain Mr. Lockett?"

"Chan to you, baby," said Mr. Lockett, still without offense.

"Chan, then. Is he to—to go to classes with me?"

The twinkle reappeared. "Might add to his education. As to explaining—why don't you just tell 'em the truth?"

"I see," Noel said, "like a black eye that you really did get by running into a door. Well, it's worth a try."

She turned to go, and paused. "Thank you, Inspector," she said, "for believing me when I said I was in danger and didn't know why."

"Oh, I believed you," Geraghty said. "You may very well be in danger, until you tell everything you know. Good night, Miss Bruce."

She went out, with Mr. Lockett at her heels. Her heart seemed to be going down slowly and inexorably like a pneumatic hoist. Until she told everything she knew...! He'd spotted something—

But I don't really know anything, anything at all, Noel told herself miserably.

"I never was a bodyguard before," said Chan Lockett from his position one pace behind her.

"I never had one," said Noel, "so we're even. What on *earth* am I going to do with you?"

"How big is your apartment, or wherever you live?"

"One room, and a sort of kitchenette, and a shower. I certainly can't ask you in!"

"We'll fix it up somehow," said Chan comfortably, and she began to feel that Inspector Geraghty hadn't, after all, taken leave of his senses. Absurd as this was, it was better than being alone and heartily afraid.

The heat of late morning woke her from a long but singularly unrefreshing sleep. Noel Bruce lay blinking at the streaked paper on the ceiling of her room, at the sun streaming in through motionless curtains, and the odd reflection where it struck the long-handled hand mirror on her dresser. She came back to realization with a painful start. In the light of morning, the melodrama of pursuit and terror seemed as remote as a screen play she might have witnessed the night before. What she was thinking of now was Tannehill, her friend, so horribly plunged into tragedy.

I've got to see her, Noel thought, swinging her feet to the floor. I ought to be with her—if she wants to see anyone.

She started coffee on the dismal little gas plate while she was taking a shower. The kitchenette arrangements in this room were odd in the extreme. What had once been a service porch, with a door to a rickety flight of steps leading to an alley, had been converted by the process of boarding up the outside door and setting an ancient cabinet against it. One end of the long narrow space had then been boarded off for a washroom with a minute stall shower. The most you could say for it was that it was compact.

She had just finished dressing when there was a rap on her room door. "It's Chan," said the slow cheerful voice. "Do I smell coffee? Are you decent?"

"You do smell it, but I can't offer you any in here!"

"Why not?" Mr. Lockett inquired through the door. "I been in once already, last night, when I made sure nobody was hidin'."

Noel thought of Miss Ibsen, next door, and then of Lockett's vigil somewhere outside the rooming house. "All right," she said. "Leave the door open."

"Swell." Mr. Lockett ambled in. His round blue eyes made a comprehensive sweep over the awkward shape of the room, the Raphael cartoon Noel's father had once brought her from Italy, and the freshness of the scrim curtains. "It's not so bad in daylight," he said. "Sun kind of brightens it up."

Noel gave him his coffee and a heated butterhorn. At intervals she found laughter bubbling up within her and suppressed it. Her bodyguard evidently wished her to be under no misapprehensions, for he was telling her in full detail about Sarah in the Nurses' Corps and pressing into her hands one after another of a large collection of snapshots. In the midst of this the footsteps of Miss Ibsen sounded outside in the hall, and the lady, descending the stairs on her way to her cashier's job in a local restaurant, gave vent to a sound of disapproval which was meant to be audible.

Chan Lockett was not so unobservant as his guileless countenance seemed to indicate. As the downstairs door closed he concluded his description of Sarah's charms, and remarked, "Now the old biddy's gone. I heard her stirrin' around her room all the time I was phonin' the Chief from that pay phone in the hall. That the only one you've got around here?" Noel nodded. "She had her ears hangin' out, most likely. Well. Last night I didn't know what I was in for, but I guess Butch doesn't think you're a murderer."

"Oh!" Noel said. "Was that what you had on your mind?"

"Part of it. You know," said Mr. Lockett, feeding a stick of chewing gum into his face, "this is the first time I ever heard of him putting a bodyguard on anyone. A tail, yes; but the other— you must have something kind of important."

"I certainly don't know what."

"He doesn't either, I guess. You must have said something that gave him a hint. Of course, he wouldn't want to work you over; he wouldn't do it to a young lady. He'll just sit tight and listen to you talk, and maybe trip yourself up. Or maybe," Lockett said, his eyes brightening, "the Chief hopes you'll spill something to me."

"I have nothing to spill," said Noel crisply. "I told Mr. Geraghty everything I knew last night. It seemed to me," she hastened on at the look of disbelief in his eyes, "that you were put on this job to save me from being harmed or murdered myself!"

"Oh, that. Yeah. Listen, the Chief says you never got a good look at these guys who were chasing you; but didn't you see the car?"

She made a hopeless gesture. "Nearly every car looks alike these days; five years old at least, paint dull, nothing to distinguish one from another."

"Any of your pals in the Art School got cars?"

"Most of them. Steffany hasn't," Noel murmured half to herself, "but Papa Gene drives a sedan around, and Hobart's got one, and the Watkinses use their family's car when they need one—"

"You look over their cars next time you get a chance."

"It wouldn't do any good. I'd never know it for sure. And some of them I couldn't count on seeing—I've heard Rome, for instance, talk about a car that a friend in the Service said he could use, but he doesn't drive it to the Plaster Works! Most of these people have just enough money to get by on, Chan. They don't drive regularly, you see?"

"Not much money?" Lockett looked surprised. "I always thought of these arty people as kind of doing it for fun, and playin' round a plenty." He shook his head. "I was just a rookie when they used to have those Art Balls up to the Fairmont. Boy! What went on!"

Noel said, "Don't expect anything like that these days. I wish I could think of something concrete about that car, or the people in it, but except for the heavy-set one's neck, I can't. They were nothing but shadows." She thought, That's not exactly true. One of them had on what looked like a Navy officer's cap, outside here in the street. None of the witnesses to the shooting had mentioned that, maybe the cap had been removed.

She narrowed her eyes, considering. There must have been some reason for that slight masquerade; someone had known that she would be disarmed, reassured, at the sight; therefore that person had probably guessed that she might have been expecting an officer—

Someone knew where she lived, and had followed her home on that night of September 12th, and had seen her and Miles kissing each other on the front steps...She stiffened suddenly; the door to the service entrance at the rear of the hall had been ajar, that night when she came up. If she had happened to be alone—

Oh, heavens, what a miserable business this could be. She had started with the intention of telling the police everything she knew, but leaving Miles out of it. That was fair enough, surely? He couldn't, certainly he couldn't, have had anything to do with it; but there was the awkwardness of his past connection with Anna. No. If anyone mentioned that former engagement, it wouldn't be Noel Bruce...But it was unexpectedly hard to get around the mention of his name! She'd had to name him once, in fact, as her companion on the Skyline adventure, because that was already on record and could be checked. That was normal enough, driving officers about was her job. But she'd forgotten Miss Ibsen, who might have witnessed more than a spoken good night, and she had had to skirt nimbly about the workman behind the cement mixer... "I dropped in four or five nights a week, Mr. Geraghty. Seems to me once there was a plaster caster there, I don't know which one—and I can't for the life of me remember which night! It was some time last week." There was another lie. She could patch it up all right when the time came, but still—the cement mixer had appeared obscurely in her dreams, with the inspector himself rising from behind it and saying "Jam," in a grave voice.

"You had nightmares last night, didn't cha?" Chan Lockett inquired idly.

Noel jumped. "I— Where were you that you could tell?"

"That balcony outside your window, over the porch. I shinnied up the post about three o'clock this morning. Felt too far away, sittin' in my car down in the street. Somebody got in here, you might yell, but by the time I got here you might've croaked."

Noel battled with mixed feelings. "You—you must have been very uncomfortable."

"Naw, I've slept in worse places. Nobody was snipin' at me with a rifle here, anyhow."

"Did I, uh, say anything in my sleep?"

"Yeah." Lockett chewed his gum happily. "You said, 'He saw us together. No use. He saw us.' You know, if I was you, I'd come clean with the Chief."

CHAPTER FIVE

SHE LAUGHED, AFTER A MOMENT. "I was trying to think what on earth I could have been dreaming about. Why, that was nothing. If you want to report it to Mr. Geraghty, I can explain it—I'll tell him I thought Peek-a-Boo Pennington was after me!"

Lockett turned to gaze at her, amazed disapproval in his look. "The private eye? Say, whose old man have you been playin' around with, a nice dame like you?"

"Oh, nobody's! Forget it, Chan, I was only joking." She was dimly aware of a fact that later acquaintance would bring home to her: the possible, the highly improbable, and the utterly absurd were as one in Mr. Lockett's eyes. She got up, and said, "I'm grateful to you for standing by on the balcony. I'll be all right for the rest of the day, though, so why don't you get your sleep?"

"What you going to do for the rest of the day?"

"I have to go and call on Tannehill—Mrs. Verney—if they'll let me."

"Where, out to that St. Francis Wood place where she was stayin'? I'll go too. Sure," he added at her look of surprised protest. "Butch'd wring my neck if I let you go *there* alone."

"Chan, this really is silly, it's broad daylight and I'm not that important! Oh, all right, I see you're going to make heavy weather of this. Come on!"

It wasn't such a bad idea after all, for Lockett had a car.

Noel's dictum about the comparative poverty of art students had not embraced the case of Anna Verney. Anna had inherited a moderate income on the death of her parents, and she also had an aunt in San Francisco who must be comfortably well off, judging by her home. It was in very good Spanish style, with tiles and balconies and a garden so skillfully landscaped that the closely encroaching grounds of the neighbors were hidden behind tall hedges with a complete illusion of privacy. On a rustic bench in the garden, almost out of sight of the windows, sat an unobtrusive man, whom Noel observed with a slight shock.

Lockett stopped, caught the man's eye and made a slight gesture of his head toward the house. The man shrugged. Lockett said, "Okay, baby, you go on in. I'll be around."

An elderly woman in black, probably the housekeeper who had been mentioned in Anna's newspaper interview, took Noel upstairs to a guest suite that occupied the rear of the second floor. The sitting room would have been all right for anybody's honeymoon, thought Noel, with an eye not only to the luxury of its furnishings but to the isolation from the rest of the house, even to the balcony with its outside staircase that led directly down to the garden.

In the adjoining bedroom, Anna Verney was lying on a chaise-longue, her head turned away, looking listlessly into the warm green of the tree-tops. She heard the steps, she said, "Oh, Bruce, honey!" and half sat up, holding out her arms. "I knew you'd come! I couldn't count on anyone's loyalty as I can on yours!"

"Oh, for heaven's sake," said Noel almost roughly, "what's loyalty got to do with it? I only wanted to tell you how sorry I am, that it—that this should happen to you, of all people."

"You're sweet, Bruce." Anna was dry-eyed, but she took one of her long difficult breaths and buried her face in Noel's shoulder. Noel looked down on the smooth gold hair, drawn into the simplest of knots low on the neck, and felt an actual pain of sympathy. She said, "You're all alone?"

"I sent the nurse away. Mrs. Fritz could do anything I needed done. I'm all right."

"Truly, Tannehill?"

"Truly." Anna lay back on the chaise-longue. She gave Noel a direct look. "I can say this to you, I couldn't to anyone else: the very—horrible qualities of this business about poor Chet are anaesthetic, in a way, because instead of just thinking that he's dead, and missing him, I have to answer questions and try to pick up obscure clues out of my memory and wonder why—why—why. It takes the whole thing one step farther from reality."

"That's rather wonderful of you, Tannehill," said Noel slowly. "You don't mind talking about it?"

"Oh, I mind. But again, the more I talk the less real it seems. Are there"—she gave a faint smile—"any things you want to discuss?"

Noel opened her lips to say indignantly that certainly there were not; instead, she heard herself blurting out, "Did Chester know about Miles Coree?"

Anna Verney's head turned swiftly. "Coree—*you* know Coree? But of course, it was you talking to him that night at the Art Center. Oh, Bruce, I lied to you about being there that time, I'm sorry—but you asked me right in front of Chester if my friend had found me, and—well, I can't explain it just now, but it was simpler all around just to say I hadn't been there... Yes, of course Chester knew I was engaged to someone else. He knew as well as I what a tragic thing we were doing, but—it was too strong for us. I haven't any other excuse. Coree understood, after I'd written to him, at least he said so, but—I hadn't known he was in port, and when I saw him without warning I just couldn't face it. I—suppose I hoped I'd never have to see him again."

"Tannehill, dear, you don't have to explain anything to me. I just—I couldn't help wondering, because none of us had known about Miles."

Anna gave her a swift unsmiling look. "I know. Probably that part of it can't be kept secret, but I—well, I wish there were some way to—pass over the fact that Coree was in town about the time that Chet must have died."

"I haven't said anything about it, myself, except in mentioning things that were already on record." Noel felt her way among disturbing thoughts. "But of course as soon as Miles gets back in town he'll talk to the police himself."

"Do you think so?" Anna frowned faintly. She glanced out the window and shifted the conversation. "Who was the young man who came in the gate with you?"

Noel grinned. "I'm telling everyone that he's my bodyguard."

"That's not a bad story," said Anna appreciatively. "I must say I can't see any reason why the police should suspect *you*."

"Good heavens! Did you think he was trailing me, that openly?"

"Well, the Law is watching every move *I* make," said Mrs. Verney simply.

"Tannehill, I can't take that seriously. Why on earth—how could they possibly—"

"Suspect me of murder?" The low voice was steady. "I don't quite know why myself. You know how things were between us."

"I suppose I do," said Noel absently. She thought of that announcement party for Tannehill's intimate friends, starting at the Plaster Works with champagne; of Red Hobart walking in uninvited and drunk and jabbing at Chester Verney with needle-sharp insinuations: "Is this the third or fourth time you've tried it, Verney?" And the unruffled blandness of Verney's heavy features, his unusually charming smile as he said, "The fourth in a lifetime. But this one's going to stick, isn't it, dear?" Anna had been thinking about something else, for at first the question had not seemed to penetrate, and then she had turned to her husband and smiled in her turn; that beautiful look she sometimes wore, that never failed to melt anyone's heart. "Yes, I know. You were in love."

"I took this marriage as a job, not always an easy one," said Anna musingly, "but it seemed what I wanted."

"And you've always had what you wanted." Noel smiled, it was a familiar small joke among Tannehill's friends.

"What possible purpose could I have had? They always think of money first." She was back to the questions. "That doesn't mean anything in this case, of course. Chet left me a few hundred dollars."

"Tannehill!"

"Oh, yes! I knew about it from the first, naturally. He lived on a lavish scale—we'd have done it together, if—things had gone right. He's always made money, but twice at least he's nearly cleaned himself out paying a lump sum to his wives when they got their divorces; he and his law partners divided big retainers, but Chet lived right up to that income. He'd have been set up again next month when the Crandall case comes to trial, with another huge fee, but until then—no, I was residuary legatee, and at this moment that gets me about fifteen hundred dollars. He had business insurance that goes to his partners, and a life policy that pays his child by his first marriage—"

"He had a child?" Noel was fairly giddy with successive amazements.

"One he never saw—from that misalliance when he was under age, when his parents bought the woman off. A horrible person, one gathers," Anna said. She gave Noel a sidelong look in which malice glinted. "But my other two predecessors must have been fairly dreadful too. I told Chet it made me nervous about myself, but he only laughed and said that his taste was formed at last, after three mistakes."

Noel said, "The last Mrs. Verney was very nice to me the one time I met her. But what about the child?"

"Oh, that. The marriage was annulled, you know, and when Chet's parents found out the baby was coming they made the woman leave town—disappear, and promise never to see him again. The child's claims were to be covered by his insurance. He had no other children, poor Chet. We—I might—" She shook her head fiercely and gazed at her hands.

"Don't say any more. I shouldn't have let you talk so much, it's harder on you than you know. Tannehill, is your hand all right?"

"Going to be. It would have to get infected, of course." The golden-haired woman got up and walked impatiently back and forth across the room.

"You were a silly not to let us get a doctor the night you burned it. Think what might have happened!"

Anna Verney gave her an appealing look. "I know, but I was afraid he'd hurt me some more! I just wrapped it up—yes, I should have known better, you needn't tell me—"

The black-clad housekeeper knocked gently and opened the door. "It's the inspector to see you again, Mrs. Verney. Should I tell him you don't feel well enough?"

"Oh, dear. I thought we'd been over every smallest detail." None of Anna Tannehill's friends had ever seen her smiling serenity disturbed, no matter what the occasion; this time was no exception, but Noel saw that the lines of fatigue deepened in her friend's face. "No, Fritz, he knows Miss Bruce is with me. Ask him to come up...Bruce, stay a few minutes, I'll ask him— oh, Inspector Geraghty, good afternoon." Anna went back to the chaise-longue and sank down. "Have you more questions for me?" She smiled with a rueful lift of the eyebrows. "Let Miss Bruce hold my hand, won't you, please?"

No man, Noel thought, had ever failed to fall victim to that soft loveliness. "Only a few questions, Mrs. Verney," said

Geraghty courteously, sitting down in the indicated chair. "We've been trying to trace the woman your husband spoke of during that telephone call on the night of the twelfth."

"And I've been trying to think of her name." The low voice held a wealth of apology. "I can't remember, Inspector. He said something about her having spotted him on the train to Los Gatos, worse luck, and having insisted on talking to him. It seems to me that she was a witness in the Crandall case, or connected with it somehow, and he'd been seeing her privately, but he'd never happened to mention her name to me before, and it simply went out of my mind. Amber? Aubrey? Sauber? Something—I wish I could think of it!"

"We haven't found any trace of her," said the Irishman, his eyes on his small notebook. He wrote down some brief notation. "Mr. Verney's partners had never heard of anyone by a name that sounded like that. Of course there are dozens of witnesses in that will case...That telephone call puzzles me, I don't mind telling you, Mrs. Verney." The deep-set eyes were fixed on some point beyond the two women. "Your husband wasn't seen in Los Gatos at all on that Wednesday; of course there was no reason why anyone should have noticed him especially. The trains are still crowded, and plenty of people get off there. But we haven't been able to trace the call."

"You don't mean that, possibly, Chester wasn't calling from there at all?" Anna turned slightly pale and looked bewildered.

"That's one possibility. Did the operator—"

"I didn't take the call at first. Mrs. Fritz would know. She heard me talking afterward, too."

"Yes, she reported on what you said," the inspector remarked, "looking daggers at us for asking her about your business. Things like, 'Yes, dear, is everything all right?' and, 'Oh, did she? What rotten luck. Of course she will have to be dealt with sooner or later,' and, 'I'll wait to hear from you.'"

"That was about the substance of what we said. Dear Fritz," said Anna Verney, smiling, "she's always felt she couldn't do enough for me. She wouldn't lie, though."

"No, I imagine not."

"She's always felt to me like a member of the family. I couldn't help being lonely after Chester went, and I got her to come up and sleep in this sitting room from Wednesday night on." Anna gestured toward the outer room from which the balcony led. "It was a comfort to me. I didn't want to go back to my studio; frankly, Inspector, I felt a little queer about having everyone know that Chester and I were taking our honeymoon separately!"

"I can see that." Geraghty's melancholy face did not change in expression. "Mrs. Fritz says she didn't see your husband at all, but she heard his voice in the evenings."

"Of course she didn't see him. We kept out of her way, and I sent her out daytimes. Chet—oh, well, we've been over all this."

"You mustn't get upset, Mrs. Verney," said the inspector soothingly. "We're just trying to trace his movements; that's the only way we'll ever get anywhere on this case."

"I know," Anna said wearily. "Inspector, haven't you found out a single thing?"

Geraghty did not reply for a time. When he spoke there was a curious note in his voice. "We've got a few things, a line on the identity of Claude Pruitt, for instance. You're sure you never heard of him, Mrs. Verney?"

She made a helpless gesture. "If I did, I've forgotten it completely. Who was he?"

"I'll tell you tomorrow, perhaps, after we've checked up a bit more. Or maybe you'd better just read the papers." The inspector looked at Noel and then consulted his notebook again. It was a plain gesture of dismissal.

Departing, Noel thought how oddly fragmentary was her knowledge of Anna Tannehill. They had talked more intimately this afternoon than ever before, and there was an indefinable difference in her impression, as if a preconceived picture had been blurred. And yet she considered Tannehill one of her real friends.

Emerging from the cool hall into a blaze of sunlight, blinking and dazzled, Noel reflected on what Anna had done for her. Tannehill's influence with Papa Gene Fenmer had not ceased when their admitted affair was over. She had used it to promote a scholarship for Noel's second year at Sherwin.

And, thought Noel, she didn't know me well at all, then. I'd never done anything for her, heaven knows, and it isn't as if she would ever ask anything in return. But what I wouldn't do—

Mr. Lockett was placidly chewing gum in the car. He said, in answer to her question, "Naw, I don't mind waitin'. The housekeeper gave me something to eat, anyhow. I guess she thought I was your chauffeur."

"Don't you have a way with you, though!" said Noel, slamming the door. "Always getting handouts from women!"

Lockett looked aggrieved, but started the car without comment. Noel looked absently through the window at the winding, tree-lined street, and found herself trying to reconstruct the movements of Chester Verney when he left the guest suite of Mrs. Tannehill Bates on the morning of September the twelfth. A short half block to the bus stop, a bench there for persons waiting—or the car line a quarter of a mile over. Any chance of picking up a cab out here? Probably not.

"I've been thinking of something, Chan. It seemed to me, considering the grisly way that her own statue was used to hide Verney's body, and the fact that her beautiful work was ruined—I've wondered if the police had thought of looking for someone who hated *Anna*. And yet I don't see how anyone could."

"Say, listen," Lockett said. "You might tell me a few things. I expect Butch knows about 'em already, but I kind of don't like to bother him or Kotock with questions, see, because I'm not official. But I've been wonderin' why in hell this guy was stripped down and shellacked!"

"That's easy enough. I don't know much about sculpture, except from hearing my friends talk, but I know the general idea of armatures, and how the clay's put on and taken off again. The clay won't stick to cloth, nor to skin; but it will to shellacked surfaces."

"Oh, I get you. The killer bumped off Verney right there, prob'ly, and then had to hide his body. I suppose they figured this Mrs. Verney wouldn't be round for a while, account of her honeymoon, is that right?" Lockett interrupted himself to dodge two jockeying cars at an intersection, beating an indignant bray out of his horn. Noel's driving experience led her to look at him with admiration as he swerved to safety by a matter of inches. "Well, look, baby," he went on, unperturbed. "How'd they know somebody wouldn't take those rags off for a look at the statue a couple days after he was killed?"

"Nobody would! No one but the student or the instructor would ever touch a clay model, it'd be worse than reading another person's mail."

"Yeah? That'd fix it up, all right. Here's this statue, life size, nobody's goin' to touch it—"

"And lying down," Noel said. "Hardly any armature."

"*Who* was?"

"The figure. The others, the standing and sitting ones, have a framework of pipe and heavy wire inside them, for the clay to be built up on. This kind of figure doesn't take much armature."

"I get it. Good enough place to hide a stiff, better'n shipping it off somewhere in a trunk. Seems that shellac and the clay slowed up the decomposing business, makes it harder to guess when the guy was bumped off. The murderer knows it's no use tryin' to keep people from identifyin' Verney, somebody'd be sure to miss him pretty soon, so he doesn't bother hidin' the wallet and stuff. The clothes had to come off, I reckon they could've been burned in one of those stoves in the Works, but they leave all the junk that wouldn't burn. Okay," said Mr. Lockett, as if communing with himself. "But what gets me—"

He fell silent for a moment, and Noel glanced at the nondescript buildings and stores of upper Market Street.

Her train of thought came back for a moment: once in town, Chester Verney could easily have slipped into the world of half-shadows, the realm of the anonymous. He had been seen, as it happened, by the woman called Mrs. Amber, but Mrs. Amber was completely a shadow. No one had heard of her...It was a possibility, was it, that Verney had not left town at all, that his mention of a fictitious person was "mere corroborative detail?" But if that were true, why on earth should he have wanted to stay in town?

"I tell you what I don't figure out," Chan said, "and that's why he had to be buried in this statue at all."

"Why, you just said it yourself; it was a good—"

"No, that's not it, baby. Listen, you have to go back to your room right off? I'd kind of like a look at the Plaster Works again. Okay?" He made for a perilous left turn at Van Ness. "It was good, for a last resort. Better'n taking the body out in your car, with chances of bein' seen either then or when you dumped it somewhere; and wherever you dumped it, there was the chance it'd be found in a couple of days, which of course there wasn't here. The delay here gave somebody time to fix up an alibi, or anyhow to gain time. Mixes up the police, and the witnesses too. Hard to say just who was in which saloon two weeks ago. Okay. But look; if you're going to kill this guy at all, why pick out the Plaster Works to do it in? Nobody's going to conk him someplace else and then lug him in there, and be cornered on a long job like puttin' him into this statue. He must have been killed there. Well—it narrows the field so darn much that you'd think the murderer would have done it any other way, any at all, if he had the choice."

"Narrows the field," Noel repeated.

"Yeah, sure. Must have been one of the sculptors or sculptresses, you see?"

"Don't call them sculptresses, for heaven's sake. Woman sculptor is the term."

"Because nobody else is going to know about this shellac, or how to get this clay off and put it on again."

"Go on!" said Noel incautiously. "I'm no sculptor, but I could have done it."

"Huh?" Lockett's round blue eyes were on her, startled.

"I don't mean I did! I couldn't have pulled that body around, actually, probably no woman could, but I'd know about the statue part. You could do it yourself, now that I've told you." She stopped suddenly and bit her lip.

The car slid to a stop in front of the familiar wooden fence. There was an afternoon wind blowing in dreary hot gusts; dusty papers shifted in the gutters, and the brilliance of the sunlight somehow intensified the forlorn and empty look of the street. One person was in sight, a uniformed policeman standing guard at the gate. He started to wave them on, and then hesitated, and crossed to the car.

"Oh, it's you, Lockett," he said. "Chief says nobody's to go inside yet. You want anything special?"

"Nope. Just another look."

"Come in the yard if you want. No farther."

"That'll do." Lockett got out; Noel debated staying in the car, and then decided to follow. She said as they passed through the gate, "What are you expecting to find, Chan?"

"I dunno." He hesitated, looked sideways at her, and then said in a mutter inaudible to the guard's ears, "I kind of want to get a line on some of these sculptors, what kind of fellows they are. The guys that are interviewin' them can tell, maybe, but I haven't got any job like that, I just have to guess, maybe by lookin' at the kind of things they carve. Now, look, this statue." He waved a hand at the block of stone in the courtyard. "Whose is that? What's he tryin' to do?"

"Will Rome's doing it, and I couldn't tell you what it will be. Some sort of kneeling figure, I think; see, here are the bowed shoulders, and a cowl over the head—he hasn't shaped the features."

"But it looks like nothing human," Lockett said plaintively. He scratched his head and absently put a stick of gum into his mouth. "What kind of guy—"

"Queer, maybe, but brilliant," said Noel. "He has some idea here, even in this unfinished state you can feel life in it. It's—straining at its bonds of stone. Do you suppose I heard that somewhere, or did I make it up?"

"I don't dig you," Chan Lockett told her despairingly.

"Rome's something of a law unto himself. He's an independent, you know—established. About forty, and rather sad-looking, and gruff—not fond of women—and with some unexpected traits about him; he's mad about jive, and he's found two or three places in town where the men from various bands get together after the night spots close up and have private swing sessions. They let him come and listen. Of all the incongruous sights, that must be the top: Rome in his shaggy clothes and his shaggy head with those great thick points of hair running down onto his neck, and that big seal ring he usually wears on his left hand—in the middle of a bunch of swing performers!"

"And he did that." Lockett gazed once more at the statue. "What was that you said, about its being sort of alive? Yeah, I guess I see what you mean."

He removed his gaze and focused it on the door that led to the Plaster Works. "Who d'you suppose went in there to meet Verney?" he murmured.

Noel saw, so clearly that it gave her a physical shudder, a vision of Chester Verney stepping through that door: the heavy, handsome, smartly dressed man, unhurried, greeting someone in those ringing deep tones that could sway a jury by their timbre alone, sauntering to his death. She saw, not hard sunlight on battered and paintless boards, but a deserted dusk.

"Chan," she said, "it must have happened at night. It had to, because people were working here every day until nearly seven. And it couldn't very well have been after midnight, because then the lights—there must have been some light for the work that was done on that clay model—would have been too conspicuous. I suppose that narrows it too?"

"Yeah, lights. Beats me why somebody didn't report lights." He accepted her premise casually, and she realized that the police must have thought that up long ago.

"I think that a few weeks ago the plaster casters were doing overtime on some sort of housing contract. Maybe if anyone in the neighborhood saw a light on—whenever the murder was committed, it wouldn't make much impression, he'd just think the plant was going again." She paused, frowning. "But for Chester Verney to come down here alone, to meet someone at night, doesn't make sense. He was a smart man. He wouldn't act like the people in the old novels who'd get a call to come to the deserted warehouse at midnight, and who'd go, and find their enemies lying in wait. What on earth got him here?"

"Yeah," Lockett said, "and when? He calls his wife on Wednesday night, maybe he comes on down here afterward; maybe he hides around somewhere and it's Thursday or Friday or even Saturday night, the coroner could make a slip up on one day. And what time? Seven, you said—"

"If he'd come any time before dark he'd have been seen," Noel said on a sudden recollection. "There was that old watchman staying around until nine or so every night!"

"Watchman?" Lockett snapped his fingers. "Not an old coot lookin' as if he was goin' to fall apart, red nose, kind of crummy eyes, around five feet six, stubble beard?"

"It could be," said Noel, smiling. "I've never had a good look at him."

Lockett looked thoughtful. "Bird like that was wanderin' around here yesterday night, asked me what went on. I told him it was murder, and he went off kind of grinning to himself. I got a notion to—naw, the Chief wouldn't miss a bet like that. I'll work it into the conversation, like, some time when I see him."

A car stopped outside with grinding brakes. A huge voice was heard: "Officer! Open the gate, if you please. I need some material for one of my students."

A brief but spirited dialogue ensued between Papa Gene and the policeman on guard, the former invoking the names of the Mayor and the Commissioners, the latter sticking to the orders of Inspector Geraghty. In the midst of it, Eugene Fenmer was diverted by the sight of Noel and Lockett, who had approached the gate with deep interest.

"Little Bruce, by all that's holy," he roared. "Returning to the scene of your crime?"

"Papa Gene, for heaven's sake don't say things like that. My friend here takes them seriously."

"Ah, yes." Fenmer dismissed his argument with the officer by waving his hand and turning his back. "And who *is* your fat friend?"

"My bodyguard. Don't you think I need one?"

Papa Gene shook with loud laughter. "With a body like that, Bruce, you need more than one. I've offered myself, d'you think it's kind to choose someone else?"

"Well, at least I get exclusive attention from Chan. Mr. Lockett, Mr. Fenmer…A lot of good you'd be, you old rip," she added amiably. "Always chasing off after a new student, or making passes at old lady Sherwin in public—"

There was more laughter. "That got us some more endowment. She loved it. Come and have a drink, young Bruce, and bring your guard along for your peace of mind. Glad to meet you, Lockett." He clambered back into his own car and started the motor, shouting, "Follow me; just around the corner to DiMaggio's."

Lockett was nudging Noel violently. "That the car?" he whispered.

She looked startled, and her eyes flicked over the car as it moved off. She said, "I'd forgotten. It could be. Papa Gene's car has just been washed and polished, hasn't it? And the license plate got a good scrubbing while they were at it."

CHAPTER SIX

INSPECTOR GERAGHTY, the unwitting object of Chan Lockett's hero worship, was spending Saturday afternoon in a state of hearty dissatisfaction. He had returned from his interview with Anna Verney looking more melancholy than ever, and by four o'clock had read and digested a staggering mass of reports, all to no good purpose.

A few witnesses, indeed, had professed to have noticed lights in the Plaster Works at night; but not one could fix the night, and on the investigation's being pressed, it turned out that most of these memories went back to August, when the plaster casters had been officially working overtime.

No one of the dozens of persons interviewed had any recollection of seeing Chester Verney after he left the house in St. Francis Wood. The housekeeper, Mrs. Fritz, had been absent for all the daylight hours by permission of Mrs. Verney, and so would not have seen his departure in midmorning. The next-door neighbor, one Sheldon Scott, was of little more help; he had seen lights in the Bates' guest wing on Monday and Tuesday nights when he drove into his own garage at ten o'clock. "Mr. Verney was certainly in those guest rooms on both nights," he said. "I, uh, know Mrs. Bates slightly and I was interested in her niece's marriage. It was with no, uh, prurient curiosity, I assure you, that I glanced up at those windows; my driveway is close to Mrs. Bates', with a hedge between. The couple were listening to the radio on one occasion, I saw Mr. Verney's head clearly outlined in shadow on the wall, very like a Roman emperor; I had seen pictures of his fine features. And on Tuesday, I think it was, there was a man's voice speaking with affection. I trust that the Verneys would not have regarded this as, uh, prying? No, I saw no one on Wednesday morning."

"Maybe it helps to eliminate his law partners," Geraghty said to the silent Mr. Kotock who was in attendance, "because Verney was the goose that laid the golden eggs in that firm and they'd be fools to kill him for his insurance; and it helps some more to cut out all the plaster casters. None of 'em knew Verney except through the newspapers, and all of 'em have families and have been home from six-thirty on, every night for the past two weeks. But that doesn't cut out everyone but the sculptors, by a long shot. Not yet, it doesn't. We got this Pruitt business on our minds, it means we've got to dig up anybody out of Verney's past who could have held a grudge against him, and an ex-D.A. has plenty of people like that hanging around."

Mr. Kotock nodded gloomily. After a silence he inquired, "Handout?"

"I suppose the Press room's bulging at the seams," said Mr. Geraghty irritably. "You can let 'em up here in a few minutes. Did you get anything out of that old bum, the one that was hired as a watchman?"

Mr. Kotock spread his hands eloquently.

"Tough, or doesn't know anything? The boys don't even know that, huh? I'll try the let-down business." He heaved up his long frame from the chair and sighed.

The ancient and grimy cubbyholes of the Hall of Justice were no more depressing than the old ruin who sat in one of them, slouched on a hard chair. His age might have been guessed at anything from fifty to seventy-five; it was possible that he shaved sometimes, for his grayish whiskers were at stubble length, but it seemed unlikely that he ever washed. He peered up swiftly out of red-rimmed eyes that made Geraghty think of a ferret.

No trace of the inspector's distaste appeared in his mild look. He sat down and said, "Hello, Dad. Have a smoke?"

Old Dad accepted the gift, peered at it closely and allowed his upper lip to curl back over the wreck of teeth as if in disappointment. He then lit it shakily and gazed at the floor.

"Soon as I heard the boys had you down here, I was afraid they'd got to feeling rough," said the inspector. "I called 'em off."

"Yeah, an' then you come round soft-talkin', expectin' to get somethin' out of me thataway," Old Dad burst out in a sudden snarl. "Think I don't know? 'S an old game!"

"Ah, you're onto us," said Geraghty easily. "No harm in trying, is there?"

"No harm, hell! Pullin' a fella in here that ain't done nothin', mindin' his own business. I tell ya I don' know no more than I knowed this mornin'."

"I didn't hear what you said when they brought you in. Go over it once more, Dad." Behind the ease of Geraghty's manner was a hint of the pressure he could exert. In spite of himself the derelict responded to it. "I know your name's Patrick Malone," Geraghty went on, "but everybody calls you Old Dad. That's good enough for me. You were in the First World War, you have a little pension that keeps a roof over your head in that dump on North Beach, you've been unemployed for some years."

"Got a job bein' watchman for that stone statue," Old Dad said. "Guy that's carvin' it hires me to scare off the kids."

He gave an unexpected and wholly dreadful grin, making Geraghty think of the Old Man of the Mountain. "Oughta hear 'em holler when they see me. Got a gun, but I don't hafta use it. Don't hafta do nothin' but jus' sit there in the yard, nights and Sundays, an' if the kids're too brash maybe kinda flap my arms at 'em, see?"

Geraghty said that he saw. "The job make you much money, Dad?" he added.

"No cash, har'ly. Fella gits me a meal ticket. Scairt I wouldn't show up, maybe, 'f he paid cash." The red eyes peered out again with an eerie effect of shrewdness. Sodden Old Dad might be, but he was not witless.

"What is it, snow or Mary Warner?" the inspector said casually.

"Huh?" Old Dad's face settled back into vacuity. "No cash, where'd I git anything like that?"

"There are ways. You might know 'em better than the Narcotic Squad." Geraghty watched him; was that gleam in the eyes one of hidden laughter?

"They all take cash," said Old Dad, with truth.

Geraghty let it drop. "You been showing up at work okay, the past two weeks?"

"Yeah, I been there every night. Yeah, an' maybe I seen lights there one night, was it any of my mix? Guy hires me to scare off the kids, I ain't got no call to go nowhere but that yard, see?"

"This is Saturday. Was it this week you saw the lights? Last week? Come on, Dad, you can remember." Geraghty's deep-set eyes were inscrutable, but behind their mask he was puzzled. The old fellow wasn't hopped up right now, but neither was he in the madly jittering state of an addict craving a shot. In the latter case he might have been bribed with a promise. Not a real hophead as yet, the inspector thought; he's had some kind of dope, enough to make him want more sometimes, enough to make him crafty and stupid by turns; and smart enough to conceal which state he was in at the moment.

"'While ago," Old Dad muttered, his eyes beginning to shift. "Not when they was workin' there nights, some other night. Don't rec'lect when. Gah dammit, how ya think I'd rec'lect?" He began to whine. "Days're all the same, I ain't got no way to know one from 'nother."

"What if it paid you to remember?" Geraghty said casually.

Old Dad shook his head. "Got no way to rec'lect. Toosd'y, Thursd'y, I dunno."

"You see," said Geraghty softly, "we could promise, at least, to protect you. Somebody's hired you to keep still, isn't that it? How long do you think that person is going to keep on paying you?"

"Who's payin' me? Ain't got a cent," Old Dad snarled.

"Then maybe the person has promised to pay you. Wouldn't it be cheaper for him just to slit your throat some time?"

The ferret eyes flickered once more, but the derelict shook his head in slow bewilderment. "Lissen, Cap, I ain't bein' paid by nobody; 'cause, see, I don't know nothin'. I never saw nothin'."

"Well, Dad," said Geraghty, rising, "in that case we've got no reason to keep you here. Can't pull you in on a vag charge so long as you've got your job. Might be, though, you'd find a nice safe cell the best place to be. You come back and talk to us when you see my point. Maybe your memory would improve too."

The shrewd look returned for a moment. Old Dad heaved himself up and added to his murky costume a sharp touch in the shape of an old chauffeur's cap. "Safe enough," he muttered as if to himself. "Can't rec'lect nothin'." He added unexpectedly, "You been white enough, Cap, but there ain't a thing."

He was almost credible. There was a queer rascally self-respect about him in spite of the shambling and hangdog gait with which he disappeared across Portsmouth Square.

Inspector Geraghty watched him out of sight. He shook his head and opened the door to the newsmen.

Noel Bruce, entering the dim cavern of the bar at Joe DiMaggio's, stopped and put out a hand to halt Lockett. "There," she murmured, "you wondered what kind of a man thought up that stone statue. That's Will Rome, talking to Papa Gene."

Across the low tone of cocktail conversation, Fenmer's voice carried easily. "It'll keep, man, it'll keep! They wouldn't even let *me* in…No, for some reason I'm unable to fathom, the courtyard is suspect as well. Don't make a fool of yourself by insisting."

Will Rome, hunched on a stool at the end of the bar, lifted his sad-shaped eyes and said something which the approaching pair could not hear. Noel slid onto the stool next to Papa Gene and said, "Hello, Rome."

"The little Bruce," said Fenmer, "is being untrue to Art. She has a new follower, Lockett by name." He gestured in introduction.

"Zat so?" Rome muttered. He looked up again, seemingly taking Chan's measure in a long slow scrutiny. Mr. Lockett chewed his gum calmly, and after a pause replied, "Yeah, she's showin' me round. Takes me everywhere, don't you, baby?"

"Fine time you pick to show anyone around," said Rome jerkily, "just after hell breaks loose."

"But that," Fenmer pointed out with an oddly deliberate tempo, "has nothing to do with Bruce."

"No matter. I guess she's in on it, like every other living soul that's been near the Plaster Works. Mean to say the police haven't had you on the carpet, Bruce?" Rome poured the rest of the drink down his throat and slid the glass across the bar. "'What were your relations with Verney?'" he quoted savagely. "'Describe every move you've made for a month. Describe everybody's reactions.'"

"Well, Rome," said Noel, taking a sip of her own drink, "they got under your skin all right. That's about the longest speech you've ever made to me."

"All one family now," Rome remarked, looking at his glass again. "Just like a family, too. Everyone thinking up reasons to suspect the other fellow, tell something on him—anything to convince the cops it was somebody else who did it!"

Eugene Fenmer said, "Have a drink, Rome, and let's turn to some lighter aspects of the artists' life. Young Lockett is a newcomer, after all."

"Yeah," said Chan in his cheerful drawl, "I don't know much about the stuff you people are doin', but I sure admire it. Say, you mind telling me what that statue of yours is goin' to be when it's done?"

"You've seen it? How'd you get in there?"

"Just gawpin' round," Chan grinned at him. "Cop at the gate let us take a peek."

"Hell! They wouldn't let me in to work!" Rome swung off the bar stool, his face once more heavily sullen. "G'by, Fenmer, Bruce—I'm leaving. Well, I'll tell you, buddy—that's a figure of Death, ready to touch somebody; only it'll be blind, as blind as justice."

"That's quite a conception, Rome," said Noel. "A war death, that takes one man and leaves another, without reason?"

"Yeah. And it won't stand a chance in this competition, I know that. They want weeping angels, or noble soldiers, or something that makes death seem sensible. I'm not giving it to 'em," said Will Rome gruffly, and went out. Fenmer's eyes followed him in an unblinking gaze.

"He feels kind of strong about it," Lockett commented mildly. "Must've been in the war."

"Not this one," Fenmer said.

"I suppose," said Noel, "that the Verney business has stirred him up. If that's a neurosis from World War One, he's kept it alive for a long time and it's riding him hard now...A blind Death. Do you think that's the kind that found Chester Verney, that he was a chance victim?"

"What," Fenmer inquired, "gave rise to that remarkable thought?"

"I knew him a little. I can't see any reason why he should have been murdered, not in his own personality at least. No, think about it really, Papa Gene. He was personally honest, he had power but nobody's ever hinted that he misused it, he had charm but he never went too far with it."

"Not with you," said Fenmer, and his black eyes sparked as he glanced at her. "Perhaps you're right, those surface indications *may* have revealed the true man. So, you have no theories at all as to motive."

"Not sensible ones," said Noel, glancing with sudden caution at Chan Lockett. Chan took a swallow of his drink and began to sing "Doin' what comes natur'lly," in harmony with the strains of the bartender's radio.

"Then you are unique. Unique," Papa Gene repeated in a silky voice, "in many ways."

Noel caught his eye and felt suddenly glad that Chan was on her other side. She had always maintained that Papa Gene was safe enough when he understood that you meant to hang onto your virtue; but she could almost sympathize with the women who had given way to the vitality in his squarely built body and to tones as kindly confidential and admiring as these. That white hair and the beard had their own *cachet*.

"So you have theories?" she said with interest. "And did you pass the buck, too? Rome seemed to think that—"

"Hold it," said Chan Lockett and grabbed her arm in a gesture for silence. "Hey, Jack, turn up that radio, will you?"

The bartender, scurrying along with an order, gave him a harried look and made no move toward the radio. Fenmer, who had listened, now rose as if electrified. "They have identified Claude Pruitt," he bellowed; and heads throughout the lounge turned in amazement as he charged through the crowd, ducked through the door under the bar, and himself twisted at the knob of the radio on the shelf behind. The announcer's voice blared out:

"—one among many aliases of the man whom Chester Verney convicted of forgery in 1936. An employee of the

Golden State Savings and Loan Company in Bakersfield, California, Pruitt had served a previous sentence in Illinois for a similar offense and presented forged references to his first employers in Bakersfield. Throughout the trial he protested his innocence of the charge, that of diverting stock certificates. The prosecution was a personal triumph for Verney, and Pruitt was sentenced to ten years in the penitentiary. Courtroom drama was added when Pruitt screamed defiance at the district attorney alleging that Verney was railroading an innocent man in order to make a showing before the coming election. Pruitt's young wife was ill at the time and did not appear in the courtroom. According to Bakersfield sources, she disappeared soon afterward. Pruitt died of pneumonia in San Quentin after serving seven years of his sentence, shortened by good behavior; he would have been released within two months... Tick-tick-a-tick...On the labor front—"

"Thank you, gentlemen," said Papa Gene, releasing the dial knob to the scandalized barkeep. With a majestic air he stalked down the inside of the bar and ducked out into the crowd. "Young Bruce, you might have kept this stool for me; never mind, bring your friend and come out."

Lockett paused outside the door to the lounge and took a long breath of the warm air scented with frying fish and popcorn from the streets of Fisherman's Wharf. "Lot of smoke in there," he said. "Have some gum, sir?"

Papa Gene refused politely. "An old enemy, by all that's holy," he said reminiscently, and quaked with laughter. "Oh, ho, ho! Butch must be hard up if he feeds the boys anything like that." He led the way to his car. "What the reporters couldn't do with that! Monte Cristo in San Francisco Bay; did Claude Pruitt die? Has he returned to wreak revenge on the man who sentenced him unjustly? God give me strength," Papa Gene roared.

"I don't get it, sir," said Lockett thoughtfully. "I know the Chief and he wouldn't feed 'em anything because he was hard up. This Pruitt would be about thirty-eight or forty now,

I figure. You're older than that, Mr. Fenmer—but of course he could have been older too. Watkins—I know Hobart, I don't guess he's been in jail in the last ten years—this Rome fellow would about fill the bill. What do you know about him?"

Papa Gene had paused, frozen with one foot in his car, to listen to this speech. He now exchanged an incredulous glance with Noel. "On my sullied soul," he whispered prayerfully, "he believes it. He's working out—"

"Humor him, Papa Gene," said Noel, herself giving way to laughter. "He's a nice guy, you know. Off the record, did you escape from Quentin three years ago?"

"Of that," said Fenmer with jocose emphasis, "I'm innocent. It can be proved. Other sins—but we will not go into that."

Lockett looked from one to the other, his large face perplexed. "How about this Will Rome?" he insisted.

"Rome? He's—" Papa Gene broke into a broad grin. "His past is veiled in mystery. He purportedly came here from New York, in—aha! You have something there, soldier, he arrived here early in 1944. He has no wife, to the best of anyone's knowledge. He is gloomy, as befits a man who is lurking about meditating revenge. If someone stepped up to him and muttered, 'Pruitt, I know you,' I would not answer for the consequences." Papa Gene settled behind the steering wheel and hunched over it, his broad back quaking with laughter. Noel thought, He's laughing too much, too easily; he's putting on an act. "Rome, of course," the old gentleman said, "was holding a one-man show in New York in 1940. His work was shipped out from San Quentin, no doubt."

Lockett said in a disappointed voice, "Well, that kind of spoils it, I guess. All the same, there might have been some way."

"Chan, get it off your mind," said Noel. "The police will have some pictures of this Pruitt, won't they? Drop in at the Hall of Justice and take a look at them." She was careful to keep the indulgent note from her voice.

"It's not physically impossible," Fenmer added kindly. "He could have done the stuff before he went to jail, but to work in Bakersfield as a forger...Listen to the old man go on. Wonderful how simple faith proves infectious. Lockett, my young friend, I found myself imagining Claude Pruitt as an unknown, skulking about; for a moment, almost, I believed that. But he is not Rome."

"He's not an unknown, either," the young man said. "That sculpture business—"

Noel felt a mounting excitement. She said, "Chan, do find out. Papa Gene can drop me—let's see; the lobby of the Sir Francis Drake. I won't stir from there until you come for me. It's safe enough, and you don't have to be at my heels every minute."

"Okay," Lockett said. "I'll drive over to the Hall of Justice and pick you up after. Goodbye, sir."

Papa Gene waved at him and let out the clutch as Noel climbed in beside him. As they turned the corner, Fenmer glanced sideways at Noel and asked, with genuine surprise, "Young Bruce, do you mean he is really your bodyguard? Connected with the police?"

"Yes. Isn't it silly? I think Mr. Geraghty was indulging him, somehow, but it's to make me feel safe—and it does."

"Good God," Eugene Fenmer said thoughtfully. He let Noel out at the side door of the Drake and drove away, looking actually nervous.

She sped to a telephone. "Mrs. Fritz, please let me talk to Miss Tann—to Mrs. Verney. It's important." When Anna's low voice sounded, Noel said hurriedly, "Tannehill, did you tell the police how you hurt your hand?"

"Yes, in a way. It was the truth, that I took hold of the handle of a heavy pan that had been in the oven and was nearly red hot."

"Not about the note?"

"I didn't mention that." Anna Verney sounded abashed. "I didn't think—I was afraid, to tell you the truth, Bruce. What if they hadn't believed I didn't write it?"

"They'd be able to tell, you silly. Tannehill, you must tell them. Call up Geraghty now, *please.* Haven't you heard about Claude Pruitt?"

"But he's dead!"

"I don't care. There might be some connection. You *do* that!"

She turned away from the booth and went up the marble stairs to the lounge. Her dark eyes were brilliant with excitement and hope. A new lead, and one that led to a shadowy figure, not to one whom she could recognize too well!

That had been on the fourth of September, in Anna's apartment on Post Street. Eight or ten of the art-school people had come in for one of Anna's late suppers: the two Watkinses and Steffany and a few of the painters; Rome, reluctant and solitary; Red Hobart because he seemed to be indispensable to Steffany; Chester Verney. Noel had been trying to help in the kitchen, and had found little to do. Tannehill had just removed from the oven a heavy cast-iron pan of Spanish rice whose aroma filled the room as the cover was removed; she was saying, "The plates are ready, Bruce honey. Yes, you can take them—" and Chester Verney sauntered into the kitchen and smiled at her.

"Before we begin, my dear," he had said, "I'd better tell you that I have to leave early. I can't stay for the games."

"But we're not going to play games, Chet!" Anna had sounded only amused and amiable.

"No?" The heavy, handsome face had changed indefinably. "I thought you were grooming me for a leading part. Didn't you slip this into my pocket?"

Noel could still see him, holding out a slip of paper, his eyes on Tannehill's face. She could visualize what was on it, too, she couldn't have helped seeing. Four words, in Tannehill's own square script: "You are a murderer."

Her friend had looked at it and gone terrifyingly pale. "I—Chet, I didn't put that—why, it looks like my writing. But I never wrote that!"

"Of course you didn't," Verney said instantly, putting the bit of paper back into his pocket. "Someone's playing a joke, no doubt. The note wasn't there half an hour ago." His eyes narrowed, and he stood considering while the two women looked in horror at each other and then at him. "Or it might be more of the same," he had said to himself, cryptically. "My friend's adding some refinements."

He had gone out, and Anna, remembering her duty to her guests, had turned to serve the food; but in her unnerved state she had not remembered the searing heat of the iron handle. Noel felt a reminiscent shudder even now, recalling the piercing cry of pain, the hastily snatched wrapping for the burn. Even in those first moments of shock Tannehill had managed to whisper to her, "Bruce, please promise me, don't tell anyone about the note. Not till I understand what it meant."

Now, thought Noel Bruce, there may really be some meaning to it. There could be no possibility that Tannehill had written that note, her surprise and fear were unmistakable. Noel thought again, If there were someone who hated her.

Forgery. All the limitless possibilities of forgery, a letter that might have brought Chester Verney back from Los Gatos, or kept him in hiding in San Francisco, or even led him to the Plaster Works in the dark of some evening.

And yet, the forger was dead, and his name had appeared on a rough tombstone of clay.

The office building at Market and Kearny was clean and echoing and uncannily bright in the stillness of Sunday afternoon. The door to the suite marked "Prince, Kelm and Verney, Attorneys at Law," stood ajar, and behind it men's voices sounded.

"I quite understand, Mr. Kelm," said the deep resonant one that belonged to Geraghty. "Mr. Prince hadn't seen the papers while he was on his hunting trip. I appreciate his telephoning in from Sonora, and your calling us at once. They had said nothing to you—yes, I see."

The suite was a long chain of rooms. Geraghty was in the last of them, a resplendent one of blond wood and discreet color, the office of the senior partner. He bent over a table under an opened safe door and looked once more at four or five notes spread out on the blotter. "They had been coming for a year, approximately, at irregular intervals. Uh-huh. This one, 'Because of you an innocent man is dead,' was the first? Block letters, h'm. No two alike. This one's typed—what?"

Kelm, a slim gray-haired elegant, made a nervous gesture with his cigar. "Mr. Prince tells me, Inspector, that Verney made some quiet efforts to trace the writer of those letters. He had, ah, unexpected results with the typewritten one. It was, ah, written on the machine of one of our stenographers."

"It was?" Geraghty said mildly.

"The investigation faded out there. No, not because Verney suspected anyone in the office. No one of us would have reason—or be so foolish. Anyone could have slipped into the girl's room and written that sentence, unobserved. Anyone in San Francisco; we have a great many clients, callers, interviewers..."

"Yes, I see. All of these postmarked San Francisco, except the last one which imitates the handwriting of Verney's wife. All different disguised hands, or typing, but the same literary style. Not a bad one, either," said Mr. Geraghty with a sort of cough. "Terse. 'There is blood on your hands.' 'Do you sleep well?' Uh-huh. Did they make Verney nervous?"

Mr. Kelm raised an eyebrow. "Our partner was an unusually fearless man, Inspector."

"I've heard so...Can you tell anything about these with the naked eye, Ziller?"

The department's handwriting expert touched the last note, in the script that resembled Anna Verney's. "A babe in arms could pick that out for a phony. Traced; sometimes two or three letters together, sometimes a whole word. 'You are a murderer.' See where they didn't even try to cover up the gaps between the u and r, and the two sets of er's? Don't need to blow it up, either, to see how unsteady the lines are. Lousy job," he concluded disapprovingly.

"That so? Almost as if somebody wanted us to be sure it was forged. Kind of a childish method to use, wasn't it?"

"You said it, Inspector. Babe in arms could have *done* it."

"And no matter who did the tracing, you'd know it was traced."

"Right you are."

Geraghty contemplated the notes with a melancholy face, and slipping them carefully into an envelope handed them to Ziller. He said nothing more until after they had taken leave of Mr. Kelm and had descended to the empty lobby of the building. Then he remarked as if to himself, "Supposing you traced your own handwriting that way, would it still look phony?"

The expert looked round at him quickly. "Sure would. Maybe we could tell, by the—"

"Never mind your technical talk. I hear enough of that in the courtroom. All you can swear is that it's a traced forgery."

Ziller gave a short laugh. "Right you are. Pretty tough if you depended on that for a conviction. Hardly anybody believes we know anything about our business!"

"I'm not thinking of a conviction," said Geraghty testily. "Just counting possibilities. That one's a long shot." He got into his car, and again seemed to be talking to himself. "That story about being afraid we'd suspect her—damn it, it sounds like the truth. Sure, she's scared. Treat these people like they were china, and they're still scared of the law. I wish I'd gone into the priesthood."

He slammed the gear lever into place and drove off gloomily.

CHAPTER SEVEN

NOEL BRUCE TURNED at the door of the hotel room and spoke in a patient tone, much the same as that in which you try to induce your dog to stay home from the excursion. "I'm safer here than I'd be anywhere else, Chan. Now for the Lord's sake, take a vacation."

The handsome blonde woman within the room looked out at Mr. Lockett with frank astonishment, and as the door closed demanded in an undertone, "My dear, who on earth is that?"

"Mrs. Verney," said Noel, "please don't ask me to explain him. I've got so I don't know what he's doing myself!" She sat down with a deep breath and tossed back the cloud of soft black hair that had blown about her face. "These two days—!"

"They must have been something," said the woman sympathetically. "Are you bored to death talking about the murder? Because of course that was one reason I wanted to see you again, I remembered you were with the art-school crowd and I'm frankly perishing to hear what went on! The other reason," she added with a nice smile, "was because I liked you that one time we met."

"When I'd just arrived in San Francisco, and you asked me to dinner. I never had a chance to tell you again how much I appreciated that."

"Because within a month or so I had flitted away," said June Verney, chuckling.

"Well, yes." Noel also laughed. "Don't think I'm flattering myself, but I worried a bit for fear you'd think I—that Chester was too much interested in—"

"In you? No, dear, he liked blondes, and more mature women than you were then. Twenty-one, weren't you? Anyhow, the shoe was on the other foot, you know. Let's have a drink."

"Thank you, Mrs. Verney, but I've been having too many drinks for my own good."

"Anything you say; iced tea? And call me June, no need to be formal...No, dear," said June Verney, interrupting herself to give an order to Room Service and laying down the telephone again, "I didn't have time to worry about Chet's outside interests. He kept me too busy accounting for my own. Look, I'll tell you." She lit a cigarette and settled down comfortably. "I was fond of Chet. He had most of the things a woman wants, and he was a sweet fellow in lots of ways. You think I'm up here from Bakersfield just for the looks of the thing? No, I came for the funeral, to—well, to be with him one more time. Milly, that was his second wife, would do the same if she wasn't tied up with a new family in L.A. Don't look so flabbergasted, sweetheart, all Chester's wives part from him with such a lot of good feeling that it's pathetic, and Milly and I never had anything against each other, nor against the latest one, either. Chet always looked around for a decent period before he tried another one. I hope the fourth Mrs. Verney would have suited him better than we others!"

"Perhaps she would."

"They'd been married how long? Three months? Maybe she hadn't had time to find out his little trouble. Oh, my dear, jealousy—pathological, no doubt of it. You couldn't pass the time of day with the elevator man without Chet's going into a broody state. Not violent, just hurt, because he loved you so much—you know? If you did go a little farther, say you danced three times with somebody else, he got livelier. Just what he'd have done if I'd really cheated on him, God knows. I never tried it. No, dear, he was fine to know but not to be married to."

"That does sound like an assignment. What about the innocent men you danced with?"

"He never accused any of them to their faces. I should think they'd have been good and mad if they'd known how he felt. B-field is kind of a conservative place," June Verney mused. "I thought things might improve when we got up here, but in a way they were worse." She rose at a knock on the door, and admitted the waiter with the tray. Visible beyond him was Chan Lockett, sitting on a chair in the hall, his round eyes fixed hopefully on the open door.

June Verney began to laugh uncontrollably. "Noel, your friend won't go away. For heaven's sake, let's have him in, I can't stand thinking of the poor guy out there—"

"He's sort of a policeman," said Noel warningly.

"Well, what of it? I think he's cute, and Lord knows I haven't any guilty secrets to reveal. You don't mind, really? Sit down, Mr. Uh—oh, Lockett? Well, have a drink."

"I won't disturb you," Lockett said in apologetic tones. He retired to a corner where he made a valiant attempt to be unobtrusive.

"Well, as I was saying, Chet had rather a different set-up here than down there. Everybody'd known him, he'd been D.A., he was a big shot in his home town. He came up here and went into private practice—and Lord, wasn't he brilliant!—but the kind of cases he had, you couldn't ever call them shady, but there was something about them—anyway, the kind of society we got into wasn't exactly what he wanted; not the top crust by any means. He was disappointed in me, too. If he got somebody who lived up to what he expected, which was plenty, he'd have been happy. He was really romantic, Chet was. Always looking for the perfect marriage. Well, so I wasn't it, and when he offered me a big settlement the first time I suggested divorce, I took it. No hard feelings." Mrs. Verney shook her head. "Poor Chet, he was so damn generous with his money—never was an easier man to divorce, I guess."

She straightened up and finished her drink. "Sweeten yours, Mr. Lockett? Now, Noel, I've been talking your ear off. I've got to have some inside dope to take back to B-field, you know. Give!"

"I don't really know much, June. I'll do my best—"

That was a job, indeed, doing her best; she couldn't mention half the things that really troubled her about the case. She would not have poured out her heart to June Verney in any case, but the presence of Lockett made her task more difficult yet.

She managed it fairly well by sticking to the objective point of view. She found herself aided, now and again, by a disembodied-sounding voice from the corner. "I don't know what sort of evidence the clay of the statue would offer," she said doubtfully, at one point, and the voice said diffidently, "No fingerprints. Murderer wore heavy gloves, they figure. Seems one of the plaster casters missed a pair of gloves a while back, but couldn't be sure when. The gloves weren't found. Wouldn't have been hard to get rid of, the Bay was right there."

"Thank you, Chan," Noel said, grinning; and in a few minutes, floundering about the undoubted fact that someone must have had a key to enter the Plaster Works at night, and that only the sculptors and their intimate friends had keys, she found her story once more augmented. "They figure that Verney musta borrowed his wife's key without her knowing. She hadn't missed it, but there it was in his case. Could be he let the fellow in, instead of the other way round."

"I didn't know that," said Noel rather faintly.

"It's no special secret, I guess," Chan Lockett murmured. "Seems to me the Chief published that; maybe it didn't get much of a play in the papers, too much else going on."

"And speaking of the papers," said June Verney with relish, "did you see what one of 'em did with the story of Pruitt's wife?" She rooted among a sheaf of news sheets. "My dear, you should have heard B-field jabbering when that bit about the headstone came out! We all remembered the case, of course, and some of us connected the false name with the right one. What? Smart? Oh, no, my dear, anyone who'd wanted to read up on Chester's cases would have seen it, the names this man went under were all published...Here it is. 'Young Mrs. Pruitt waited in hospital for the verdict, herself so near to the time of childbirth that she could not appear to give some slight comfort to her husband. Nurses at the Bakersfield General Hospital describe her as apathetic throughout the ordeal—' I'd be apathetic, too," June Verney interpolated. "Toxic edema of pregnancy, phew! We heard she was so puffed up and bleary you couldn't have recognized her—"

"Did you know the wife?" Lockett inquired solemnly.

"No, nobody did really, they kept themselves inconspicuous—you know, hoping to make a big killing and then disappear. She was a mousy little thing, I heard. Chet went to see her once, just out of kindness and I suppose to say he was sorry, and he said she looked like nothing on earth and wouldn't say a word."

"You suppose he'd have known her again after she got her looks back?"

"Why, of—" June Verney stopped and looked at him. "No, maybe not. That's a—funny idea."

"He's full of them," said Noel. "What else did the sob sister dig up? I know that newspaper!"

"Let's see. Apathetic—oh, here, '—until three days after her baby was born, dead; and the news came that her husband had been convicted. It is alleged that at that moment her eyes took on such a malignant light that the nurse attending her was afraid to remain in the room.' Isn't that a lovely story?" said June, grinning and casting away the paper. "Can't you see how those things get started and nobody can bear to let 'em drop?"

"How old was the wife?" Lockett inquired diffidently.

"I couldn't say. A nurse who took care of me once later, Bostwick her name was, was a probationer on Maternity when all this went on, and she told me something about it; seems to me she did say the girl was quite young."

"Eighteen or twenty, maybe. Well, look, baby," Lockett addressed Noel, "how old are these sculptr—lady sculptors?"

Noel looked at him fondly. "Chan, you're becoming the light of my life."

"Listen," said Mr. Lockett, alarmed. "Sarah—"

"Sarah couldn't be safer than with me. I'll answer you, Chan, with pleasure. Anna Tannehill is about twenty-eight, and Daisy Watkins rather younger—twenty-five at most, I'd say; and Rita Steffany is about the same, maybe nearer Anna's age—that's what I'd guess, but she's told me so many conflicting facts about her past life that I could never be sure of any detail."

Lockett meditated, and the two women exchanged a guarded glance. He said, "What happened to the wife?"

Mrs. Verney entered into the spirit of the affair, sinking her voice sepulchrally. "She disappeared! No one ever saw her afterward! There was a father, or brother, or something, who came and spirited her away."

"A father, huh? It does seem as if any of those dames would be kind of young; of course this one could fix up the way girls do, and you couldn't tell."

"And appear in San Francisco, take up sculpture so that if Verney happened to work his art-patron stunt she could meet him and worm herself into his confidence?"

"Or marry him," Chan said simply.

"Oh, Chan! that's—well, no, it's no sillier than the rest of your idea. She would then nurse her revenge for years, presumably, three years in fact; Pruitt died in 'forty-three, didn't he?"

"Well, layin' for her chance," said Chan reasonably. "But the father, there's another idea. The two of 'em could work together. Sometimes I think this job was worked by two people, they could do it a lot quicker and not take such a big chance of being caught at it. Father or brother. This Rome fellow could be her brother, I guess he's not old enough for anything else."

"I'm fairly sure it was a father," said Mrs. Verney helpfully.

"That old bird who bought us the drinks last night; he'd do."

"Does he suspect everyone who buys him a drink?" Mrs. Verney asked. "Let me have your glass, Mr. Lockett."

"Yeah, and he was nervous, too; laughin' and ho-ho-in' all the time, especially when the stuff about the forger came out."

"I love this man," June Verney murmured. "How about Noel, you're not going to leave her out?"

"Too young," said Lockett regretfully. "I'd sure like to know where that wife went."

Noel regarded him with rather more respect than before. Chan had interpreted Fenmer's mood; he was observant if nothing else. She said, "Would the department have pictures of her? Maybe not. That seems to be my solution for everything, and you were disappointed last night in Pruitt's, weren't you, Chan? Oh, I've thought of something else. How about the forged note in Anna's handwriting? Would the wife or father have introduced that motif—"

"That what?"

"The—the idea of forgery, cropping up again—just to remind Verney of his past cruelties, warn him that revenge was waiting?"

"Oh, that." Mr. Lockett turned thoughtful.

"Or was the wife a forger in her own right?" Noel prodded gently.

"Sa-ay." The blue eyes lifted to hers with admiration. "I never thought of that angle. *She* was the guilty one, and Pruitt took the rap for her. He could've taken those stock certificates home with him—"

"Unluckily," said June Verney, "Pruitt was the forger. He had a record a mile long, and he was guilty, and he really did die in jail—your police department probably knows that."

"He could've taught his wife how," Chan persisted hopefully.

Noel and June Verney rocked with joyous laughter. "How to while away a pregnancy," June murmured. "Sitting around the dining table of an evening, taking a forging lesson."

"Go on," said Mr. Lockett amiably. "You ladies are kidding."

June wiped her eyes and recovered. "Look, Chan—I must call you that—I'll do something for you. Seems to me Miss Bostwick got married and came up here; she may be nursing right now. I can find out where *she* is, and you can interview her."

"I bet you the Chief's thought of that," said Lockett, but his face lit up.

"And it's dinner time, I'm going to order up some food, you two must stay with me. This—takes all the horrible part out of poor Chet's death, somehow," said June Verney, her handsome face sobering momentarily. Then she grinned again. "Let's you and I get tight together, Chan, and leave Noel to her iced-tea bender."

"I got to stay sober, thank you just the same. Got to take care of Miss Bruce."

"Don't let that stop you," Noel said. "There wasn't a sign of my villains last night, was there? I think you scared them off. In fact, I'm beginning to wonder if I didn't imagine most of it."

She thought she meant that, and in the next moment her physical nerves reproduced the terror of her hunted flight through the alley. A prickling shiver went over her. No, she had not imagined the man with the thick neck, nor his companion. They were shadows without features, but they meant active evil.

"Yes," she said almost feverishly, "let's stay to dinner. Let's make an evening of it, Chan."

The postman came late to her narrow street. It was well after nine on Monday morning when Noel unlocked her mailbox at the street door with the renewed lift of hope that she had felt daily for the past week. Surely there would be something now. There had been no word, no letter postmarked St. Louis, nothing except the brown orchids that had arrived on September 13th, and the card that said, "From the way I feel, it really happened."

She had a letter from her mother, and an invitation to someone's exhibit of paintings, and a card from a furrier. She let her arms drop with a gesture of disappointment and turned to re-enter the house. Chan wasn't in evidence; maybe he'd decided she was safe enough in daylight.

"He's not much of a correspondent, is he?" said a deep voice from within the hall.

Noel gave a violent and guilty start and looked up into Geraghty's mournful face. She stuttered, "I d-don't know whom you mean."

"Never mind, my daughter Patricia used to look just like that when her young man's letters didn't arrive. Just a long shot," said Mr. Geraghty with his remote twinkle. "Hope I didn't startle you, coming in the service entrance. Too easy to walk in there. I don't like it much."

"We have locks on our inner doors."

"Good. Well, Miss Bruce, I'd like a little talk with you. Okay to go up to your room?"

Noel sighed and then laughed. "By now, the custom is justified by usage." Geraghty nodded and remarked, following her up the stairs, that it was quicker and quieter than asking her to come to his office.

He sat down and began politely to take her once more through the history of herself and her family which she had sketched during their talk on Friday night. It was several minutes before she caught his emphasis on date and place of birth. She broke off with a gasp in mid-sentence.

"Mr. Geraghty," she said firmly, "it's not the slightest use your trying to make out that I'm Chester Verney's long-lost daughter. You can check on this information, I suppose. I was born in 1922, and Verney certainly wasn't under age then, so that his first marriage could be annulled. Seems to me he mentioned that it was in 1919 that misalliance took place."

Geraghty looked at her quizzically. She added, "Do you really have to follow up all those remote possibilities?"

"That insurance was the only chunk of money he left, and the child who was the beneficiary hasn't turned up from anywhere else. It was called Marion Smith, by the way; could have been a boy or a girl. Sure, we check on everything."

Noel chuckled. "Have you tried Daisy Watkins? She's twenty-five, I think. She has a nice plump comfortable mother who doesn't know anything about Art but wants Daisy to have her chance because it's so wonderful that a Watkins should show any talent. And isn't Daisy Watkins a good false name? It couldn't be Mary Smith because that's too near the real one. I'm sure Daisy is lurking under a cloak of disguise."

"I'm sure," said the inspector mildly. "Now I'll hand you a real laugh. We checked on Miss Watkins and her parents, too."

"No! Would you mind telling me what happened?"

"The old lady," said Geraghty with a far-away look, "waved a marriage certificate and a baptismal record in our faces and told us, in a nice way, to go to hell." He paused, glanced down at the blank page of his notebook, and added, "In the course of conversation it came out that Daisy's cousin Paul was adopted."

"Sinister, isn't it? Are you going to make something of it? All this sounds so like Chan Lockett that I'm quite at home." Noel looked at Geraghty consideringly, and blurted out, "He's as nice a watchdog as anyone could want, but do you really think he'd be useful on the Homicide Squad?"

"I'll tell you, Miss Bruce," Geraghty said, "there are worse things than a cop with no sense of the ridiculous. Chan believes in some screwy things, but while he's tracking them down and finding that they don't fit the facts, he turns up some useful details on the side. And he notices things." The sharp gray eyes met hers. "He's no spy; but he's aware of the times when you get nervous about the investigation."

"Oh, indeed?" said Noel politely. She matched his gaze, stonily.

"It's connected with Anna Verney; not directly, perhaps, but there's something you know about her that hasn't been mentioned."

"I'll tell you what I know about her, Inspector. She's lovely and serene and kind, and whatever indiscretions she might have in her background she was never the wife of a forger."

"I didn't say anything about this Claude Pruitt business," Geraghty observed. "It's beginning to look like a fancy red herring, anyway. Didn't cost anything to put that name on the headstone."

"Very well, and she never sent her husband any threatening letters. One more thing I know about her, she's not a complete fool."

"You're right of course, Miss Bruce. About the letters, I couldn't be so sure. Might be a nice touch to have the final one in her own hand, but looking as if it'd been forged."

"Oh, for heaven's sake! And then be so convincing when she acted shocked about it that she gave herself that dreadful burn?"

"That would be convincing, but assuming—I say, assuming that Mrs. Verney planned to get rid of her husband, she might fix up a real good act in advance to make us think it was impossible."

"Look here, Mr. Geraghty, Anna couldn't stand pain. I know that. She could no more deliberately inflict a wound on herself than I could—well, torture anyone else. And even in the last event, if she nerved herself to anything that extreme and out of character, do you think she'd ever burn her *hand*? A *sculptor*? No, that was real surprise and shock, and a real accident."

"Good case, Miss Bruce." Geraghty nodded. "Speaking of the letter, do you happen to have any specimens of her handwriting?"

"No. Why should she write to me, or any of us, or if she did why should the note be kept? I can't remember her ever writing anything but—oh, well, of course, if it were a recipe or something like that, you'd keep it."

"She ever give out recipes?"

"Now that you mention it, I think she did," said Noel slowly. "Not to me; I don't do much cooking here. Steffany rather fancies herself as a cook, though, and Tannehill might— you ask Steffany."

"I will." Geraghty rose and stretched unobtrusively. "Miss Bruce, on which nights did you visit your friends at the Plaster Works, week before last?"

"I don't remember exactly." The answer came fast enough, but her mouth had gone dry. The way he got you to talking about something else and then slipped in a catch question! "Monday and Friday, I'm sure of, because we all went to dinner and on to Life Class." Even as she spoke, memory whispered a quick warning. She had already mentioned that Wednesday evening, because then she had expected that the workman would report her being there and perhaps mention Miles. But if he'd reported that, Geraghty had never spoken of it. Something queer—

"You mean when the sculptors were there, don't you?" she added quickly. "There was that one time when they'd all left early, the night of the twelfth. I did go in for a minute, but there was no one on hand but one of the plaster casters."

Geraghty did not move, and for a moment he said nothing. She heard the restless stir of wind outside, and the sound of church bells ringing the Angelus somewhere far away, carried on the dry north wind. Her room seemed very hot.

When the Irishman spoke, his voice was milder than ever. "One of the plaster casters. You know them by sight?"

"Some of them. I didn't see this one's face, though. Why, was it important?"

"That wasn't a plaster caster, Miss Bruce. For the past two weeks they've all gone home at six sharp. I believe you said it was after seven when you dropped in that night."

So he'd remembered. He never forgot anything, Chan had told her. Because she was not surprised at the news, she had her reactions ready. "It wasn't one of the workmen?" She caught a sharp breath. "But—but then—who?"

"That's an interesting question," said Geraghty dryly. "Just where was he when you saw him?"

"Lying on the floor with his head behind the cement mixer, as if he were repairing the mechanism. I remember thinking he'd probably jimmed it up himself during the day and had to stay overtime to fix it. I never did see his face. He was gone when—when I came out of the other room." She had nearly said "we." Watch it, she told herself.

"He was gone. H'm. Miss Bruce, did you see him move?"

"No! Oh, but—you're not thinking that he could have been Verney—already dead, and lying there waiting for—for—oh, no. I wish I could say that, it would explain so much and simplify things for you, wouldn't it? But I spoke to him as I went in, I said 'Hello, Mike,' because about half of them seem to be called Mike, and he answered—sort of a surly grunt. And I think he was in the telephone booth later; I have a vague sort of recollection—"

She had not seen him. It was Miles who had stepped back into the yard, meaning to telephone in the little enclosed office, and who had emerged at once saying that it didn't matter; the workman was using the phone. But that was only a shade off the truth.

Geraghty, who had been standing with his hands in his pockets, took them out and sighed. He sat down again. "I want you to search your memory, Miss Bruce," he began.

But it was no use. He took her through the story, the description, over and over again; she could be entirely truthful when she said that the workman was unrecognizable, only his legs showing; that she had noticed nothing out of place, nothing significant in the sculptors' workroom.

Geraghty gave it up finally. He said, "I suppose it could have been a man or a woman. Now we'll have to check on where every one of 'em was between seven and seven-thirty on that night. If we get anything, it may help; timing is so damned important in this case. But—" He shook his head.

"They'd all have been getting slicked up for the Sherwin party," Noel said. "Unless someone was right in the room with them, I suppose you couldn't accept that as an alibi. Anyone could have slipped over to the Plaster Works and got into one of those sets of overalls, some of the workmen always left theirs hanging on the wall. But why? Was that man waiting for Chester Verney right then?"

"I don't know," Geraghty said. He rose, really to go this time. "I don't know what it'd prove if we did find out who was there. Plenty of lies in the information your friends have given me; funny how easy it is to spot them when you've been in the business as long as I have: a hesitation here, or a look straight in the eyes to impress me, or some detail repeated over and over when there's no reason for it." He did not look at her, though he may have known that she was wondering which of those slips she had made. "But even when you catch 'em lying, you don't know what the lie indicates. Well, we'll find out."

He was gone, and Noel told herself that he certainly liked a curtain line; but weren't those lines effective! She sat here feeling as guilty as if she really knew something about the murder—

And she did not. She had not one scrap of evidence.

The inquest on Chester Verney ended with a verdict of "Death caused by a blow from some blunt instrument, delivered from the front, crushing the temporal bone. Murder by person or persons unknown."

"He could of fallen down and bashed his head on something," one of the jurors suggested, but his colleagues rounded on him with scorn. "Then why'd anybody bother doing him up in that statue?" they asked with some reason. Nobody insisted on viewing the body, since all those big words about extravasation of blood had been explained. They seemed to mean that the face was blackish and all out of shape; it made you queasy just to think about it. The skin wasn't broken anywhere, was all you could say for it. That wasn't much.

Nobody had found the weapon, either. They figured anything really hard, like an iron pipe, say, would have left some other mark on the crushed temple. Of course after all that time, if any of the sculptors' tools had been the weapon it could have been cleaned up or taken away. Seemed like it had a broader surface than any of those tools, too. "How the hell did a big man like that stand up and let somebody bop him sideways on the head?" one of the jurors had demanded, but there was no answer to that one, either. If he'd been sitting down, talking to someone he knew—but even then he'd have seen the blow coming from the front. He hadn't been doped. "Too deep for me," the juror said. "I bet it's too deep for the cops, too."

The inquest was on Monday afternoon. On Monday evening Inspector Geraghty was in possession of a recipe for chowder in a characteristic square hand, and of a set of newspaper clippings relating to a cause célèbre dating back to late 1943 and early 1944. The case was that of a Mrs. Able, accused of murdering her lover. Chester Verney had defended her, had obtained her acquittal on technical grounds, and had seen her released and re-established in her own home. Seven months later Mrs. Able, palpably insane, had killed her husband and shot herself. The stories on Able's death had run for three or four issues, the first one violently indignant in tone and accusing the law and lawyers of letting an insane criminal run free. The following ones were written in a different spirit and made no mention of lawyers.

"Okay, Kotock, send him in," Geraghty said.

Red Hobart swaggered into the office and sat down uninvited. The uneven contours of his face were spread with an unaccustomed pallor, but his manners were no less brash than ever. "Get on with it, Aloysius Cletus," he said. "Where's the big boy with the rubber hose?"

Mr. Geraghty had no fondness for his baptismal names, unused even by his wife. He looked at Red, however, unperturbed. "Kind of fond of needling people, aren't you, Hobart?" he murmured.

"Simple pleasures of the poor," Red said, smirking.

"I've been talking to Cleveland." Walter Cleveland was owner and editor of the *Eagle*. "He says you're something of a crusader. Get started on something you believe is a crying shame, and it's kind of hard to hold you down."

"Somebody's got to speak out. I've worked on plenty of papers besides this cheap sheet, and they've got one thing in common—the publishers are always scared."

"They're no fonder of libel suits than anyone else," said Geraghty dryly. "Cleveland's had to muzzle you more than once, hasn't he?"

"Sure. Think I'm ashamed of it?"

"You knew Mark Able, didn't you?"

"Who didn't? Great old sportsman."

"You're right. Fine fellow, too." Geraghty took up the sheaf of clippings. "You wrote this first story on his shooting, didn't you? Made it look as if Verney was to blame."

"He was to blame. I'm not ashamed of saying that, either. He knew that woman was guilty, she ought to've been put away. It was all of a piece with some of his other dirty cases. Look here, Inspector, we went over this ground on the night Verney's body was found. Sure, I didn't like him, professionally. Personally, he may have been okay, I barely knew the guy."

"Maybe not. Interesting correspondence you carried on with him, though, beginning about a year ago—soon after Able died. It seems to work up in intensity," said Geraghty smoothly, "to this last note: 'You are a murderer.' That one didn't go through the mails; you slipped it into his pocket at a studio party. Maybe that was a smart trick, forging his wife's handwriting, and maybe it wasn't."

The long hammering began.

Denials. The proof of fingerprints, of handwriting tricks evident in the printed note. Denials growing weaker. The production of that recipe for fish chowder in Anna Tannehill's hand: "Miss Steffany had kept it. She tells us that you asked to borrow it once, and she was amused at your being interested in a recipe. The word 'mussels' and the word 'chowder' could be traced in part to form 'murderer.' The whole thing has a schoolboy flavor, Hobart, but you're no schoolboy."

The red-veined eyes grew ugly then. "That stinking little black-haired—"

"You can cut the description, Hobart."

"She hands it over just like that, does she? Selling me out in half a second, to save her own hide! Have you looked into her affairs at all, or did she get you too, with that come-on look?"

"Never mind that now. You admit you wrote these letters?"

"There's not a goddam thing in 'em you could prosecute for, not a threat, nothing that couldn't be sent through the mails. Just needles under that bastard's thick hide. Okay, okay, I wrote 'em, I copied that writing to make him look twice at somebody in his own house—shake him up—"

Progression. What else did you have against him? Where did you know him before? What did he do to you?

The jerking open of the shirt collar, the deepening of the red streaks in the eyeballs. "Jesus, you think I'd be ass enough to write those letters if I meant to conk Verney?"

The deep voice dry and hard, saying, "That headstone—a touch of poetic justice, or something, in the name written on it. You're a great one for poetic justice. What did he do to you?"

"That headstone? Don't give me that! You know as well as I do that the Claude Pruitt business was a red herring, somebody knew about Verney's career in Bakersfield and dug that name up, went all through the headstone business to throw you cops off the scent. It seems to've worked! What are you trying to pull on me? I didn't kill Verney! I never touched him!"

Reiteration. Where were you on the night of September 12th? The next night? Friday? Saturday? The alibi for two nights, the sullen refusal to speak about the others. The pressure. Where were you? What did Verney do to you? When did you work in Bakersfield? Where were you on the night of September 13th?

The final breaking down. "All right, check it, check it. No, I don't give a damn about her good name; her husband'll find out, that's all, and spoil the best lay I've ever—"

"You mean you have trouble finding 'em?" Geraghty, having at last achieved something definite in answers, was almost jocose.

Red Hobart settled back in his chair and defiantly lit a cigarette, sucking in deep drags of smoke. His eyes grew small and ferocious. "If you're thinking about that black-haired bitch, there wasn't much doing there. Her heart belonged to Daddy, she said. Yeah, I wondered who Daddy was. Ask her! Talk to some of the people in that studio building, ask 'em how many nights she was away from her room. They'll say it was none of their business. Maybe it wasn't. I should complain if they live free in the art colony."

"I'll make a note of that, Hobart," said Geraghty. He also leaned back, his deep-set gray eyes cold. "Sure you wouldn't like to tell about some of your successes down there?"

"Okay, okay, they're all as pure as lilies. Lay off me, can't you? Haven't I told you what you want to know?"

"I can't promise to lay off you. Plenty of things about this story of yours that don't satisfy me. People don't remember one man in a cocktail bar on one special night two weeks ago—unless they've been encouraged, and reminded, and maybe confused about which night it really was."

"If I'd killed Verney I'd have done better than that for an alibi—all four nights."

"Or maybe you wouldn't. Innocent men sometimes don't have good alibis; guilty ones are afraid to make 'em too perfect."

"Leaving you up a stump and looking round for a scapegoat, which is me. Well, you can look around for another! Get somebody with a real record!" Hobart paused with a sly sidewise glance at the Irishman. "Listen, Inspector. Forget about this letter stuff. I'll give you a tip."

"I can't make deals." Geraghty waited uncompromisingly.

"Okay, I'll give it to you for free. I've done a bit of research on this case myself, for a gag, looked up a few of the people. A pal of mine in New York dug up something. You got any records on a fellow called Wilson Cromartie?"

Geraghty waited. Hobart dragged on another cigarette, and talked.

At the end of five minutes Geraghty nodded brusquely and said, "You can go, Hobart."

"Go on," Red jeered, rising. "You're trying to make out you knew the story. Follow it up, then. The witnesses got bought, or turned yellow, that's what happened. Want to bet on it?"

"I don't bet, either."

"Okay, sit there looking as if I was a slug. Why didn't I come out with this earlier? I'm for the underdog, haven't you heard? But not at my own expense, brother. Not at my own expense."

Geraghty waited until Hobart had disappeared. He shook his head as if to clear it of fatigue, and said, "What time is it? Ten? Kotock, you might see if you can get hold of Will Rome. There are a few points in Hobart's story that don't jibe with what he told us the other night. The New York records aren't clear on them either. Better have him up again."

Rome was not available. He had sought solace in a private jam session, it seemed; Mr. Kotock reported with the single word, "Jive."

CHAPTER EIGHT

ON THAT SAME MONDAY about noon, Noel Bruce came out of her last morning class and stood about in the lobby of the Sherwin School for a few minutes with an irresolution far from her usual habit. The school was a large old building on Buchanan Street which had once been a home, and its entrance hall was still impressive. She paused by the front door and peered through its plate-glass panel as if half expecting to see Chan Lockett stationed on the porch.

That business about taking him to classes had been a joke, after all. She wasn't quite sure any more of what was a joke and what wasn't; association with Chan, maybe. At any rate, the inspector seemed to feel that she was safe in daylight and in a crowd, especially since she had assured him that she no longer had the sense of being followed. She had not mentioned that sharper sense of uneasiness, the feeling that someone she knew, one of her friends, had been living with the memory of murder.

"Hello, Bruce," said Daisy Watkins at her shoulder. Noel managed not to jump, and instead gave Daisy her warmest smile. "Not in such a rush as usual?" the tall girl went on aimlessly. "We hardly ever see you around here after the whistle blows."

"I've taken a week's leave from my job."

"Oh, good. Are you—do you have to go anywhere in particular this afternoon? I mean, you don't have to—to testify at the inquest?"

"No, why should I? Do you?"

Daisy shook her head. "Come back to the studio with me, will you, Bruce? I'll give you some lunch. Please, come on. I feel sort of lost these afternoons while they won't let us work at the Plaster Works."

Noel hesitated. "I was half expecting to see someone. Tell you what, I'll leave a message with the secretary to say where I've gone."

Daisy gave a pale smile. "And if you don't come out within an hour, call the police?"

"That's a touch I hadn't thought of," said Noel brightly. She thought, This is a fine state of things. The mildest kind of joke seems to send me into gooseflesh. Nobody in his senses could suspect Daisy of killing Chester Verney, or chasing me in disguise.

They caught a Union Street car which rattled and clashed over hills with such abandon that conversation was impossible. Daisy didn't try to say anything, at least. She looked straight ahead of her, her angular plainness so intensified by strain that she reminded one of a death's head.

"How's Paul?" Noel said idly, when at last they were approaching the studio on foot. "I haven't seen him for days—but then, I haven't seen any of you except Tannehill and Papa Gene."

"He's all right, I guess," Daisy said. "I haven't seen him either."

"Oh?" Noel blinked. The Watkins cousins had been virtually inseparable since Daisy had talked Paul into enrolling at Sherwin.

"He may have gone over to Oakland to stay with the family. I didn't feel like going home." Daisy unlocked the door of her studio with its incongruous air of tidiness. "Sit down, Bruce, while I start the coffee." Her voice came back indistinctly from the kitchen alcove. "Funny feeling to have the police tell you to stay put. I don't know anything, I'm of no use to them, but just the same they have to keep a finger on me. *Lord*, if only they'd get this thing—" Water clanked in the antique pipes of the sink, and her words were lost.

Noel looked around at the prim arrangements of the studio. There was an old-fashioned marble fireplace, which in anyone else's quarters would have been treated as something wildly amusing; here it seemed to be accorded respect, for Daisy had placed several framed photographs on its narrow ledge. Noon sunlight blazed through spotless window panes, and the cast of Daisy's bas-relief in abstract, the best work she had done, was unsullied by a single grain of dust.

There was something missing. Noel glanced about her again. She hadn't been here often enough to catalogue the room's contents, but there was something she'd noticed.

The water was turned off. Daisy Watkins said, "So what do you think, Bruce?"

"About what? I couldn't hear you."

"Don't you think the police are completely inefficient?" She emerged wiping her hands. "Because if they had any idea of what was going on they'd have made an arrest by now, instead of pestering people who don't know anything. I told them I didn't, over and over."

"I hope not too many times," Noel said, smiling. "The inspector gave me a tip about that, he says if a person insists on a minor detail it's likely to be a lie."

"Oh, did he?" Daisy looked away. "Well, my ignorance doesn't seem like a minor detail to me." She was silent a minute, and then said unexpectedly, "I did my best. Nobody could say I didn't. If only it was the right thing to do!" An anxious frown creased her forehead; she stood spreading sandwich mixture on bread at her neat blue-enameled table, looking all at once grotesquely out of keeping with the careless world around her. Noel thought, Daisy ought to be looking like that because her second child has been exposed to measles, not because she's been interrogated about a murder in the art world.

She said, "Never mind, Watkins. We've all had our share of wondering that, I imagine." Hadn't we, indeed! "You want to hear something funny? I know a man who's been following this case, and he dwelt lovingly on the fact that you could have been Chester Verney's child who bumped him off so you could collect the insurance."

Daisy gave a sniff of laughter. "I know the police thought that, or something like it. They talked to Mom. What did they think I'd do, step up innocently and say I'd been around all the time and now I'd take the money, thank you?"

"Better than that. You might have had an alter ego prepared in some place far away, another personality with hair dye and lots of make-up and a character unlike your own; then you'd disappear from here presently, and pretend to discover proof of your parentage all at once, and collect as Ermintrude Vanderventer, or something."

"Your friend must be nuts," Daisy said. Then she smiled oddly. "I hope he hasn't checked up on me too closely. I used to spend lots of time visiting out of town."

"Not really! Where?"

"You think I'm going to tell you?"

"So you are the murderess. I might have known. Good thing I left that note for the police." Noel felt more comfortable. This was the old cheerful Daisy.

"What's more, I was thinking of skipping out as soon as the police would let me, and going to visit Aunt Clara again."

"Right in the middle of the term?"

"I'm sick of Sherwin," Daisy said with sudden intensity. "I haven't got a chance in that competition, and I'm not good enough to go on studying, and I know it. I've known it for a year...Here, have some coffee...Up to now, I've sort of stayed on hoping, I guess, and feeling that—that the life, and the people I knew, were enough to make up for my own failure. But now I—"

She left the sentence unfinished, and began to eat a sandwich, palpably without appetite. "Who do you think killed Verney?" she blurted out.

"I'm baffled," Noel said. "And if *I* feel that way, how can you blame the police for being slow to solve the case?"

"No, I mean it. You must have some idea."

Noel said, "I don't. Not the faintest. One minute I really believe there was a forger who came to life and planned revenge, and the next I think that one of Verney's law partners will turn out to be his long-lost son. But you know—under it all, I can't help feeling that—with all those anonymous letters, and the choice of the statue, and one or two other things, it might have been somebody who wanted to see Tannehill involved; someone who would have been glad to make trouble for her, even if she couldn't be really accused."

"Couldn't she be?" Daisy said. Her eyes were on her coffee cup. She stirred its contents zealously.

"Not possibly, I should think. Look at all the physical limitations, her hand, and the fact—which couldn't be foreseen—that she was nervous after Chester left and had the housekeeper sleep in her sitting-room every night from Wednesday on. Look at the entire absence of motive. No money coming to her, and if her marriage didn't click she could certainly have divorced him at the drop of a hat and stayed friends with him afterward! And then, she's just not that sort of a person."

Daisy stirred her coffee. She said in a low voice, "I see what you mean. But how about—someone who didn't dislike her, and knew that she couldn't get into serious trouble, and—" She let the sentence trail off.

"That's too involved for me, just now. I think somebody hated her. I don't see how anyone could, exactly."

"She might have been envied," Daisy said, "from the bottom of somebody's soul. That's not quite the same as hate.

She's always had everything she wanted, all her life. It might seem rather unfair to—somebody."

"Tannehill's always earned her good luck! You think of the things she's done for everyone she knows, and realize that she never expects a thing in return, she doesn't demand homage, she doesn't care if the person thanks her or not—she's got something coming to her. I might have envied her myself," Noel said, half laughing, "if she weren't always so simple and pleased when things do go right for her!"

"She's pleased, all right," said Daisy. "Anyone would be." She picked up her sandwich and wandered over to the window with it, munching absently. "Well, anyone who looks like that can afford to be simple—and generous. In fact, I've heard that she's so good-hearted that she 'cain't say no.'...Don't pay attention to me, I'm being nasty. The heat, probably. She's been generous to me."

Noel said, "Now I know what's different in this room. You've taken away the model of Tannehill's head. Did you send it to be cast?"

"No," said Daisy. She put down the sandwich and leaned out the window. "I thought—yes, it is! Paul! Come on up, I'm home! Why didn't you ring the bell, silly, instead of mooning around down there in the street? Of course you've got time!"

She turned back into the room, smiling. "That sap," she said, "wondering if I've been mad at him, I suppose." There was still a touch of anxiety in her look, and Noel thought, There's the child who's been exposed to measles!

There had been that note in Daisy Watkins' voice, exasperation and indulgence mixed, that had the true maternal ring.

Paul Watkins came up the stairs with his deliberate and unyielding step. He paused in the doorway, and said, "Hello, Bruce. How've you been?"

"Nervous as a witch," said Noel. "And you?"

"The same, the same." He glanced at Daisy, eyes sliding sideward in his unmoving head. "I was kind of hesitating on your threshold, Daze, because I have an announcement to make. The ceramics department at Sherwin is going to be shy one student."

"You quitting?" Daisy said. She looked alert and worried. "Going to look for a regular job? Paul, you can't! You're not—" Daisy stopped and bit her lip. "We won't discuss it now."

"I'm leaving," Noel said, getting up. "Discuss away."

"Don't you go, Bruce," said Paul Watkins. He gave her a sincerely imploring look. "Daze is going to jump me, I can see it in her eye, and I need support!"

"Jump you, what nonsense, as if I ever tried to—to—"

"Are you trying to say dominate? Because of course you don't, Daze. Nobody's ever thought that. But look here—no, please stay, Bruce; I've wanted you to hear this, too. I think a lot of you, and I'd just as soon you didn't go on thinking of me as a spineless kid or a neurotic."

"I never have, Paul."

"People who take all the time they need over their convalescence don't become neurotic," said Daisy quietly. "It's the ones who try to get well too soon who develop inferior feelings."

"I've taken plenty of time." Paul's hand, surprisingly powerful, reached out and held Noel's arm. She sat down unwillingly. "I've enjoyed it too much, playing around with clay and glaze, and being in the Sherwin crowd, and having you take care of me. There are people who like being fussed over, and told to wear their rubbers when it rains, and I may be one of them."

"You also like being near Tannehill," Daisy said in a dead voice. She was sitting back in her neat blue upholstered chair, her eyes the indeterminate color of cheap marbles, and with no more expression.

"Sure. Who doesn't? What's that got to do with my taking stock of myself?"

"Just about everything, I'd say. What you call taking stock doesn't sound like any of your expressions. You've been repeating something that was said to you. And it's come on rather suddenly, seems to me. When did Tannehill give you this fight talk? *Which of those nights week before last?"* Daisy almost spat the last sentence at him.

"What—" Paul began, and stopped short. Noel took one hurried glance at him. That smooth, boyish face of his had never had much expression; even his months of pain had not marked it noticeably; but now something queer had happened, as if it had fallen in, as if life had gone from the flesh.

"Never mind. Forget it. I shouldn't have said that." Daisy twisted uncomfortably, her strong big hands interlaced. "Bruce, you may be getting the wrong idea. I'd just as soon have this relationship cleared up, too. I'm not in love with Paul, and I don't—I give you my word, I don't—feel possessive about him. If he wanted to marry someone I'd be completely happy. I do know something about his physical and—and nervous condition, though. It's no easy job to persuade a man to do less than he thinks he can for a while, just so he'll be sure of getting completely well in the end, and I can't help resenting it when a woman who doesn't know a thing about him thinks it's time for his therapy to end, just on general principles!"

"Tannehill knew enough," Paul said quickly. There were small white spots by his nostrils. "The Army doctors told me I was all right, that ought to be enough for you! They told me I could take off that cervical collar—"

"If you felt comfortable without it! And look at you, still holding your head as if it hurt, afraid to move your neck—"

"I can move my neck all right. It's just habit to hold it this way. I can do anything I—"

"Up to about three weeks ago you wore that collar off and on, took it off when you felt rested, put it on again when your neck got tired. And where's it been since?"

"Oh, around," Paul said. Noel, in an agony of embarrassment, tried again to leave, but his hand shot out and restrained her.

"Around the Plaster Works somewhere, I suppose. You took it off the night of Tannehill's announcement party because she asked you to, so sweetly, saying it'd spoil the dinner party for her if she thought you weren't well. For her, you haven't worn it since then. You don't know what you're risking, what nerve pressure—"

Daisy caught a sharp breath as if she were going to cry, or as if she were trying to recall her last words; but if she had meant to go on, there was no opportunity. "The thick neck," Noel said involuntarily, in a half scream. "The neck—in the car—"

It had come to her in that moment; the silhouette had worn the curiously rigid look of a high leather collar under a turned-up cloth one. She had seen Paul looking like that on congealed winter days, sitting in the corner of the sculptors' workroom, kneading away at his chunk of clay. Paul—no, it couldn't be—

Arrested in mid-argument, the Watkins cousins were silent with surprise, and above the cheerful street noises below the room was thick with their silence. And then a small thing happened that illogically enough sent Noel into a chill of terror.

Paul Watkins turned his head and looked straight into her face.

She was on her feet, jerking her arm away from his touch. "I have to go," she babbled. "I shouldn't have stayed, you'll wish you hadn't let me hear all this. I must hurry—"

"*Wait*," Paul said. The word snapped out like a "Halt!" to a column of marching men. "Don't let her go for a minute, Daze. We've said something to upset her, I want to know what it was. Bruce, what's the matter?"

"Nothing! I told you I'd been nervous." She backed toward the door. There was Paul's face, round and inscrutable and blank as a schoolboy's; there was Daisy's, all its pleasant home-liness out of focus with emotion. She didn't know what to look for in either; she only knew that she must postpone thought until she got away.

"You don't mean—something to do with the murder?" Daisy blurted out. "You look as if you thought—" She jerked her head awkwardly from one side to the other, looking at her cousin, looking at Noel.

"I don't mean anything."

"Listen." Daisy Watkins lunged forward as if to get between Noel and the door. "You were looking for somebody who hated Tannehill. You said someone like that might have tried to implicate her. All right, you can go to the police and tell them I hated her! That bust—I smashed it, I took a hammer and smashed it, I didn't want it near me! I didn't want any reminder of her helpfulness, taking away the one thing in my life that was anywhere near successful, something I was doing without any thought except for Paul—"

"Well, you can stop doing it now, Daze," Paul said. There was a queer gentleness in his tone. "I'm grateful to you, but from now on—let's each of us be on his own."

Daisy looked at him. With a visible effort she controlled her breathing. "You don't mean—tell them—"

"Of course. I played along because I thought it was *you* that needed—but now I see what you think. You tried, but—don't do any more."

Noel had the door open. She turned blindly to leave, the quick sentences still rattling about her ears, half understood. Paul Watkins came after her, adding an expressionless "Goodbye, Daze," to his last remarks. Daisy stood in the middle of her neat room, with the hot sun pouring in through the spotless windows, and began just audibly to cry.

"Sorry we let you in for that, Bruce," Paul said, closing the door behind him. "I didn't quite see where it was leading. How we learn things!...May I take you somewhere?"

Noel's feet clattered on the stairs. "No, thank you," she flung over her shoulder. She didn't care if Paul realized that she had suddenly been afraid of him; in a minute she would reach the blessed heat and noise of the street—

On the second landing a man stood, speaking through an open door. "Say, is Miss Bruce—" He turned. "There you are, baby," he said in a relieved voice. "You might 'a' waited for me at the schoolhouse!"

"*Chan*," Noel said weakly. She could turn now and watch Paul Watkins as he came down the stairs, his head rigid, his steps regular and careful. As he went by he gave her an odd smile of understanding and something else indefinable. His round young face still wore that lifeless look.

"Well, so we've got one more detail," Inspector Geraghty said wearily to his assistant. He tilted back in his chair and sent one of his melancholy glances out the window at Tuesday morning's sunshine. "I guess the little girl honestly didn't remember about that collar, no reason she should hold out on *that*. Doesn't get us much of anywhere, though. It was kicking around the office in the Plaster Works for a few days after that party, and then disappeared some time, nobody knows when. Any of them could have walked off with it. Watkins himself could've done it; maybe he needed it to bolster him up after all."

Mr. Kotock busying himself in a corner of the room with an appearance of not listening, gave an expressive sniff.

"Sure, murderers slip up just as conspicuously as that; you know it. The rest of the business—well, it's not out of line; decision for the murder, sort of a fantastic nervousness for the rest of it. It's looked to me as if two minds were at work, but they might just be in the same body."

"Why?" Mr. Kotock muttered.

Geraghty appeared to understand this ellipsis. "Darned if I know. His parents are dead, so we're having a tough time tracing his origin. Maybe he's telling the truth when he says he doesn't know his own real identity, and maybe—"

His telephone rang, and he lifted the set to his head. "Yes...Yes, I see; you can't count on her...Well, Mrs. Verney, since you've been so cooperative, we can stretch a point this time. Do you need any help in getting there?...Yes, that's right, you have the car. I remember. Goodbye."

He hung up. "Mrs. Verney's aunt can't get here, she's recovering from an operation at the Mayos'. The lady wants to go back to her own studio, it's lonesome where she is. This way her friends can drop in and cheer her up." He glanced sideways at Kotock.

Mr. Kotock looked at his watch and seemed to calculate.

"Yeah," Geraghty said. "The funeral's over; just barely over, I figure." His deep-set eyes held their far-away look; for a moment he tilted in the swivel chair, whistling almost soundlessly. "You know, Al," he said suddenly, "things'll be coming to a boil before long. We haven't been so hot on this case, plenty of suspicions but no way to pin 'em on, the unlikeliest things taking up our time and the likeliest possibilities turning out to be impossible…But I've a hunch that these people have been stewing about long enough. There'll be a break."

Mr. Kotock nodded. He left the room for a few minutes and came back with a bunch of reports. Geraghty glanced through them and brought his chair to an upright position.

"Right you are," he said. "I'll start with the Steffany girl. The breaks may be coming, but I'd better help 'em along a bit."

The sculptors had been given permission to return to their section of the Plaster Works on Tuesday afternoon. This meant that they had missed only one actual work day, though from the universal griping on Monday one would have thought that the police were throttling the whole future of art. Today the urge to return to clay and stone were not so marked.

"I'd sure like to see 'em working," Chan Lockett had said wistfully to Noel. Noel, who herself was suffering from a strained sense of emptiness in the afternoons, had said after reflection that she didn't see how it could do any harm.

They walked in on a scene of lethargy. Steffany had arrived, but was sitting on an upturned bucket smoking and contemplating her statue, which was still covered. Paul Watkins sat in his accustomed corner, kneading away at his accustomed ball of clay. He was not looking at Daisy, who was moving back and forth in an aimless fashion collecting her tools, now and then stopping to look about her as if she couldn't be sure what she was doing. Only from the mold-making sections next door and the courtyard outside were there any sounds of activity. Rome was chipping away at his stone, the chisel making hard, hot, grating sounds in the still air.

Steffany was talking, her rich voice sullen. "I don't see what else I could have done. It's unbearable to have them come prying and poking into your life, asking the damnedest silliest questions, and if you wait one minute to answer they look at you as if you'd committed the murder yourself. I was so glad to have one simple little question I could answer that I came out with it before I thought. And how was I to know about that anonymous letter that Verney got?...Oh, there you are, Bruce." She broke off and gazed warily at Lockett.

"This is the gang, Chan," Noel said easily. "Steffany, Watkins, Paul Watkins, my friend from out of town, Mr. Lockett. I'm telling people he's my bodyguard."

"I think we've met," said Paul Watkins coolly, raising his eyes for a moment. "He's from the police, isn't he, Bruce?"

"I sure wish I was," said Chan humbly. "Nothin' I'd like better than to see all the inside workings of a murder case."

This unexpectedly tactful evasion eased the atmosphere. "I wish you were in with 'em, and could tell 'em to lay off," Steffany said. "None of us could have had anything—"

"Nuts," Paul Watkins said. "Don't fool yourself, Steffany. It was one of us, of course, or someone we know. Else why would they be calling us back over and over?"

Daisy caught a breath as if her throat were raw, and glanced at him. He went on as if he hadn't heard her. "Trouble is, we've all held out some of the details. I didn't think my, uh, omissions would count as lies, but it seems they did."

"*I* didn't hold out anything," said Steffany indignantly.

"The hell you didn't," said a husky voice from the far end of the room.

Steffany jumped and whirled around. Red Hobart had opened the rear door that led to the alley and was leaning

against the jamb, his hat pushed back from a perspiring forehead in a peculiarly disheveled effect.

"They let you out early," the dark woman said uncertainly.

"They let me out, period. Yes, boys and girls, my connection with that cheap rag known as the *Eagle* was severed as of
last night. But I see you're all back at the old stand; very pretty,
ve-ry gratifying."

"I wish you'd be quiet," said Daisy Watkins dully.

"Pardon me, pardon me," Red said. He was on the verge
of being drunk. There was an ugly edge to his voice.

"You still speaking to me, Hobart?" Rita asked, with a fair
attempt to be casual.

"Sure, sweetheart, sure. No hard feelings at all." He sent
her a barbed look. "We're even, anyway. I had kind of a hunch
that I'd be leaving this burg before long, so I celebrated by
handing out a few tips. Hot ones, sweetheart." Red laughed
unmelodiously. "No, no, not all of 'em were about you." He
strolled over toward the clay bins and mounted one of them to
look through the high windows toward the yard. The window
was open, and he called out, "Good afternoon, Mr. Rome—or
should I say Cromartie?"

The hammer and chisel stopped short.

"Watch me needle him," Hobart said over his shoulder.
"Say, that's a nice statue you're making out there. Are you sure,
though, you haven't cut too deep under the arm? The left arm."

He grinned, still perched on the clay bin and hanging
to the windowsill. "Okay, sweetheart," he said, cutting off an
expostulation from Steffany, "I don't know anything about art
except that I don't like it. It's his statue, sure, I know that. Just
the same, you see if he doesn't go back to that statue after a
while and look it over and kind of worry. I've been watching
that guy. You just have to touch him up a bit—"

The door to the plaster section swung open and Will
Rome came in. His sad hound's eyes held a queer light. He paid
no attention to the other occupants of the room, but went up
close to Hobart.

"Come down off that box," he said in a low voice. "What did you mean, calling me Cromartie?"

"It's your name, isn't it?" Red descended with insolent deliberation.

"It was my name once. Any law against shortening your name for professional purposes?"

"Did I say there was?" Red laughed again, in a pleased way, and added, "Shortened your name, and shortened your mane. Hey, that's not bad. Look, boys and girls, Rome's got a haircut. All the time I've known this guy he sports a shag of hair halfway down his neck. It took the police to get him spruced up!"

Rome had been talking in a rough undertone during the last part of this speech. Now his words could be heard: "—thought you'd buy your way out of trouble. You didn't tell them anything they didn't know. Think I'd hold out on that myself?"

"Sure, fella," said Red soothingly. "Safest way, when you've got a record."

"Record, hell. I was innocent, and you—"

"Listen, bub, are you sure you told the cops *all* about it? You were pretty free with that story about the saloon brawl, and how the nasty man kept badgering you till you just gave him a little push, and he up and died of heart failure."

Will Rome's arms were rigid at his sides. "That was about the way it happened," he said. "Were you a witness?"

"Newspaper pal in N.Y. wrote me about it." Red was elaborately careless, talking around his cigarette. "He said maybe you didn't know your own strength, throwing that left of yours around, but that there was more to it than that. Sure, the guy you killed had a bum heart, but there was some business that was hushed up about what started the quarrel, and how many times you hit him."

"Hushed up. That what you told the cops? You listen," said Rome, in an ominous low tone. "You suppose it wasn't hell enough for me to dig it up again, myself? You think I brushed

the whole thing off twelve years ago—that I haven't seen that
guy lying there, dead, a million times since? You think I can't
see his face when he went down, and feel my left hand aching,
and remember that it took a—took a life? Why, you cheap tale-
bearing sot," Rome added, and moved his feet in a cautious slide
along the floor, "why d'you suppose I'm not whaling the guts out
of you right now? You tryin' to make me out a murderer?"

"Red, look out!" Steffany shrilled. The four other occupants of the room had been petrified in their places since
Rome had come in; now Lockett half rose and then sat down
again, as if realizing that he had no authority. Red Hobart,
uneasiness seeping through his alcoholic bravado, stepped
quickly out toward the open portion of the room.

Rome turned and followed him. Now the craggy, weathered face was in full view, the eyes glinting, the thick brows
drawn down. "So it was you gave 'em the tip there was more to
it than what was true. You, gettin' me back there to be ques-
tioned, to start through that hell again!—and then coming
round to needle me about it. If you weren't as drunk as a skunk
you wouldn't have the guts to do that. As it is, you yellow-
bellied rat, you—"

"Cut it, Rome!" The command cracked like a mule-driver's
lash from the corner where Paul Watkins sat. "Quick, Steffany,
get him out—" Rita was on her feet, pushing a suddenly
sobered Hobart through the door to the alley, and Chan
Lockett, without seeming to move at all fast, had managed to
plant his stocky body in Rome's way.

The big man stopped short and looked around. For the
first time he seemed fully aware of the company. He said, "I
wouldn't have hit him—I guess. I'd never be able—I couldn't
take—" His tongue went over dry lips, and he raised a hand
and rubbed it, palm outward, across his eyes. It was his left
hand; at the base of the middle finger a patch of shiny skin
showed whiter than the rest.

Noel, her heart settling down from the startled pace it had
assumed, told herself that it was Rome's ring, the heavy square

seal that he wore except when he was working that had made that patch. His left hand—she wondered if the ring had some meaning to him; if it were worn as a sober reminder.

"Sort of provocation that's hard to take," Rome said dully. He drew a deep breath and started heavily toward the door, only to stop in his tracks. His craggy face went gray.

"Good afternoon," said Inspector Geraghty from the doorway. "I'm sorry to interrupt you. Miss Steffany here?"

Rita came back through the alley door. "Yes, I'm here," she told him. Her black eyes were wide, but she managed a slow smile.

"Could I see you for a moment?"

"Here? Well, really, Inspector, there's no place to talk, unless it's something you don't mind the others hearing—I mean, that you think *I* wouldn't mind—"

"I'd rather say it in private," said the inspector gravely. "Perhaps my office?"

Rita cast one wild look around her, caught a crimson lip between her teeth, and started to follow the inspector through the door. Outside, her feet stopped. She called, "Bruce!"

Noel got up, feeling rather unsteady, and went out. Steffany said almost inaudibly, "Look, Bruce, do me a favor. I'll get out of my working clothes, I've got a dress on underneath. Hang the overalls in my locker at the school, will you? Here's the key."

"Yes, of course."

"I won't go down there in this rig," said Steffany passionately. "I guess I know what he's going to—to try and find out. I'll not stand a chance unless I—"

She slid out of the voluminous overall and stood up, slim and curved in a thin blouse and cotton dirndl. "Yes," said Noel, "I see what you mean." She took the key and the overall, bundled them up and went back to the workroom.

Chan Lockett's round blue eyes were following Rome as he moved slowly toward the door. He said to Noel, "Wait round for me a minute, will you, baby?" And as the sound of Rome's slow footsteps was heard in the plaster section, dwindled as he went outdoors, and became audible again outside the window, Lockett climbed to the perch which Red Hobart had recently occupied and gazed through the window.

Daisy Watkins was taking the wrappings from her statue of the airman. She worked slowly, and once she looked up and met Noel's eyes. "You see?" she said in her dulled voice. "It'll never be the same again."

Paul's eyes moved toward her. He stopped kneading his lump of clay, though he held it caressingly in both hands. "She feels bad, Bruce, because she lied for me," he said, "and I can't be properly thankful." He glanced down at the clay and then tossed it unerringly into one of the open bins. "Too bad we couldn't stick to the story, Daze, in a way—it's unhandy to try proving alibis. But you know, that evening of the Sherwin party I really was lying down with a gin-fizz headache upstairs in one of the studios. Nobody disturbed me. And the night before that—though that doesn't count, of course, because Verney was still alive—I went out to St. Francis Wood to see Tannehill."

"So that was when she gave you the fight talk," Daisy said remotely.

"Well, Daze, she didn't call me out there just for that. Her husband had gone back to his bachelor quarters for something, and it seemed like a good time for me to do an errand for her. I guess it's all right to say it now, when Verney's dead. She wanted some things destroyed at her own studio that she hadn't had time to clear out. Seems he sprang this announcement and honeymoon business on her suddenly, and she didn't specially want him wandering into her studio and seeing the stuff later on. She said it would hurt him to know she'd kept it. She wanted that bust of him taken back to Post Street, too; she'd thought she could work on it at her aunt's house, but her hand wasn't healing right." Paul was talking easily, but his eyes were fixed on his cousin's drooping head, as if he hoped these details would convince her of something. "I wasn't there more than half an hour, it was nine-thirty before I found the place and at ten we heard him driving into his garage and she said I'd better slip out down the stairs from the balcony. She asked me not to mention it to anyone for fear he'd find out what the errand was. That's the only reason I didn't say anything before."

Daisy gave a faint but audible sniff. Her clay model was uncovered now, and she stood gazing at the pilot's upturned face. "And Thursday?" she said harshly. "I know where you were Friday night, because you did turn up for our movie date—that one time."

"Thursday's one of those times I can't prove," Paul said, half jocosely. "It's awkward, but it's true. I didn't know Verney had left town, of course, but I—I hadn't wanted to telephone, and I sort of hoped I might catch a glimpse of her alone. But I saw the car in the driveway, and so I just came away again. I had my family's car for a few nights. Funny thing," Paul said conversationally, "you know that bench where people wait for the bus? Well, there was a fellow sitting there looking half dead, and I offered him a lift, but he wouldn't take it."

From the window, Chan Lockett said in a ruminative tone, "Hobart called the turn. Rome's stopped work, he's lookin' at the place under the arm of that statue, kind of worried."

"And I'd seen his face before," Paul went on, "or somebody exactly like him. It was the man in those photographs, the ones I burned for Tannehill. I wondered if he'd managed to see her, or if he'd gone out there and just found out she was married, because it was that Navy officer she was engaged to before he went overseas. He looked," said Paul, "as if he'd seen a ghost."

CHAPTER NINE

NOEL CAUGHT HER BREATH. Her finger flew to her lips in an instinctive gesture; and Chan Lockett chose that moment to turn around.

She thought faster than ever in her life. "The door to the alley," she whispered. "I thought I heard someone out there."

Lockett went to the door and opened it. No one was in the long passageway. He moved back into the room, remarking, "You sure got the twitches, baby. Wouldn't have done much harm if somebody *had* been out there." Noel thought, Did that fool him or not? And is Paul telling all this on purpose because he thinks Chan is connected with the police? And why? *And what made Miles look so terrible?*

The faces around her wore expressions of blank candor. Daisy said without much interest, "I didn't know she was engaged."

"Didn't you? Some of the old guard knew Steffany, I think, and Papa Gene. I suppose it was broken off when she met Verney. Pretty trick for a man to play, wasn't it? Working on a woman's kindness and affection so that her loyalty was submerged. If that had happened to me," said Paul reflectively, "I wouldn't have cared very much for the man who did it."

"The man, the man!" Daisy said. "It was all his fault, wasn't it?" She gave Paul a brief look. "You make me sick," she muttered, suddenly pale and on the verge of tears, "and yet I—I can't help—I wish I'd stuck to my lies! I don't know what I've done, I'm going to get out of town the minute they'll let me, I wish I was a million miles away. There isn't a thing left!" She turned swimming eyes on her statue, and with an abrupt gesture picked up a clay-cutting tool and dragged the wire across the pilot's face. "I wish I was dead," she added in a quiet tone, and, leaving her tools and the wreck of the statue behind her, went on a blind rush through the door.

There was a moment of silence. Then Noel said, "I suppose it's no use your going after her, Paul?"

"None, I'm afraid. You see, she thinks I'm crazy, that those broken vertebrae of mine pinched a nerve, or something." Paul was quite matter-of-fact about it, he was smiling, but the smile sat oddly on his still face. "I was so inflamed by love, she figures, that when I heard Tannehill and Verney were married I went off my rocker. Maybe I'm his son, too, or something."

Noel got up. "Don't be silly," she said. "Chan, we'd better be leaving."

"Why, Bruce, you're not afraid of me too, are you?" said Paul.

They left him sitting alone in the corner, still smiling.

"Quite a day," said Mr. Lockett, outside. "I guess it isn't always like that."

"Not always. Will you take me over to Sherwin, Chan? I'm ashamed to be using you as sort of a taxicab, but—"

"I don't mind goin' around with you, baby. You're all right," Lockett assured her, cheerfully grinning. She accepted this as a high compliment, with an absurd feeling of warmth and pleasure.

"Too bad the girl busted up her statue," he said regretfully, sliding behind the wheel. "I thought it was pretty good; looked like something. But I guess she was upset."

Mentally handing him the palm for understatement of the week, Noel nodded. She got out quickly as the car stopped before the Sherwin School and performed her brief errand. For a minute she paused outside the office door, thinking she would leave Rita's key with Mary Porter, the secretary; but Miss Porter was deep in a telephone conversation and Noel slipped the key into her purse and ran down the stairs again.

Lockett began to talk the minute she re-entered the car. "Spooky joint, at that, I should think it'd get on their nerves even when there wasn't a stiff around. All those wet rags, makes you think of dead people, somehow. You know, I been figuring. The guy who bumped off Verney wouldn't 'a' turned on those overhead lights for the statue job; prob'ly had a flashlight or something. Could you do it with that little light?"

"I think so."

"Well, look," said Chan Lockett, turning west on a one-way street and immediately stepping on the gas, "if it was me, and I was alone, no matter how used I was to the place I'd be scared. I'd want to get out of there fast, stuff the body in a car trunk or something, think of a way to get rid of it later."

"Unless," Noel said, "it had been planned for a long time, and you'd nerved yourself to do it."

"Well, it doesn't seem as if it could have been planned. I don't suppose," said Lockett rather shyly, "that you'd remember all that stuff I said when I was figurin' why the killer picked out the Plaster Works to hide the body in?"

"Yes, I do. Every word."

"About how it was kind of crazy, on account of narrowin' the field? Well, look, baby; if the killer had a chance to plan, why didn't he pick out a better place right at first? Why didn't he arrange to kill Verney at that bachelor flat of his? The houseboy had been laid off for two weeks, and there's a separate entrance, nobody'd see him go in and nobody'd find him there either, and then it might 'a' been anybody on the Pacific Coast who bumped him off. But suppose you just happened to get him at the Plaster Works, see, and it's a good chance to murder him when you'd been thinkin' about it for years and hadn't been able to get at him, and you bop him right then—it might explain things. And if there was two of you—" said Lockett meaningly, and brought his car to a stop at the mouth of Noel's street.

"That's a thought," Noel said respectfully. "Chan, do some more figuring. Come up a few minutes, the household must be used to you by now—anyway, my landlady hasn't handed me any eviction notice."

"All right." He followed her up the narrow sidewalk and the gray steps, softly continuing his train of thought. "Two. Let's see; the Chief doesn't much like the idea of accomplices. One of 'em always cracks, and a smart murderer—and this one looks kind of smart—wouldn't take a partner unless he had to. Well, look, you know these folks, how would they pair off, who'd take who for a side-kick? There's Miss Steffany and Hobart, I guess they were pretty thick before they got to tellin' tales on each other."

"You've got to link them up with the two men who were chasing me. I can't believe that one of those men was a woman in disguise."

"Yeah, that's right. Take two men. The old boy, Fenmer, and who? Hobart?"

"I don't know why you lead off with Papa Gene, but he'd be unlikely to choose Hobart. He despised him."

"Fenmer and Rome?"

"They hardly know each other. Rome doesn't go around with any of the men from Sherwin. That's out."

"Fenmer and Watkins?"

"If Papa Gene were planning to shoot at me," said Noel slowly, "he'd be too smart by far to let Paul Watkins appear in his own cervical collar. You have to protect an accomplice, don't you?"

"Hobart and Watkins? Hobart wouldn't care if his pal gave himself away, as long as Hobart got out with his skin."

"Maybe. But Hobart thought Paul was a sissy. I can't see that combination."

"Well," said Mr. Lockett, quite undaunted, "that second man must 'a' been someone we haven't had a sight of yet. Maybe the old father."

"The old—you mean Mrs. Claude Pruitt's sorrowing parent?"

"Yeah, sure. How's about that old watchman?"

"Fine, except that he's falling to pieces. I do love that story," Noel admitted. "Sorrowing parent stays around to watch over his daughter, who's disguised as an art student, he in turn being disguised—or doing a sort of Stella Dallas, peering through the window at the Plaster Works."

"I don't dig you. You mean the dame in the soap opera?"

"I'll tell you about it some other time. Chan, not one of those combinations sounds right. There's something out of drawing."

"Something screwy about that statue deal, too," Lockett mused. "You know what? Butch can't get it either. He says there's somethin' more behind it than just hidin' the body... Well, how about the dames? One of those workin' with a man, and then keepin' out of it afterwards." He fed a stick of gum into his mouth without interrupting the flow of words. "Mrs. Verney, now, most of these men are kind of hopped up over her."

"For heaven's sake, Chan, leave her out," said Noel wearily. "She had no reason to kill Verney, she gained nothing!"

"Okay, leave her out," Chan agreed readily. "I guess you'd have to be pretty cracked over a dame, even a blonde like that, to bump off her husband and then never get anything out of it yourself. Unless she had a lover—aw, look, baby, I got to think of all the angles. I know, they ain't proved anything on her... Well, the Steffany one?"

"She'd work with Hobart, maybe. No one else." Noel thought suddenly, if there were anything in this absurd idea, Rita could just possibly have worked it. If she'd been Verney's mistress—and she'd claimed to have been before his marriage—if he'd been with her in some hideout for a night or two, and then had been taken to the Plaster Works on some pretext so that he should not be connected with the hideout—and *if* she thought that Noel had some knowledge of the truth—she could have tipped off Red on that night when the two of them had discussed the murder, in the Tavern; she could have let him know that Noel would be going home alone.

"Miss Watkins?"

"Nobody but Paul. But they've been at cross purposes ever since, and he made her tell the truth about those nights when she said he was taking her places or staying in the studio."

"Well, that'd fit. Wouldn't be the first time people have fought after they'd been partners in crime. I kind of like—"

A moment since the telephone, outside in the hall, had rung. Now Miss Ibsen's voice was heard, calling from afar as if she feared contamination through Noel's open door. "Miss Bruce, it's for you."

Noel excused herself and went to the telephone. Miss Ibsen was on her way downstairs, muttering audibly about people who let other people do all their errands. The voice in the telephone said, "It's Mary Porter, Bruce. Are you coming in tomorrow?"

"Wednesday? I haven't any classes until eleven."

"One of your colleagues from the Twelfth Naval District left something here for you. Said she'd had no luck getting you on the phone, and happened to be passing by."

"What is it, Porter?"

"Looks like one of your sketch pads, it's in an envelope—yes, I can see your signature on the top drawing. Seems the car you were driving one night cracked up, is that right? And this pad slipped down behind the front seat and wasn't found until the mechanics took the car apart."

Noel, who had been leaning against the wall, stiffened suddenly. She said, "Porter, will you look—"

Miss Porter, however, had been distracted. She was saying to someone whose agitated voice quacked in the background, "No, sorry, but I don't know where he is." She returned to Noel's ear. "Naturally they thought it didn't matter, so they didn't return it until the car was all repaired. Sounds suspicious; what did you do to the sedan?"

"Never mind, I'll tell you some time. Porter, hang onto that, will you?" Noel in her turn was distracted by a conversation at the lower door. Miss Ibsen was telling someone, "Up there, but I don't think you'd be welcome, she already has a man in her room."

Noel said, "Oh, heavens—I'll try to get over, what time is it? After five? If I don't make it by the time you're ready to leave, stick it through the letter slot in my locker, will you? Yes, I do want it, it's important!"

Miss Porter was indulging in another aside. "Get out, children! Go 'way, boys, you bother me—Honey, I don't care if you've just spent two *weeks* at the police station, he's gone, and I don't know where—No, not you, Bruce. Right you are, maybe I'd better just stick it in now, you'll never make it here by six. I don't want valuable works of art kicking around my desk."

Noel thanked her and hung up hastily. She was curious to see the person to whom Miss Ibsen had been talking, and as soon as she got back in her room she wandered to the bay window and glanced down the street.

A man in a white-topped cap was just turning the corner, going away. There was no doubt about his identity. She had picked him out once from a crowd of two hundred other Navy men.

She turned hurriedly from the window. Chan Lockett sat placidly on her brown slipper chair, masticating his gum, his round blue eyes gazing into space. She did not underestimate him any longer. It was unlikely that he had missed the colloquy at the door below, and he was sure to have glanced out himself.

Lockett could believe impossibilities, he could look with the utmost seriousness for a sorrowing father of a forger's widow. What couldn't he do with a naval officer who was calling on Noel, and who might very well be the same one who had sat on a bench in St. Francis Wood the night after Chester Verney disappeared, looking like death? Who, in fact, *was* the same one?

Noel sat down. She was in a position, of her own making, in which she scarcely dared open her mouth for fear of uttering a revealing lie. If the man with whom she was in love should be ready to doubt her virtue, she had just seen the last of him. The end of her quandary might be in sight if she could get out alone for an hour; and her every move was the object of interest to her faithful bodyguard. Her mind swept all these considerations aside, and told her only, "Miles Coree is here. Miles has come back."

"Go on, Chan," she said decorously, "where were you?"

"I guess I was about through, on account of I got to thinkin' about dinner. You going out?"

"I'm going to have tea and toast here, and go to bed early. That scene at the Works took it out of me more than I'd realized."

"Yeah. Well, I'll go out and grab a bite and come back."

"Chan, you know, this is ridiculous. I can't tell you how much it's helped, especially that first night, to have you guarding me, but it can't be necessary any longer. If I'd had any guilty secrets to get off my chest, you'd have heard them long ago." She grinned at him and Mr. Lockett gave her a pleasant smile in return, his round eyes candidly on hers. "And certainly those two villains aren't still pursuing me!"

"How do you know?" he asked reasonably.

"There hasn't been a sign of them, has there? You know what I think? They must have believed I knew something, so they took that shot at me last Friday; and then when I got to the police and told my story and there wasn't anything revealing in it, they must have realized they were safe."

"Could be." The blue eyes still met her own. "I've got so I kind of like this job, though. There's more to it than just takin' care of you. It wouldn't hurt, see, if when I do get back on the Force I had a leg up on account of helping Butch, unofficial."

"Chan, if you want to squire me to any more hair-pullings in the Plaster Works, you're welcome as you can be; but I really don't think you need to lose any more sleep."

"I'll talk to Butch. He got after the landlady to lock up those service doors at night. Maybe I could just arrange to be in my car, down below your window, the way I started out."

Noel made a gesture of defeat. "Thank goodness the nights are warm," she said. "I'd hate to have a case of pneumonia on my conscience."

She breathed more freely after he was gone. In spite of Miss Ibsen's helpful hints at the front door, she had every expectation of hearing Miles Coree's voice, there or on the telephone. If she didn't hear from him—that was that; but she wasn't going to get into the shower until late in the evening, just in case.

Six; six-fifteen; six-twenty-five; she sat smoking with deliberation, her eyes on the clock. Miles. Somewhere in the blazing September streets of the city, in a hotel, in a bar, he was moving with that easy carriage, that air of race and courtesy. His deep voice with the laughter in it was speaking to someone...There was the telephone!

"Noel," the deep voice said, "this is Miles Coree. Are you all right?"

"Of course I am! Miles—when did you get back?"

There was a brief hesitation. When he spoke, it was in a peculiar tone. "I never left," he said.

"You—"

"Tell you all about it later. Noel, I've got to see you, I—it's all I've been thinking about for nearly two weeks. I was at your house an hour ago, but some old harpy scared me off, and I didn't want to break in on anything. Can you talk now?"

"Yes. The man was—connected with the police, informally."

"I guessed something like that. That's why I wondered if you were in any difficulty. He's gone? May I come out now?"

"No, please don't come here. We'd—we'd have to sit on the front steps. Entertaining the police in my room is one thing, but you'd be something else."

"You realize that, do you?" Coree laughed, that heart-warming sound she remembered so well.

"Don't start any double-meaning game, Lieutenant Coree. No, Miles, truly I'd rather meet you. Where are you now?"

"Staying at the Clift."

"Supposing I come there—well, as soon after dark as I can make it. After eight, that would be."

"I wish," said Miles Coree, "that there'd be a good long eclipse of the sun right now. But, as you say; eight. I'll be waiting for you, Noel."

She clicked down the receiver. There was no time to lose; if she hadn't dared an attempt to slip out now, Chan Lockett would be sure to choose that time for his return. ("Go *home*, Fido," she thought with exasperated laughter.) She went swiftly down the hall to the service door. Not only was it locked, but the landlady had removed the key.

There was one possible way. It had been in the back of her mind ever since she had seen the white-topped cap at the corner. Noel went back to her room, locked the door and shut all the windows in spite of the stifling heat, and, after a precautionary glance at the street, set up the screen with which she masked the entrance to her kitchen quarters.

The old-fashioned cabinet had been built to last, but it could be moved. She pushed it at right angles to the wall for an additional sound-break, and went through its drawers for tools. There had been a straight key in that top drawer once, and she had left it there...Yes, there it was.

With a tack-hammer and a thick-bladed kitchen knife, Noel began to remove the boarding from the disused door of the erstwhile service porch. That door, as she had noticed idly long ago, was boarded over on the inside only.

The nails came out with squawks of protest, but they came. If Lockett should return and hear and guess what she was doing, she was sunk—except that he couldn't get into her room; and if she heard him banging on the door she would simply finish the job and skip out into the alley while he was occupied, damp and dust-covered as she might be. And if the key doesn't fit the lock of this door, Noel told herself fiercely, I'll take the door off its hinges! But I'm going to see Miles alone, without any danger of getting him involved, and put the whole thing in his hands.

This seemed to be her night. The key did fit the door; there were no knobs but the latch had rusted and stuck back in its socket, and the door itself was not nailed shut. Noel stacked the boards in a corner and got into the shower, filled with self-congratulation. She had just emerged when Chan tapped on her door. "Hey, baby," he said, "it's okay. I'll be down below, just in case, but I guess you're safe."

Her lights went decorously out half an hour later, when the sunset had died. She was out on the dry boards of the old service stairs, tiptoeing down the long-disused steps; they rattled, but they were still safe. Down the alley, over two blocks to Geary, onto a loaded streetcar that stopped to let her squeeze herself into the midst of a perspiring but good-natured crowd. She had not been seen. The car stopped not twenty yards from the entrance to the Clift Hotel.

Noel walked into the lobby with an unhurried air that was a minor triumph, considering the state of her circulation. She glanced deliberately right and left. Unerringly her eye found the tall figure it sought.

Miles Coree was at the entrance to the corridor that leads to the Redwood Room, moving slowly along—to the bar, or to the smaller hotel entrance that also gave on Geary? It was almost as if he were trying to urge someone along with him.

He moved a step farther, and his companion became visible: dull black pumps and bag, a black linen dress of superlative cut, a subdued if knowing black hat on shining hair; a beautiful face with serenity in its every line, earnestly upturned to the man's. Tannehill.

Noel's first impulse was to turn around and leave unseen, her second to treat it all as a matter of course. She told herself with painful firmness, It isn't as if we were engaged, I have no claim on him; and why shouldn't he see a woman who meant a great deal to him in the past?

She went forward, smiling, and Miles Coree turned and saw her. His eyes shone under their heavy brows. Anna Verney looked around, caught her breath at the sight of Noel, and smiled in her turn, radiantly, welcomingly.

"Bruce, honey!" she said. Both her hands caught Noel's in a warm clasp. "So it's you that Coree was expecting! I stole half an hour of his time, but I'm just leaving. You know," she added with her lovely direct look, "I've been calling the Clift shamelessly, every day, to see if he'd come back yet. My friends have been wonderful, but it seemed to me that I had to see Coree before I could—begin to pull myself together. If you know him, you know why."

Indeed, Noel thought, I know why. There was something so comforting about him, the quiet and assurance under the surface gaiety.

She said, "But you mustn't go yet, just because I've come."

Lieutenant Coree had been looking attentively at them both. He spoke for the first time: "May I offer you a drink, Anna? I'd meant to invite Noel to the cocktail room."

Tannehill hesitated. "Perhaps just one. I shouldn't be out at all, but it's done me good already, seeing you." She went with her graceful step down the corridor. Miles Coree touched Noel's arm in a formal gesture of escort, but the light contact went through her like fire. He bent his head and murmured in her ear, "No privacy anyway. Where *could* we go for the sort of thing I want to say?"

Noel gave him a fleeting smile. "Only a park bench for the likes of us," she murmured in return, and followed the blonde head.

"Never mind," said Miles, behind her. "There'll be time. I keep telling myself that."

There would be time. Or would there? She had delayed, temporized, for all these days, waiting only until he returned. Now—there was a queer feeling behind her breastbone, that had been there held in abeyance ever since his telephone call. He'd been here all the time. He had not let her know.

When their drinks came, Anna Verney said repentantly, "I've been doing all the talking this evening, Coree. It isn't like me. Now, I do want to know about your family."

"They'll be coming out here in a few days," Miles said, his eyes on his drink. "They went East to meet my younger brother, the one who's been in the occupation forces in Germany."

"I should love to see your mother again. You never saw a more utterly beautiful person, Bruce. But perhaps she won't want to receive me," said Anna wistfully. "This—all this dreadful business about poor Chester, and the newspapers—"

"I doubt that she'd mind that." Miles Coree glanced at her. "It scarcely reflects on you."

"I still don't understand," said Anna, "how you could have been completely ignorant of what had happened until yesterday. Don't you even read headlines?"

"It happened that I didn't." Miles' mouth twitched, and he became absorbed in his glass again. "I wasn't in a position to use my eyes for some time."

Here I sit, thought Noel, like a bat in the daylight—except that I'm right side up. Or am I? I might as well be asleep, or invisible—

"You see," said Lieutenant Coree, with a slight cough, "I was on Treasure Island in a contagious ward. Just by chance there wasn't anyone else there with my particular variety of plague, and I was in no state to gossip with the nurses."

"Coree, you poor angel! What happened to you?"

He looked at Noel, with that same unexpected shyness and embarrassment that she had seen in his face at their second meeting. "I had measles," said Miles Coree sheepishly.

Noel's lips parted in surprise. "But you've had them before! The time you listened to *Little Women*—"

She caught Anna's quick glance, with a sharpness in it that changed at once to raillery. "My dears, did you get to the childhood-memory stage?" Anna murmured.

"These were the other kind," said Miles, unheeding. "They used to be called German and now they're five-day. Only for me they were eight-day and came back for a second whack at me." His eyes met Noel's again. He said softly, "First I'm rude to you and then I meet your enemies and can only make faces at them. And now—!

"They let me out of the T.I. sickbay on the twenty-first, supposedly cured. I came over here early in the afternoon, called you, Noel, at the Twelfth Naval District and of course couldn't reach you, and began to collapse again about five. Just missed the extras, I suppose. I wrote you a note," he added to Noel, "and left it for the chambermaid to mail. From the look in your eye I suppose you never got it?"

"No. I suppose my letters to you in St. Louis haven't caught up with you yet? There were a whole lot of questions in them."

He shook his head. She thought suddenly, Measles make you wretched before you know what they are. I wonder— "Miles," she said, "when did you come down with your variety of plague?"

"About two days after I saw you last."

"Then you must have been feeling ill on that Thursday night when you'd been out to St. Francis Wood."

Lieutenant Coree blinked once. Anna Verney said, "How on earth did you know Coree had seen me?"

"Funny thing: Paul Watkins drove out there and saw Miles on the bench by the bus stop and recognized him from some photographs he'd seen."

For the fraction of a second there was a curious tension about the small table. It enclosed the three of them in something like a globe of clear plastic, while outside people laughed and glasses and money clinked. Then Coree said easily, "Was that the young man who offered me a lift? I'd been out there, as you guessed. That was the unfinished business I told you about, Noel; I felt that Anna and I must come to a clear understanding—"

"To part friends," said Anna Verney softly. "I couldn't bear to be anything but friends with you, Coree."

"And I was in something of a fog even during the visit, you remember, Anna? The headache hit me just as I got to the stop. I thought I'd better sit there for a while, because," said Miles candidly, "I was afraid I'd be sick in the Good Samaritan's car."

"I wish I'd known," Anna said. "I did notice that you were *distrait*, Coree, but I thought you were—well, formal because I was a married woman. And all the time—" She smiled at him ruefully. Her eyes suddenly glistened with unshed tears. "It's odd how comforted I feel, just to have you so forgiving, standing by me, and yet it's broken through the unreality. I'm not—not numb any longer. Do forgive me," she added in a low voice, and bent her head over her purse, searching for a handkerchief. "What a place to make a scene!"

She was in command of herself within a minute, and her clear gaze searched out Noel's. "I wasn't doing much crying earlier, was I, Bruce? Did you think I didn't care for Chester, because I said there were difficulties about the marriage? But I meant to make him a wonderful wife, the kind he'd always hoped for. Even after we lost the baby—"

"The baby?" said Noel in a startled whisper, and remembered Anna's unexplained illness at her aunt's home in mid-August.

"Oh, he was barely started, no more than a medical term to anyone else, but he was awfully real to me." Anna's white eyelids were lowered. "I've never been denied anything I wanted, people have been so wonderful to me, but—Nature saw to it that I shouldn't have everything."

Miles Coree was looking at her in a new way. Earlier he had been formally courteous, so much at ease that it seemed he had no feeling for her. Now his eyes held a limitless compassion, and something else which Noel could read only as intentness. He said, "I'm very sorry, Anna."

Noel thought, with a dart of physical pain, "He could love her again."

"I wish," Anna said, looking past him with a set face, "that if Chester had had to die anyway, he could have gone knowing that he was to have a child he could acknowledge. Well, there it is...Bruce, honey, there's something I've been wondering. Didn't you do a portrait sketch of Chet, at that party in the Plaster Works? I saw you looking at him, and your pencil going—did it turn out well?"

"Rather well. I meant it for you, Tannehill, but somehow the moment was never right for giving it."

"Do you suppose I could have it now?"

"Of course," Noel said. "I don't know what state it's in. It was lost for a week or two and it's just been returned."

"And you didn't look at it?"

"It turned up at Sherwin, and I told Porter to put it in my locker. You'll have it, or a copy."

"You're a darling, Bruce," Anna said, with her soft warm smile. She glanced down at her watch and uttered a startled "Oh! You'll never forgive me. It was the last thing I wanted, to intrude on your date, but—you'll never know how much this has helped me."

Miles Coree was on his feet, helping her out from behind the table. He was looking a little beyond her, and when his eyes fell on Noel she was startled to see how remote his whole bearing was. A million miles away, and receding farther at jet-propelled speed—

She said, "I think I must go too. This has been very pleasant, Miles," and waited.

His look focused on her with effort. For a moment she thought he would say, "No, please, stay." She could see his intention change. "It's been my pleasure," he told her politely. "I appreciate your coming, more than I can say."

Oh-oh. That for you, Bruce. The brush, the speeded parting, the congealed congé. She had not asked Miles Coree one of the questions that had been so painfully stored up against his coming; she hadn't even found out if he'd talked to the police; all that she knew was that she had no claim upon him and could not try to assert one while Tannehill needed him. And if he still loved Tannehill? Then the whole thing was over, it could be erased like a faulty line in a drawing.

But *if he doesn't*, thought Noel moving with composure down the short corridor to the lobby, I'll wait till this mess is cleared up and *then* see if Bruce does any graceful bowing out!

She caught a glimpse of herself in a mirror. She looked much the same as usual except that the creamy olive of her skin was delicately flushed. Women are wonderful, Noel told herself politely, and sketched a nod to her reflection in the glass. "Thank you, Miles," she said, "but I couldn't think of taking you out in the night air. If you'll just put me in a cab?"

She had almost forgotten that sense of being followed. It was not with her now. The cab-driver, lavishly over-tipped and paid by Miles, would have taken her to her very door, but she redirected him to a point near enough to her alley entrance. There was no one watching, no one in the dark length of the alley, no one to see her as she went quietly up the wooden stairs and let herself in at the newly opened door. So easy, she thought with a faint smile, so lucky—and what did it get me?

The night was still and hot, one of the rare moments in San Francisco's seasons when a chilly sea breeze was lacking. She was still cautious, she would not open the bay window that led to the small balcony. Chan might have changed his mind about guarding her; and if he were actually in his car below, she would not leave herself vulnerable to any possible villains. "They've probably forgotten all about me, too," Noel whispered to herself, "but just the same—"

She locked the dismantled door and managed without too much noise to push the cabinet back into place. The boards must be replaced tomorrow. She raised the one window she dared open, a small one on the same wall as the kitchen, but at a safe distance from the outside stair. Fortunately her bed was beside this window. She undressed and creamed her face in the dark and got into bed.

Then for a long time she lay awake, looking somberly at the silhouetted corner of the house next door, gray and ugly even in the clarity of moonlight.

The moon had gone down when the sound awakened her, something like tapping close beside her. She was hazy with sleep, in the state when waking events seem only the continuation of a dream. For a moment she was still, gazing up at the double glass of the raised window. A point of shadow appeared against it; someone was knocking to waken her—with a long stick? What was it?

"Bruce," said a hoarse soft voice outside. "Bruce. Wake up."

"What is it?" she said clearly, still half in the dream. "Who's out there?"

The dream began to melt away. She half sat up in bed, leaning on her elbows. "Who are you?" she repeated, her throat beginning to tighten.

"Call me Claude Pruitt," the hoarse voice said.

CHAPTER TEN

HER STIFLED GASP was heard outside, for there was the sound of a curious chuckle. She could place the voice now, obviously at the top of that flight of steps. She shook her head, still half drugged with sleep.

The voice came again, soft, slurred, unrecognizable. "That Navy man that was with you at the Plaster Works—you listenin'?"

"Yes, but what—"

"He was back there the next night."

Noel thought, this is part of the dream, I'm imagining a voice talking nonsense. Miles couldn't have—No, of course not. That Thursday night was the beginning of his illness.—And at once another thought crowded in: *he might not have known.*

"You want the cops to know that?"

"No!" She let it fall sharply. If Miles had done anything suspicious, the revelation must come from him.

"Quiet!" the voice warned her. She thought, Chan must be out of hearing. If he'd only come, and get one look at that man—but if I scream, the man will escape. If I could just see, myself—I'll have to stall for a moment—

"What do you want?" she muttered, and raised herself cautiously, inching toward the window. Against its dark gray the tip of the rod that had tapped the glass showed black and quivering.

The answer came pat. "Key to your locker at school."

"To my locker?" This was fantastic. Her mind wasn't clear yet.

And then she remembered Porter, on the telephone, talking about the locker and the sketch pad, and breaking off to address someone in the background. She said, "I—don't have the key," and turned without sound, getting into position.

"That's a lie. Get it."

She was near enough now. She leaned forward quickly—just one glimpse—

The rod slashed at her face. There was something sharp on the end, for quickly as she jerked away, it had grazed her hairline with a lash like a sting-ray's. As she put up a hand, dazedly feeling the scratch, the voice came again.

"Could 'a' got your eye with that," it said, and chuckled.

The dream broke wide open. She was broad awake now, her whole body prickling with needle-sharp reaction, a cold sickness climbing slowly in her chest. There had been relish in that half-audible laugh. *Could 'a' got your eye.*

"Get that key," the voice said, "or I'll come in."

She tried at last to call out, and no sound came. She got to her feet somehow, stumbled on her way to the dresser and groped in her handbag. Her thoughts ran vaguely, smothered by terror: That key must be important to him, but it is to me too, I didn't think I'd give it up—what was it I thought of when he first mentioned it? Something—a way out—

Her fingers closed on a small cold strip of metal, loose in a pocket. So that was it. Cheat to win. But hurry—he might really get in.

She got back to the window, her keys jingling in an unsteady hand. In a stifled croak she said, "How—"

The tip of the rod jiggled. "On here. No tricks. Don't drop it!"

The sharp thing at the end was a hook of wire. Noel's hand went out slowly, rigid with carefulness. She tried twice before the wire went through the hole in the key. Then it hung and swayed and was withdrawn.

"Okay," the man said after a second's wait. The steps creaked faintly, and his voice began to recede. "Back to bed, and keep still, or—" The creakings were farther away, and lower.

Noel thought dimly, Still, hell! I can't even swallow!

In the next moment she had to swallow, to grit her teeth and draw a long hard breath to fight down nausea. After another moment that passed, and she crouched shaking and spent on her bed; but coherent thought had returned.

She knew that nothing was lost as yet, for the man who called himself Claude Pruitt had taken with him the key that opened Rita Steffany's locker and not Noel's.

They had given away something. She knew now what they wanted, why they had been after her all that time. If she had not been unusually cautious she might have been caught and searched—if no more. Her pursuers had not been sure, until today, where the sketch pad was.

She thought, There must have been something in the drawing of the legs and the cement mixer, something I don't remember that I saw and transferred to paper. But how would they know that unless they'd seen the drawing?

And if they wanted the key to my locker, they must be people who can walk into Sherwin unquestioned, and they'll have to wait until the school's open. Well, let them, if they can get away with it! It won't matter if Rita's locker is searched.

Her own, lacking a key, was safe from anything short of dynamite. The late Mr. Sherwin had made his money in steel furniture, and his own products equipped the school.

Noel waited for her physical weakness to subside. She told herself, There must be a salient clue of some kind in that pad. The murderer shan't get it; I'll trust nobody, I won't show it to a soul until I've seen Miles. And then we can pool our memories of what happened on that Wednesday night and go to the police, and hand over the clue. It might even solve the whole case. Until I've seen Miles—because I'm going to see him again, whether that was a brush-off or not. He's got to tell Mr. Geraghty his part of the story. He owes me that much at least.

She sat up straight, pushing aside her other thoughts to face one that had been quietly asking for attention. Who knew that the sketch pad was in her locker?

The person who had been in Mary Porter's office while that conversation was going on might easily have seen the sketch block. What had Porter said?—"I don't care if you've spent two weeks at the police station."

She hadn't been speaking to Papa Gene, judging by her tone. Maybe Steffany, maybe any of the other sculptors.

Of course, Noel thought feverishly, I told Miles and Tannehill this evening. But it could never have been Tannehill in overalls behind the cement mixer, she couldn't have ridden around with the man who shot at me—she couldn't have had anything to do with it. Miles? Certainly not Miles. Certainly not.

And which of the men she knew had crept up the unused outer stairway, risking recognition, to get that key? It was more by luck than cleverness that she'd been able to cheat him…A thought brought her to her feet with another surge of terror. What if he'd detected the substitution and should come back? Did he know about the unblocked door to those stairs?

She felt her way, dizzily, to the front window. She leaned out and said, "Chan?" in a voice that had no carrying power. What if he'd relaxed his vigilance too much, and gone to sleep—or decided to stay away altogether?

She had underestimated him. His head was out of the car window in the fraction of a moment. He looked up at her and around at the sleeping houses, and then crossed the sidewalk and without visible effort swarmed up the fretwork pillars to the balcony outside her window.

"I'm so glad you're there," said Noel faintly. "I—maybe I was having a nightmare, but I thought there was a prowler down in the alley."

"Nobody toward the front," Lockett told her. "I been keepin' an eye out. What'd it sound like?"

"I thought steps, and a kind of rapping."

"Want me to come in and look round?"

"No!" Those boards, still stacked in the kitchen—She said, "If there was anyone, he couldn't be in here. But would you stay on the balcony?"

"Sure, baby," said Mr. Lockett comfortably. "Here. Have a stick of gum."

Noel burst into laughter, half affectionate, half hysterical. "I will, Chan, I will. It's just what I need. I hope Sarah deserves you!"

She fell back into bed, managed to think dimly about Miss Porter's hours at Sherwin—must get there before eight-thirty tomorrow morning and find out who—get that sketch block out of the locker—hide it—

And was at once deep in exhausted slumber, and did not awaken until well after nine.

That was all hooey about your subconscious telling you when to wake up, Noel thought crossly, hurrying to get dressed in the unwelcome heat. This was going to be another broiling day. The shantung dress was the coolest one she owned, and the linen sandals that went with it were all right, but the matching bag was on its last legs. Well—no matter. She drank coffee so hot that it brought tears to her eyes, and ran downstairs. Snatching the mail from her box was an automatic gesture, for letters were unimportant now.

She stepped out into the morning shadows of the narrow street and found Chan waiting for her.

Her recoil of dismay must have been obvious, for he said uneasily, "Yeah, I'm here again. Look, baby, I let up on my job too soon. This business ain't over by a long shot. I'm goin' to keep on stickin' close until the Chief's made his arrest!"

This would happen, Noel thought. Go home, Fido, home, sir! She said, "But I'm just going to classes this morning, Chan."

"I'll drive you out to your school. I'll be around."

Experience had proven that there was no use in trying to dissuade him. She got into his car, thankful at least for the lift.

He parked so carefully, in an unrestricted side street, that she realized he meant to come into Sherwin with her and "be around." Like as not he'd see fit to follow her to the locker room. I don't know why I ever started this, Noel grumbled silently. If I was going to do the police-deceiving act I should have said I wasn't afraid, and then taken whatever was coming to me.

She started ahead as he locked the car, hoping to gain a few minutes at least, and defeated herself by hurrying. The underarm bag slipped from her grasp and Lockett had caught up before she could retrieve its contents. What was worse, the fall had finally ruined the bag's weak clasp.

Noel set her teeth and walked on grimly, cursing herself for carelessness. That accident could happen again, and shoot out incriminating papers along with her lipstick.

Miss Porter's office door stood, as usual, hospitably open, and the secretary was briskly typing inside. Noel said with the emphasis of desperation, "I want to talk to Miss Porter alone, Chan," and closed the door behind her. Through its glass panel the round eyes regarded her.

"You get your package?" the secretary inquired.

"Not yet. Porter, can you by any chance remember who was here, in the office, last night when you telephoned me?"

Miss Porter stopped typing to consider. "I was on the phone solid for about an hour yesterday afternoon. Let's see— one of the students, Watkins from Sculpture Four, was in taking out her honorable-discharge papers, but I don't know exactly what time."

"I heard you say that the person had been with the police."

"Oh, that. Steffany, in a state of drama. Was that while Watkins was in, or after? Anyway, Steffany had to find Gene Fenmer without a minute's delay. Well, my dear, you know Gene leaves at four sharp every day, and how could I know where he was? In fact," said Miss Porter, rolling a small eloquent brown eye at Noel, "if I tried to keep track of *him* outside of hours, I'd have another full-time job on my hands. Why people should think—"

"Thanks, Porter," Noel cut her off. "And you were grand to take care of my masterpieces."

She went toward the locker rooms no wiser than before. It still might have been anyone, anyone! And yet she was sure that the voice outside her window had been a man's.

"Kinda gloomy and lonesome back here, ain't it?" said a cautionary voice over her shoulder.

"Not at all," Noel snapped. "I'm perfectly safe here— thank you, Chan."

He escorted her to the door just the same. He stood there, looking around; he stood there and stood there. "You hear they had a prowler here last night?" he said. "Yeah; window busted, somebody got in. Nothin' missin' that they can find out."

Noel said that it was a funny coincidence. She leaned against the closed door of her locker with fine unconcern and looked through the mail she had taken from her box. A hopeful note from the financial committee of her sorority at Michigan—how long ago *that* seemed! An advertisement; a letter from someone in Bakersfield.

"Chan, maybe there's a message for you in this," Noel said, visited with an inspiration. She tore open the letter and found that she was in luck. June Verney had written, "Miss Bostwick's name is Shields, now, and the last her old pals had heard, she had gone back to nursing at Children's Hospital in San Francisco. They said she lived in an apartment out near there, somewhere. I only hope this will do something for Chan. Give him my love, if you think Sarah won't mind."

Chan Lockett read the letter. "She wouldn't mind, I guess," he said, and stood considering the information, reflectively chewing. "Heck, I guess the Chief musta checked up on all the leads in this part of the case. Just the same—"

"You don't know if he saw Mrs. Shields?"

"He might 'a'."

"But if he didn't, what a neat little scoop for you—just supposing she knew anything."

"I ought to have pictures of all the dames in the case," Chan said, hesitating, "and I don't know where—"

"That's easy," Noel told him. "I'll draw them for you." She opened her locker, took one brief and exultant glance at the package under the letter slot, and got out a fresh sketch block. She could do Tannehill and Steffany and Watkins from memory, so often had they been her subjects; she took a few steps to a mirror and drew her own face, gazing at the reflection, her pencil moving swiftly and with decision. "Here, give me one of those snapshots of Sarah," she said. "Any one. We ought to have a few odd sketches in here, so she'd have more to choose from. And—come on out in the hall." Her footsteps rapped down the polished boards to the office door. "Porter, look up a minute, will you?" Miss Porter, used to this sort of thing, obligingly complied while continuing to type.

Noel turned to Chan and handed him the sheaf of sketches. They were rough, but she had an amazing knack for catching a likeness. Chan looked them over and then gazed at her, almost bug-eyed with admiration. "How do you do 'em so fast?" he said reverently. "Say, you know—these look like something!"

"All right. You ask Mrs. Bostwick-Shields if any of these could be her patient, ten years older. I suppose she'd know enough to discount the color of the hair, or—"

"I can tell her all that stuff, blocking off the features and all that. Children's Hospital, huh? I wish they'd all be as easy to find."

Chan took the sketches and trotted down the steps to his car. Noel watched him lovingly through the glass of the door. Good Fido; that's a good dog. And thank Heaven!

She was back at her locker; there was no one in the dusky length of the room, and she risked a quick glance at the drawings. Chester Verney—the unfinished sketch of Paul Watkins' hands, manipulating his ball of clay—the one taken from the unsuspecting rear of three guests at the party, seated side by side on upturned boxes and buckets: Steffany's sleek head with the earrings, Papa Gene's white poll with the fringe of beard catching the light at either side, Rome's shaggy head with the points of hair growing low on the neck and his left hand raised to rub his ear. Here was the one of the legs sticking out from behind the cement mixer. Now!

It was exactly as she had remembered it. There was not one new feature, nothing at all that would reveal the man's identity. *Nothing.*

She raised her head quickly. Someone was coming through the hall or down the stairs; she had delayed too long. If she were to hide the drawings and get out before Chan returned, she couldn't wait in such a well-frequented place for her chance. She listened; that deep voice was familiar. Inspector Geraghty, asking about the prowler! She looked at her purse, rejected it as a safe hiding place. "Somewhere on me would be better," Noel muttered, tucking the sketch pad nonchalantly under her arm and moving into the hall.

The inspector's deep voice was coming from around the bend of the stairs. If he saw her he'd want to know about *her* prowler, he'd delay her—She slipped lightly toward the rear of the hall, and looked into Fenmer's office. No one there.

Once inside, with the door closed, she was faced with another problem. Those heroines of costume novels who put incriminating letters in their bosoms had probably worn low décolletage and plenty of lace frills; anything that happened to their bosoms was the work of a moment. She had chosen—like a dimwit, she thought furiously—to wear this dress with the high round neck that fastened up the back with a zipper and was too thin to conceal several sheets of bond paper, even if the paper wouldn't at once slip right through the belt and cascade downward. It would have to be the bra; and that necessitated taking off this blasted dress.

Noel looked at the large windows and then despairingly around the room. She had never been here before; there was a door, would it by any chance lead to a private lavatory? She jerked it open without hesitation. No; but it had concealed a closet in which were hung three or four of Papa Gene's huge white overall costumes. She was inside, glancing at her watch as she closed the door. Almost eleven, and people would be coming out of classes and streaming about the building; better step on it.

She was out of the dress and had folded the used sheets of her drawing pad to a size that could be wedged into the cups of her brassiere—the stiff bond paper insisted on sticking out in peaks, and the problem was driving her to stifled giggles— when the door to Fenmer's office opened and two persons came hurriedly in. The door closed. She could hear a key turning in the lock.

"Now, for God's sake!" said Papa Gene's voice testily.

The other person began at once to pour out words. "You've got to help me, Gene, you've got to tell them there was nothing in it! You tried to make me yourself, and you never got anywhere, can't you sink your vanity and tell 'em the truth, to get me out of a jam—the worst jam I've ever been in? They don't *believe* me!"

Noel, still with her dress off, was held unmoving for a moment; then she grasped the closet doorknob and called out through a four-inch crack, "Hold it! I'm—I'm in here!"

The woman—Steffany, surely?—gave a loud shriek. There were heavy footsteps outside and the door was wrenched wide open. Noel had just time to retreat into the folds of the overalls, swathing herself modestly. "Bruce!" Papa Gene said incredulously, peering at her face. "What in the blazing hell do you think you're doing?"

Noel, who had begun to laugh helplessly, stopped at the sight of his face. It was lowering, congested, angrier than she had ever thought the jovial-seeming old man could look.

She began to speak, caught herself, swallowed. "Nothing but fasten my bra! It got unhooked and I had to take my dress off. Can't a girl have a minute's privacy?"

"And what's wrong with the little girls' room upstairs?" said Papa Gene with ominous dryness. He searched her face, his dark eyes hard and suspicious. "Come out of there. No, never mind your dress."

Noel jerked two of the overall suits from their hooks and draped them across her shoulders. She stalked out of the closet with what dignity she could muster, her sense of absurdity entirely quenched by Papa Gene's expression.

He said, "Is this a frame-up? Do you have a friend with a camera hidden under the desk? If so, he's welcome to take shots of the three of us, but I'd like to know who put you up to it—you, of all women."

Steffany was standing, leaning against Fenmer's desk, her color high and her breath coming quickly. She cut in, "Skip it, won't you, Gene? Never mind why she's here, maybe her bra did come unhooked! *She'll* help me. Bruce, you can tell the police where I was on most of those nights when my neighbors thought I was hiding out in some sort of love nest. I was staying with you! We can work out the dates somehow, can't we? Bruce, you've got to stick by me!"

Noel got her mind into focus, with some difficulty. "What nights? Not last week, or the week of the murder? There was only one night—"

"No, no, for months past. You know I stayed with you once a week anyway. I—I didn't tell the people in the other studios where I was going, I let them think—" She broke off, her breath coming jerkily, and turned again to Fenmer. "Gene, for God's sake, you've got to help me prove I wasn't as easy as I said I was! If I have to go to every man I—and ask them to—" She began to cry.

"Let's get this straight," said Fenmer wearily. "Do you want to convince the police you're a virgin? If so—"

"Well, I'm not—exactly," Rita sniffled convulsively, "but hardly at all! I mean—oh, you *know* what I mean. Anyway, I wanted to make people believe—I hinted about one man or another, and I sort of strung the boy-friends along, I suppose they always thought there was hope, for a while at least, because I look so—so—" She groped in her pocket for a handkerchief, found a piece of Kleenex on which lipstick had been blotted and used it, leaving a remarkable smear of pink across her upper lip.

"I begin to see," said Fenmer dispassionately. "Your reputation may not be as lurid as you seem to think it is. Some of those boy-friends are in the habit of referring to you as Deep-fr—Ah, h'm." He glanced at Noel. "The story about your being Chester Verney's mistress was your own fabrication?"

"Every bit of it! And if I can prove that the rest of the stories were lies, maybe the police will believe me! Most of the nights when I told the crowd—or let them think—that I was going to be with him, I went to sleep with Bruce."

Noel closed her eyes for a despairing moment. Those nights—! filled with Steffany's murmured confidences about the Bohemian life—"Vissi d'arte, vissi d'amore—" And all, it seemed, for the sake of a dubious effect!

"I hardly knew Chet Verney," said Rita, her eyes overflowing again. "I just picked him out to brag about because he was a glamour character, and rich and kind of notorious, he seemed like a safe choice. And he belonged to Tannehill. Believe you me, I'd never have said anything at that party about having slept with him if I'd known he was going to be killed! I—I just hoped it'd get back to her after a while, make her think he hadn't been giving her all his attention those months they'd been going around together. D-do her good," said Steffany in a loud wail, and wept afresh.

"You make me tired," said Noel. "What did you have against Tannehill? She'd done *you* plenty of favors, and never expected any thanks."

"I didn't want her damned favors. I didn't ask her to find me a studio, and railroad me into taking it, and shove her cast-off furniture into it. I couldn't seem to help taking the stuff once the thing was started, but I've hated every minute that I was under an obligation to her. I hate *her!*" Rita said with a spurt of venom.

"But for Pete's sake, *why?*"

Fenmer stood a little apart from the two women, his fingertips resting on the top of his desk, his bright dark eyes going from one to the other. He began to caress his short, well-groomed beard.

"She had everything. She's always had everything. Her parents never denied her a thing, she was such a sweet loving child, and she has an income of her own and a rich aunt and looks—Lord, hasn't she got looks!—and she's miles ahead of the rest of us in sculpture, and she had every man she wanted and all the love and admiration and—slavery of everybody who knew her. Except me," Rita said, her eyes glittering. "And finally she got Chester Verney, and *he* had everything and was prepared to give it to her. It's *too much!*"

"I hope you remember that all of Tannehill's luck came from herself?" said Noel angrily. "If people are crazy about her, it's because she's lovely and generous. She fostered her own talent. If she has everything, she's earned it."

Rita Steffany blew her nose furiously. "Well, she oughtn't to have everything on earth, nobody ought to. You can't get it by being sweet and giving people handouts they haven't asked for, any more than you can by having tantrums or committing a string of crimes. Some time you come up against a wish that people *won't* jump to satisfy for you, and then where are you? It ought to be like that, anyway, but it wasn't for Tannehill. She kept right on, time after time, always something better—"

"Steffany," said Papa Gene in that dry, harsh voice that was so unlike his usual one, "you've made some rather acute observations there; but I believe we were discussing your own situation. I shall be glad to do anything I can, but it's possible that the police will take my denials for chivalrous lies. I know nothing, after all, about your private life, nor your past. Bruce can't very well know the whole of it, nor account for all your nights."

Rita Steffany sat down, looking utterly fatigued, in the chair by his desk. "I suppose not," she said forlornly.

"You're not the first, I imagine, that has been caught in her own romancing. But what I should like to know is," said Fenmer almost pettishly, "why in the devil's flaming name did you tell all those lies in the first place? Woman With a Past— hot stuff in the studio world—"

"You're pretty dumb if you can't see that," said Rita harshly. "I came into Sherwin on the strength of my submitted work, didn't I? And I got to San Francisco, and it was just the sort of life I'd d-dreamed of, the atmosphere—and how was I to know that all of the art crowd weren't just like they are in books? I didn't want to wander in all wide-eyed and virtuous like somebody from the country, I thought they'd laugh at me. I've—I had to—those men at the police station went into every minute of my past, and I suppose everyone'll have to know, but I think I'd die—I'd rather have died a hundred times over, these two years, than tell anybody the truth." Her black head went down on the desk, and she succumbed to weeping interspersed with hiccoughs. "W-would you want to tell 'em your name was Marvel Shump, and your father kept a feed store in Alturas? And you'd been brought up to be *good*?"

Fenmer blinked, and waited a minute to make sure he had caught the sense of her words. When he spoke, his gentleness was almost startling. "My girl, nobody would have given a damn about your morals, good or bad. Furthermore, with your latent talent you could call yourself Frau Goering, if you chose, and make it into a proud name. And now, will you blow your nose and get out of here?"

"You can just wait, Steffany, until I get my dress on," Noel put in crisply. She hitched at the sagging folds of the overalls, and began a retreat toward the closet.

"Not 'Steffany,'" said Papa Gene. "I believe complete honesty is the best line for you, my girl. Not Steffany. Shump— Ah. H'm—I confess you may have a slight case there. Shump," he repeated dreamily.

"All right," Noel said in a strangled voice from the closet. "I'm through. Wait for me."

"You may go now," said Fenmer coolly. "I want a few words with Bruce."

"I haven't time now, Papa Gene, and I don't want any of your little talks. There's—what are you *doing?*" A key had turned on her.

In darkness she rattled the doorknob and shouted crossly to be let out. Papa Gene was herding Steffany into the outer corridor and his footsteps were rapidly receding. Noel yelled again, and kicked the door, but only once; she had on open-toed shoes. This was an inner door, on the rear of the building—

She stopped trying to make herself heard, and with a sinking heart considered the situation. She could not be sure what the old man had in mind, but he was a notorious rake, and—was it possible that her presence, half-dressed, in the closet of his office, had misled him completely? But not in broad daylight, she thought, scandalized. He couldn't...Might as well be prepared to fight it off; if I only had something to defend myself with!

She felt around the walls of the closet for some forlorn hope in the form of a weapon. Did Papa Gene ever carry a penknife in his overalls pockets? Papers, a handkerchief—here was something hard. Noel felt the small heavy object with a sense of familiarity. A ring with a great square seal—Well, she thought hardily, it will do as a knuckle-duster.

She clutched it and nervously rearranged her concealed sketches, which crackled in an alarming manner, as she heard returning footsteps. There were two sets of heavy ones, marching ominously into the room. The closet door was flung open.

"She's dressed now, naturally," said Eugene Fenmer in a glacial voice, as Noel emerged. Inspector Geraghty stood surveying her with his customary mildness, but she thought she could detect a twinkle in his deep-set gray eyes. She said, "Mr. Fenmer has been drawing unwarranted conclusions, Inspector. I don't care for his methods."

"I'm taking no chances this time. I had enough trouble with those creeps from Smithers and Bush, earlier this summer." Fenmer eyed Noel grimly; then his eyes dropped a few inches and a tinge of astonishment entered his look.

"And who would Smithers and Bush be?" Noel snapped. "And how am I supposed to be connected with them?"

"They're a firm of private inquiry agents, Miss Bruce," said Geraghty, "specializing in divorce cases, and some blackmail on the side, like as not. So they were after you, Gene?"

The old man's eyes sparked. "They weren't secret enough. I found out what they wanted—some dirt on my relations with Tannehill. Anything that had been between us was far in the past, but it's to be presumed the creeps did not believe that. Questioning my students, trying to bribe my housekeeper! *Slugs!*" Papa Gene very nearly spat the word. "I caught one of them. He did no business for two or three weeks afterward."

"So that's what happened to Brady Smithers' nose," said Mr. Geraghty, pleased to be enlightened. "Back in July, wasn't it?"

"It was. He threatened me—*me!* He promised to bide his time and catch me in a scandal that would ruin the school's reputation. The last person I expected to play in with him, however," said Fenmer, "was the little Bruce."

"She wasn't in with them. I'd vouch for that," Geraghty said. "Did you ever get a line on who hired Brady to spy on you?"

Papa Gene gave a loud snort. "No trouble about that. Verney."

"Chester Verney?" Noel caught her breath. "He was collecting evidence against Tannehill after they were married?"

"Verney didn't always fight clean," said Fenmer. "Well, I may have misjudged you, young Bruce. If Butch is sure of his ground—perhaps I owe you an apology."

"It's accepted," said Noel quickly. She was in a fever to be gone and rid of his penetrating glance. If only this dress were decorated with a heavy fall of lace! She added, with an attempt at a grin, "I meant to sell my virtue dear. This was in your pocket."

She unclenched her hand and the two men gazed at the object presented. "I thought I'd recognized this," Noel added. "It's Rome's ring."

"Will Rome's, is it?" Geraghty said. "How come you had it stashed away, Gene?" He turned a suddenly level look on Fenmer.

"Where in the hell did I get that?" said Papa Gene in obvious bewilderment. "I can't have—Ah. I remember. I picked it up, thinking it had been lost, and planned to return it to Rome; but it so happened I didn't see him for several days, and the ring must have stayed in the pocket of an overall I was not wearing. In short," said Fenmer, a hand caressing his beard, "I forgot the damned thing."

"Rome didn't notice his loss? He made no inquiries?" Fenmer shook his head, and Noel murmured that she wouldn't know, she seldom saw Rome. "Where did you find it, Gene? Here in the school?"

"At the Plaster Works, I believe. Yes; behind a bin of clay that was being moved."

"Behind a bin of clay. Queer place for a person to lose a ring without noticing it."

Fenmer shrugged. "Rome doesn't wear the ring when he's working. Perhaps he dropped it and someone else did stash it away."

"Meaning to keep it? Why not carry it off, a small object like this? And there were no inquiries—" Mr. Geraghty mused. He lifted his head. "From the position of the bin, could the ring have been thrown there?"

"Could have been." Fenmer looked at him with sudden attention. Noel glanced from one to the other; her desire to be gone was momentarily submerged.

"When was it found?"

Fenmer thought again. "Not last week, not the week before. Early in the month, I should surmise. There were several days when Rome was not at work. Off on a binge, without doubt. It would have been then; the first of the week after—after the announcement party." He nodded his white head with vigor. "Monday of that week. I had postponed my visit of instruction the previous Friday."

Geraghty's brows drew together. He took the ring in his hand. "A square seal," he remarked, and for some reason sighed.

Noel began to edge toward the door, and Papa Gene sprang, with his amazing agility, to open it for her. "You have developed enormously since I last saw you," he said with a pointed glance.

"What's that? You don't make cracks without some reason, Gene." Mr. Geraghty was interested.

There was a teasing spark in Fenmer's eyes, Noel saw with horror. He could throw reticence to the winds when he chose; it wouldn't be impossible that he should explain.

"I've just thought of something interesting, Mr. Geraghty," she said sweetly, turning in the doorway. "You know that we'd decided the man who pursued me in the car was wearing Paul's cervical collar?"

"Yeah. It's been found, by the way, in that heap of rubbish in the Plaster Works courtyard. No prints," Geraghty remarked.

"Oh? Well, you know, I've thought about that disguise. It seemed as if it had to be used to conceal some physical characteristic that couldn't be changed in a hurry."

Geraghty eyed her, and now the twinkle was more pronounced. He knew what was coming, but he was playing up to her. "Yes?"

"For instance," said Noel with a sunny smile, "a beard. Why don't you check Mr. Fenmer's alibis again, if I may suggest it?" She turned smartly and walked out.

CHAPTER ELEVEN

SHE HEARD THE DOOR close behind her, and hoped, as she raced down the hall, that it would take Papa Gene a few minutes to kid Geraghty out of that one. She burst into the secretary's office. "Porter," she said, "you've always been an angel to me, be an extra special one now. Let me hide in the file room, and you call me a taxi. And while it's coming, telephone the Clift for me. If you will, I'll stand in the next nylon line I see and get you a pair."

"I wear tens," said Miss Porter obligingly, reaching for the telephone. Her bead-brown eyes fell on Noel's breast, and she paused. "You in falsies? What for? I can't say they're very good ones."

Noel burst into irrepressible laughter. "Papa Gene just loved them. Look, Porter, I'll be in here—"

"You want your visitor to come in too?" Miss Porter inquired.

"Visitor?"

"Navy man, and quite a dish. He's in the exhibit room. Shall I tell him you left without my seeing you?"

"No! Skip the whole thing!" Noel dashed out again in the middle of a remark from Miss Porter. There was not much time even if she could dodge Mr. Geraghty again. Everything would have to be done on the split second for the next few hours. She reached the archway to the exhibit room breathless. When Miles Coree turned and saw her she could only smile questioningly.

He came toward her, saying, "Is there any place around here with a door that shuts?"

"Some that I don't recommend," said Noel, again giving way to laughter. "For about ten minutes, we could have the locker room."

"Where is it?" said Miles Coree.

The steel products of the late Mr. Sherwin were about them in the gloom. "Noel," Miles said, and pulled her to him.

Presently he released her. "And now, my darling girl," he said, "will you tell me the meaning of that performance you put on last night?"

"The performance *I* put on—"

"'I must be going now, Miles. Oh, no, don't come out in the cold'—What happened to you? Did you suddenly get to thinking I'd murdered Chester Verney?"

If she had ever had any creeping sensations of doubt, they were stilled now. "No," she said. "No! But you didn't know I existed, toward the last."

"I didn't know—! Well, let it pass."

"Pass, nothing. I felt as if I were intruding on Tannehill's date with *you*, sitting there with no more to say than a bottle behind the bar."

"Hell, my darling, you could have outsat her! *I* didn't urge her to stay when we first met."

"I couldn't outsit her, I couldn't. Miles, she's done so much for me, I couldn't flaunt the situation in her face; that is, if there was any situation to flaunt."

"There is indeed. I hope you'll flaunt it for all you're worth. But may I say, Miss Bruce, that with another man—one not gifted with my mental powers and pigheadedness—you might have nipped a situation in the bud?"

"I took that risk," said Noel. "Of course, I rather hoped you were pigheaded. Miles, we've got to talk fast. Have you been to the police?"

"Hadn't thought of it. I never saw Chester Verney in my life, and I had no evidence to offer."

"Maybe you have. Maybe they've been looking for you and hadn't heard you were in town. They might even suspect you. I've been—leaving your name out of it completely, until I saw you, I wasn't going to tell them that you were with me at the Plaster Works that night and that I told you in detail how a statue was taken down, and about the shellac. You didn't go back the next night, did you? Oh, I know you didn't! I've been through the most absurd maneuvers last night and today, trying to keep them from seeing that sketch I did of you standing on one leg among the covered models. I've—"

"You've been shielding me," said Miles Coree. He leaned back against a locker and burst into laughter. "You bat-brained little nincompoop. Oh, Lord. Had she but known!"

"Had I but known, I'd have done the same thing all over again. You weren't here. I was the only one who knew you had any connection with the case—except Anna, and she kept still too."

"Really."

"And do you think that while you weren't here to speak for yourself, I was going to turn you in, give the police material for a lot of absurd suspicions, *the very first thing?*"

Miles Coree grinned at her. "Now that you describe it that way, I can see that it might have made our third meeting a bit awkward. Now what do we do, get our stories to coincide? You haven't told any major lies, I presume."

"I'll show you the evidence," Noel said. "It's hidden; you don't know what wrong ideas the police can work up.—Dear heaven, it's ten minutes of twelve. In no time there'll be a mob in here…" She was walking to the far end of the room as she spoke, unfastening her bra through her dress, loosening her belt. She gave herself a lively shake, and the crumpled sketches came sliding to the floor.

From a chair in the dim corner behind the last locker, Chan Lockett rose to confront her. "I'll pick 'em up, baby," he said.

Noel, stock-still, looked at him with unconcealed horror. "Chan," she cried out accusingly, "you were supposed to be out near Cherry Street!"

"I telephoned before I left," said Lockett amiably, "and they told me this Mrs. Shields wouldn't go off duty till two this afternoon, and was busy till then."

"Aren't you even ashamed of eavesdropping?"

"Well, it's the first time I've heard anything useful since I started bodyguardin' you. Hi, buddy," Lockett added casually as Miles Coree came up.

"Hi," said Lieutenant Coree gravely. "All is discovered, I take it. I'd better give myself up without a struggle."

"Well," said Chan Lockett, "it saves them haulin' you off in bracelets. I'll drive you down to the Hall of Justice if you want, but I'd like to be sure that there won't be no tricks."

❀ ❀ ❀

Here was the dingy office again, with the scarred plaster walls and the rolltop desk, and the oblique view of Portsmouth Square its only redeeming note. The look on Inspector Geraghty's face could not be considered in the latter class.

"Okay, Lockett, you can go," he said as the younger man finished his recital.

Chan said nothing, but his round eyes expressed dismay and longing.

"Yeah. Find yourself an errand if you want to. This may take some time."

When there were only three of them in the office—besides Mr. Kotock, as usual so silent as to seem almost nonexistent—Geraghty leaned back in his swivel chair and gave Miles Coree one of his penetrating glances. "Well, Lieutenant," he said, "I'd have been interested in meeting you earlier. We knew that Mrs. Verney had been engaged to a Navy man several years ago; it was not until yesterday that we found out that you had been in town, and in communication with Mrs. Verney, at about the time when Chester Verney died. Possibly you're telling the truth about not having heard of the murder until the end of your, uh, second convalescence. You've been off T.I. for more than twenty-four hours. You made no effort to contact us."

Miles Coree's long face was inscrutable, his hazel eyes steady. "I felt that I had nothing salient to offer, sir."

Geraghty said wearily, "There was a man on her at the Clift, of course. Kind of an interesting conversation you had in the bar."

Noel's face flamed; she made a convulsive movement in her chair, but neither of the men looked at her. "I might not have chosen to discuss those matters in public," Miles said, "but since Mrs. Verney did, their being overheard can't matter."

"And after that," said Geraghty musingly, "you did not feel free to volunteer your part of the story to us."

"I still felt that there was no story to tell." Miles' tone was even. "If there had been anything you wanted to know, I assumed that you would ask me directly."

"It was my idea," Geraghty said, "to give you a bit of rope."

"I doubt that I could be hanged by it no matter how much you gave me."

"Very well," said the inspector, flicking a glance at his assistant. "Let's go back over the story. You met Miss Tannehill in Chicago in 1941, and became engaged to her. When you went overseas in '42, she came out to the Coast to continue her studies and to be near the probable place of your leaves."

"Correct."

"Did you get any leave?"

Coree shrugged. "A spell or two in Honolulu. I had a year's extra service, but I didn't get Stateside until now."

"And in July of this year you heard from Miss Tannehill that she had married Chester Verney; is that correct too?"

"Yes. She seemed to have acted under some sort of mysterious compulsion, and didn't realize for a time that"— Miles was choosing his words carefully—"she would feel so remorseful about the, uh, unceremonious breaking of our engagement. That, at least, was what I gathered from her letters. She offered to ask Verney for a divorce at once, possibly with some confused idea of making up to me for what she had done. She figured it would be cleared up by December, when I expected to come home. Naturally I wrote to her that the idea was not to be considered. I had one more letter, written early in August, in which she said that I was right; that she had changed her mind and meant to do the best job she could with her marriage. It was a very touching letter," said Coree quietly. "She asked if I wouldn't continue to feel friendly toward her, and perhaps come to see her when I got back."

Geraghty nodded. "Then you returned—when?"

"My ship docked on September eighth. My leave did not begin until the fourteenth; I wasn't sure at the time, by the way, whether it would be extended into terminal leave. I was on duty daily until sixteen hours. The time after that," said Miles with a faint smile, "I spent daily in trying to reach Anna. At the time, I planned to go East as soon as my leave started, and I wanted to get the job of our meeting over with as soon as possible."

"Mrs. Verney avoided you, I take it?"

"She was frank about saying so. It seemed that her husband would have been badly hurt if a suitor from her past had turned up. I didn't know that at the time, of course, or I shouldn't have pressed the matter. What I had in mind," he looked fleetingly at Noel, "was to assure her once more that the break was clean, that my friendly feelings would be—felt at a distance."

"And you didn't succeed in finding Mrs. Verney until the night of September thirteenth?"

"I had no idea where she had gone until I had a message from her that morning."

"So. And you told her what you've just described to me."

"That's what we talked about, Inspector," said Miles. "*And nothing else,* Inspector. It was a short meeting, I was feeling fairly ill already, and I got back aboard ship in a rocky state. I don't remember much about the rest of that evening."

"H'm. Did you have a cabin to yourself?"

The heavy black brows went up. "I shared it with another officer. He wasn't there on any night that week. Several nights, I wasn't there either, until two or three hours."

"Which nights?"

Coree considered. "I was on the town, alone, Saturday, Monday, and Tuesday. Sunday I spent with some old friends at the Fairmont. Wednesday—Miss Bruce and I had a job to do together. Thursday you know about, and on the following morning I was carted over to the contagious ward on T.I. in, I am told, a stupor."

"I see. And you were at the Clift on the night of the twenty-first?"

"I was, Inspector, and paying no attention to the newspapers. All I wanted was to be left alone. The next morning, they got me back to the ward again." He looked at Noel again and noticed the intensity with which she was avoiding Geraghty's eyes. "Was there anything special about the twenty-first, besides the discovery of Verney's body?"

"Will you tell your story again, Miss Bruce?" Geraghty said.

Noel told it. She included for the first time the detail of the white-topped cap, and her theory about why it had been worn. Resolutely, she avoided Miles' eyes also.

"Good God," he said explosively as her last words were spoken, "you went through all that, believing it was because of some secret you were keeping that those men were after you?"

"That was about it," Noel murmured. "Except that I really didn't know then what they wanted of me. The only thing I could imagine was that something had actually happened on Wednesday night, and they planned to—they knew we'd been together until well after midnight, and—"

"I repeat," said Miles Coree affectionately, "you were a bat-brained nincompoop."

"It was my risk," said Noel sharply, "and I chose to take it."

"One interesting point, Lieutenant Coree," Geraghty said, "is that Miss Bruce saw no more of her pursuers after that night."

"Until last night," Noel said with a bravado born of guilt.

Geraghty sighed heavily. "All right," he said. "Tell me about last night. God Almighty, if people 'ud only learn! Right at the moment is the time when we want to know these things."

Noel told him about last night.

He pounced; he took her over and over the story, dragging out every detail. She could tell him nothing except that the voice had been a man's, and unrecognizable.

After the final reiterations, Geraghty gave up. He said, "Okay. Let's get back to these drawings. It seems fairly clear that those were what the men wanted. Which ones did you do on the night of the twelfth?"

"These last two," said Noel, taking the sketches from his desk. "This one of Verney—I'll keep that, Anna wanted a copy—and this one of the hands, and this of the three heads—those can go in your wastebasket, if you don't mind—were all done at the engagement party. Here's the one of the legs. You can see for yourself, Mr. Geraghty, they're nothing but legs; there isn't a thing to identify them. And," she gave Miles a slanting, rueful look, "immediately after the legs, and obviously done on the same occasion—I'd dated them, heaven help me—comes the one of the Cursing Lieutenant."

"Go over the events of that visit to the Plaster Works, if you please."

"All right, if you'll fill in any gaps, Miles. We got there a little after seven, and found the door unlocked, and went in."

"I had asked Miss Bruce where the sculptors did their work when they weren't at their own studios," Coree said. "At the time I was trying to find Anna. When we got there I felt curious as to the set-up—in fact, not knowing how the clay was preserved, I imagined that I might see what Anna had been working on."

"The man," Noel took it up, "was behind the cement mixer and stayed there. He hammered once or twice and made scraping noises as if he were repairing the machinery. You didn't see his face, did you, Miles?"

"No more than what you've drawn there. I went into the sculptors' workroom for a moment and looked around. Then I looked back through the door and saw that Miss Bruce was sketching the legs. I asked permission to glance over her shoulder, and made some remark—by George," Coree said, his eyes suddenly glinting, "I said, 'You certainly can catch a like-ness,' or something of the sort."

Geraghty nodded. "That did it, I expect," he said.

"Then we both went into the workroom. Miles, I think you said something about what a cheery spot it was, like one of our better graveyards."

"Anything special to make you feel a graveyard atmosphere?"

"Only the look of those figures, sir, like malformed monuments."

"It felt queer, too," Noel murmured, "but then I'd never seen it empty before."

"And then, sir," Miles Coree went on, "I asked Miss Bruce a dozen ignorant questions about armatures and clay and how they got the clay to stick on. I wandered around behind the statue, and barked my shin, and found Miss Bruce doing a disrespectful cartoon of my anguish. I also," Miles added levelly, "mentioned her drawing of Chester Verney, and asked who it was."

"You did ask, if you remember, if we could look at Anna's work, and I told you the coverings were never disturbed."

"That's correct."

"And here's the drawing. I've been looking at it for several minutes, Mr. Geraghty, and I can't see anything about that—aside from Miles' presence in it—that would be revealing. It must have been the other one."

"I see." Geraghty glanced at it again. "By the way, Lieutenant, what did you fall over?"

"When I hacked my shin?" Miles grinned. "Just a bucket full of water and rags. I—"

"A what?" Noel fairly shrieked, half out of her chair.

"A bucket, Miss Bruce. Pail to you."

"Full of *water and rags?* By Tannehill's statue?"

"Yes. What—"

"Good heavens, can't either of you see what that means? When a clay model is uncovered, the sculptor keeps a pail of water by him and drops the covering-cloths in as he removes them. Then when he wants to fix it up again, he wrings out the cloths and puts them on damp. Someone had been starting the job right then, and we interrupted it! He slung the oilcloth back over the model and got into those overalls—there were several pairs hanging up on the partition—and got behind the cement mixer when he heard us talking in the courtyard. We were out there for two or three minutes. Mr. Geraghty—you thought that workman might have been the murderer, didn't you? But I couldn't imagine what he'd have been doing there. Now I see. He was preparing the clay ahead of time. Doesn't that mean the whole business was premeditated, or—maybe Verney was already dead and his body was to be brought in later? *Then* it could have been done by daylight!" Her ideas came so fast that she could hardly get them into coherent words. "It was light until after eight. And—you remember, Miles, we came back by the same route after we'd been to Montara, it was nearly eleven, and I still felt creepy—somehow all the things that happened that evening seemed to stem from the feeling the sculptors' workroom had given me—and I looked over at the Plaster Works and it was dark. That—if Inspector Geraghty had any crazy suspicions about you, that ought to dispose of them, because the murder must have been committed Wednesday, and the body put in the statue, and we were together almost every minute of that evening until after twelve!"

She paused for breath, and looked with shining dark eyes at Geraghty's dubious face. "What's the matter?" she asked.

"Means the old watchman must have been in on the whole thing," he said slowly. "Means I guessed wrong about him. If the concealment was done in daylight, and the door was unlocked, he must have known what went on. I'd have sworn he wasn't toting a load of knowledge that big."

Mr. Kotock put down his pad and slipped out of the room.

"The old watchman?" Miles Coree said. "Is that the one you said wasn't right in the head, Noel?"

"I thought he wasn't."

Geraghty said, "He's smart enough when he wants to be. Hell, I knew I'd slipped up somewhere. I didn't have a tail put on him, didn't have the extra men. We had him in the day after the murder and a couple of times after that, and got nothing at all."

"The old man was in the courtyard talking to himself," Miles said. "I'd gone back to use the telephone, the one in that glassed-in office in the yard, and it wasn't free. The workman was using it—the workman we'd seen inside, I suppose."

Geraghty interrupted him. "You saw him there?"

"Only the back of his head. No, I can't remember any details. I've been trying to think ever since Noel mentioned him. There was a white cap like a painter's, and the overalls, and that's all. His back was toward me."

Inspector Geraghty looked at the floor and said nothing. The door opened and Kotock came in. He caught Geraghty's eye, and said, "Powder."

"Oh, God Almighty," Geraghty said in a despairing roar. "Between the two of you—Miss Bruce, I hope that'll show you what a damn-fool trick it is to hold back information of any kind. If you'd let us know that Lieutenant Coree had been with you at the Plaster Works, we'd have got in touch with him at once, measles or no measles. He'd have told us his story, we could have got hold of that old fellow and beaten the truth out of him if necessary. That *proves* he was witness to something; before, we only thought he might have been. Four days lost. Now, of course, he's disappeared. Four days, spent in wild-goose chases, when that one fact would have meant a direct line to the murderer! If you'd use the brains God gave you—"

"Inspector," said Miles Coree mildly, "take it out on me, if you please. On *me*."

Geraghty paused, took a slow breath, and looked at him. "Perhaps I will," he said. "There are some holes in your personal story. Miss Bruce, is there anything more you've been keeping back?"

"Nothing," Noel said. "It's no use saying I'm sorry, but— what harm did it do to leave Lieutenant Coree out of it? I know, you've explained about the old man, but you had plenty of chances to question him, and Lieutenant Coree wasn't here to speak for himself! Supposing you'd got the wrong idea from the little I had to tell about him, and had haled him back here—if he'd actually gone to St. Louis—what do you think it would have done to him as an officer in the Navy?"

"Nothing, so long as he was innocent," said Geraghty wearily.

Noel looked at Miles. He nodded, his eyes kinder than ever.

"Then, to your family, Miles, that's been so badly hurt by scandal already?"

"Same answer," he said.

"Okay, Miss Bruce," said the inspector, "you've made it clear that you had reasons for keeping still. The only thing I'm not sure of is this: are those the actual reasons?"

She looked at him, startled.

"I'd like to see you again, alone, perhaps tomorrow. For this afternoon, you're excused. Leave word with one of the men outside where you'll be. If you please," Geraghty added with a fatigued courtesy that descended on her feelings like a blackjack.

Miles Coree got up and took her gently by the arm. "And no remorse from you, Noel," he said with a grin. "Our fifth meeting won't be awkward, I'll promise you. This won't take long."

So that's what I did, she thought, standing alone outside the closed door. That's the kind of loyalty I showed!...Well, how did I know he didn't go to St. Louis? I still say I'd do it all over—

She glanced down the corridor and saw Anna Verney sitting on a straight chair, gazing as if without hope at the door of Geraghty's office. Noel moved toward her.

"What are they doing?" Anna said huskily. "What's happened, Bruce? I telephoned Sherwin to see if I could get in touch with you, and Porter told me—I came down here, I've been waiting for two hours. What is it?"

"I don't know," Noel said. Her strength suddenly deserted her and she slumped onto another chair. "Miles said it wouldn't be long, but—I don't know."

Anna took her hand with a quick warm pressure. "You love him, don't you? Oh, honey, I know—I know what it can be like. He meant a lot to me, once."

They sat in silence. Men went up and down the hall; occasionally a door opened, but Geraghty's did not. They sat on and time inched by. Now and then their eyes met, and now and then Anna Verney looked at her watch.

It was after five o'clock when she rose with sudden decision. "Bruce, let's not wait any longer."

"You go on, if you like," said Noel. Something in Anna's look made her reconsider. "What is it? Do you think Miles might be embarrassed to find the womenfolk sitting it out?"

"You come home with me," Anna said. "We'll have dinner, and leave word for him to call us—you, I mean—at my studio.

Yes, come on." Noel thought it over, reluctantly nodded, and rose. "I have the car outside, it probably has a tag on it by now," Anna added as they went down the stairs together. Noel said, "*Your* car? Go on!" in an aside as she left her message.

"Well, Chester's car," said Anna, smiling faintly as they reached the parking place and found no tag. "Perhaps his reputation still means something." She allowed Noel to get into the driver's seat. "I wonder how long I'll have the use of it."

"Isn't it yours now?"

"Oh, no. All Chet's personal property went to a brother in New York, big business. He flew out for the funeral."

"Not even the car, nor the furniture of his apartment," said Noel half under her breath.

"Not even those," Anna agreed, again with her faint smile.

The car crept along between stops in the stream of home-going traffic. Neither of them spoke again until they reached Anna's apartment.

Anna opened the door of a small sitting room, removed from the rest of the studio, and pushed Noel gently in. "Bruce, honey, you look exhausted; lie down on that couch and don't move until I call you." She waited until Noel had complied; then she went out with her graceful step and the door closed behind her.

Noel leaned her head against the arm of the couch and shut her eyes in utter weariness. She's taking it better than I am, she thought. But then Tannehill didn't make an utter mess of things; she doesn't feel about Miles the way I do, not any more. How could anyone stop feeling that way about him? Right now I love him so much that I ache, physically.

She heard soft movements in the larger rooms of the studio; she had been hearing them for some time. Once she thought she had heard Anna's voice, but it was not calling her, and she relaxed. Footsteps sounded in the quiet shady court below and from time to time someone came up the outside stair, passing on to the upper apartments. People going home tired and at peace, to supper; and here we are, she thought, the widow of a murdered man and the woman who's in love with a prime suspect, shut into another of these apartments together.

She heard Tannehill calling her to supper. She opened the bag with the faulty clasp, and searched for her comb and powder. The crumpled sketch of Chester Verney was there, too; she went into the big studio living room with it in her hand. "You wanted this," she said to the golden woman who had been Chester Verney's wife. "I wish you'd let me make you a clean copy."

"Oh, no," Anna said, taking it. "I want this one. It still has—his life in it. Oh, Bruce, honey, you did a good job."

The face looked out at them, sensuous, experienced, compelling. Behind it, lightly sketched in, was the plaster cast of the Roman emperor, like a remote ancestor cynically waiting for his counterpart to join him in the shadows.

It gives me a cauld grue, Noel thought suddenly. She was relieved when Tannehill took it into another room to put away, but something about it kept teasing at her memory until she was on the verge of asking to see it again. The puzzling thought persisted while she tried to eat the exquisitely prepared supper, while she and Anna sat together afterward, smoking, saying nothing.

A bell shrilled through the thickening dusk and both of them started as if at a physical stab. "The telephone?" Noel breathed.

"Someone at the door," Anna Verney corrected, moving with swift eagerness. From the hall a moment later, in a changed voice, she said, "Bruce, it's your friend." She came back with an expressionless face and busied herself with clearing the table.

Chan Lockett's round blue eyes were apologetic. "Listen, baby," he said without preamble, "you aren't mad, are you?"

Noel did not invite him in. She said wearily, "I don't know how you expect me to feel. You, acting as if you'd caught me and Lieutenant Coree in an actual crime, rushing us down to the Hall of Justice just so you could ingratiate yourself with your Chief—when we'd have gone there ourselves in fifteen minutes anyway!"

"Now, baby, don't be like that," said Chan humbly.

"I'm grateful for your taking care of me for those first days, but you certainly fixed me up right this afternoon. You don't know what you stirred up!"

"Yeah, I guess the Chief was kind of upset. Kotock said he swore twice. Well, listen, I kept tellin' you to come clean before, didn't I?"

"Oh, yes, yes, I know you did." She took a quick breath. "What happened after I left?"

Chan shifted his feet and began to chew on a wad of gum which materialized from his cheek. His eyes grew vague and troubled. "I dunno exactly."

"Yes, you do," said Noel. Her heart went into a plunging dive. "You look as if you were carrying a death telegram. What is it, Chan?"

He tried twice before the words would come out, and then their loudness seemed to startle him. "He's in the clink."

"Miles Coree?" Noel looked at him steadily. For the past minute she had half expected it, but now she felt the blood draining from her head, her hands growing cold. "You don't mean arrested on a charge of murder?"

"I dunno much about it," Chan disclaimed hastily. He looked hideously embarrassed, his eyes searching the air behind her left shoulder. "They've clammed up on me."

She caught at the door for support. "They can't do it," she said. "He—he was telling the truth. He had nothing to do with Verney's death. Chan, what'll happen to him?"

Lockett said helplessly, "Maybe some new evidence'll come in. If it doesn't—" The sentence dangled ominously. He seemed to be listening for something besides her answer.

"Oh, Lord, if only I knew something more! What can I do?"

"Aw, baby, I feel bad about it, but don't try to do a thing. You go home. Come on, I'll see you—"

"No, you won't," said Noel violently. She struck at the door-jamb with the side of her fist. "*You* did this. You made it come all wrong. I'm sick of your spying and your idiotic suspicions. You were going to stick to me until an arrest had been made, weren't you? All right, go on back and hang around the police station and lick Geraghty's boots. I don't need you!"

In the instant before the door slammed shut she glimpsed the hurt in his dismayed eyes and the deeper pink of his face. She almost regretted her unkindness. Then the door was closed and she walked away.

The living room was ordered now, and softly lighted. Her eyes swept it quickly and came to rest at the window where Anna Verney stood with bent head, looking out.

She said, "Tannehill, you heard him."

The golden girl turned slowly to face her. Anna's blue eyes were dark with emotion, her skin fine-drawn over the high cheekbones. After a moment she said tonelessly, "Yes."

"It mustn't happen! I've done everything I could, wouldn't *you* know of some way—?"

The scarred hand and the perfect one spread in a hopeless gesture, and dropped. Anna's voice was level, and there seemed to be warning in her glance. "Bruce, dear, there's nothing I can do."

"I think there is," said Noel steadily. "You've been concealing something, haven't you? I've felt it—something out of drawing in your manner ever since you lied, the first time I ever knew you to lie, about being at the Art Center that night before your announcement party. There have been other things since that you've held back or changed a little, haven't there? Haven't there, Tannehill?"

Anna said nothing. Her breast began to rise and fall with deep difficult breathing.

"I know why, I think," said Noel. She reached back to grip the edge of the table, stilling her shaking hands. "You've been kind to all of us so many times—I believe you're being kind again, lying for the sake of one of your friends." The blue eyes shifted. "That *is* it. Well, whoever it is must surely take his own chances now. This is Miles in trouble, Tannehill."

"I know, I know. Do you think it doesn't torment me?"

"Then you must tell the police the truth. Now."

"Bruce," said Anna Verney steadily, "you don't know what you're asking."

She waited a long moment. Noel did not breathe before she spoke again. "Just stop now. You can't be sure that I do know anything. Leave it at that, and forget it."

Noel released her grip on the table. Her hands were numb, all of her flesh seemed to be losing sensation. She said, "You're not saying that what you know *wouldn't* help him?"

Miles had been in town, he had been in communication with Anna during the week when Verney died—or perhaps before. Perhaps he had, after all, caught up with her on that night at the Art Center—but if that were so, nearly every word he had spoken to Noel was untrue. He could have got away with it, considering the state I was in, she thought with a curious lack of bitterness.

She said aloud, "It couldn't have been that Wednesday"— and caught her breath. Something shifted and settled in her mind. "Tannehill, *was* it Wednesday morning when Chester left you? Was it he who called you that night? Is that what you're holding back, the real date when you saw him for the last time?"

Not a muscle of the beautiful face moved, but there was an almost imperceptible change in Anna Verney's posture.

"So that's it," Noel breathed. She shut her eyes for a moment and saw imprinted on darkness her own sketch of Chester Verney's head.

When she opened them Anna had faced about again, gazing out at the dark courtyard, her back rigid with strain.

"It's just surmise on your part, isn't it?" Noel's voice had to be forced, so that it sounded harsh. "You're not sure who killed Chester?" The golden head moved in negation. "Then what you do know might help. Listen. Chester wasn't there on Tuesday, was he? I heard about that professor that used to come home at ten every night. It was his car that Paul heard driving in, wasn't it? There's only a hedge between those driveways, it could have sounded as if the car were in your aunt's garage. And it was Paul's voice that the housekeeper heard—Paul, doing his errand for you, taking away that bust of Chester you'd made— Tannehill! Did you use that the night before to throw a shadow on the wall, or on the curtains—" Her voice gave out at last. The final words were scarcely audible.

Anna straightened her slender back and turned, smiling. "Bruce, you don't realize what you're doing. I don't so much mind being called a liar, because I know you're overwrought; but—you must forget all this before something comes out that you'd regret saying, regret for the rest of your life."

"But Miles could prove—there was one night at least when he was with friends—"

"Stop it, I tell you." The blue eyes were wide and hard. "Don't go any farther."

"I will," said Noel over her rising dismay. "As long as there's the fraction of a chance, I'm hanging onto it. Anna, what will become of him if someone doesn't?"

"He's in a better spot than most of us. The Coree family have tremendous power in St. Louis, they'll have some influence—oh, yes; didn't you know? The very top of old-family society, and the uncle's money—it all helps. Let that work for Coree. No matter how we feel, you and I would do better to keep still. To keep still, Bruce."

She spoke with composure, but behind it was a driving force that struck Noel almost palpably. Her own urgency began to drain away. She made one last effort; she said hotly, "Even if I believed he was guilty, as it seems you do, I'd fight—" and stopped.

It was Anna's husband who had been murdered. She remembered that with an incredulous shock; of course Tannehill couldn't—but how could it have gone so completely out of her mind?"

"All right. I shan't ask you to say anything," she said list-lessly. "It's—I wish I'd never—"

"So do I, Bruce honey," said Anna Verney gently. "This has been too much for you."

"I want to go home."

"If you like. I'll drive you."

"Thank you very much. No. I'd rather not have company."

Anna looked at her for a moment, her blue eyes dark with compassion. "Oh, my dear," she said, and went swiftly to put her arms around Noel.

Noel stiffened and pushed her away. She turned in a sudden spurt of energy, picked up her hat and bag from the sitting room and went swiftly down the stairs and through the courtyard. Not until the faint coolness of the night flowed against her face did she realize how close it had been in Tannehill's studio, a drugging and stupefying heat.

She thought, I can't give up yet! I can't just go home and wait! With no plan in her mind she found herself boarding a car that went toward town, transferring at Stockton, walking up the steps of the Hall of Justice and straight to Geraghty's office.

It was dark and empty. The uniformed men in the halls could, or would, tell her nothing. A man named Coree in jail? They didn't know; she could ask that officer, maybe; he didn't know either. If a man was in on a murder charge they wouldn't let you see him anyhow, you get it, lady? Wait till morning and call up the inspector. No, they didn't know where he went.

"If he wanted me to report on every move I made, he might at least have stuck around to get the reports," said Noel, with a last weary flash of spirit. "If he telephones in a tizzy, tell him I've gone home."

"Who're you, lady?" the sergeant asked simply.

Nobody. I'm the girl who was supposed to have information, and was chased all over town by a pair of men, and was suddenly safe and a nonentity when the information turned out to be worthless. She stood on the broad steps watching the

Thursday night traffic stream past. It was all over—over in the wrong way, and nothing to do about it.

That queer numbness was getting worse, as if an anesthetic were taking hold. She started walking, threading the crowded sidewalks with remote singleness of purpose. The faces that passed her, the gaudy neon signs around Union Square, blurred and whirled like a color-top until she had to fix her eyes on the ground. There was no B car in sight, and she turned and began plodding up Geary.

A voice spoke beside her, not for the first time. "Hey, babe," it was saying, "this isn't a pick-up. You know me, remember?"

With an effort she turned her head and focused her eyes. Red Hobart's knobby face swam into clarity. He was walking along beside her, his head cocked sideways so that he could look down into her face. He was rather drunk, and he was grinning.

He went on talking for a moment longer, but Noel did not hear what he said. Those slurred consonants of his had struck an uneasy chord in her memory. Had it been he, last night—? Yet there was a familiar tone in his voice that had been missing then.

She said, "Weren't you planning to leave town?"

"Guess I can now," Red said with a darting glance at her. "Haven't asked permission, but the watchdog's been called off, near's I can figure. My de-ar li'l shadow doesn't go in an' out with me, or 'f he does I don't see him." He bumped into a young soldier and gave him a dirty look. "Maybe they've run out o' cops, what with investigatin' that flophouse fire south o' the Slot. Yeah, free as the air, tha's me. Where you been by yourself, this time o' night?"

"Hall of Justice."

"Hah! Pulled in again, like poor old Steff?"

"No. Are you feeling sorry for Rita now?" Noel remembered yesterday's events as from an incredible distance.

"Bygones 're bygones. Once I've got even I don't hold a grudge. Once I've got even," Red repeated with satisfaction.

He grinned again to himself, squinting around the smoke of his cigarette. "I guess they'll be makin' an arrest b'fore long, way things look." He glanced at her again. "Or have they made one?"

"Yes." Noel plodded on wearily, without thought. She would have crossed against a red light, but Red caught her arm. "He didn't do it. I know he didn't." A sob of utter fatigue rose in her throat, but she forced it back. "I *know*." She would convince herself at least, by saying it over and over.

"You do?" Red murmured absently. "Smart li'l chick, knows everything. Who got pinched?"

Far behind her preoccupation a warning bell seemed to be ringing. She glanced automatically to her left, hearing a streetcar stop at the crossing; it was hers. She looked at Red, whose head was turned toward a bar at the corner. Then without a word she slipped off the curb and swung herself onto the car's rear platform, where packed bodies immediately concealed her.

There was a faint sense of relief, as if she had escaped something, but she could not analyze it. She stood with closed eyes for most of the trip, got off from blind habit at her stop, and once more traversed the dim streets and the stale shadows of her own narrow lane, once more climbed the gray wooden steps of her rooming house.

Her room was a solid block of stuffiness. She raised the windows, all of them, and as the moving air of outdoors began to infiltrate the dead heat, stood swaying and blinking with her hand on the light switch. She flipped it and the darkness returned. Her hat and bag went down on the floor where she stood. She managed to get across the room to her bed, and in an access of overpowering fatigue lay down as she was.

Dimly in her mind, as sleep came down upon her, was the thought of something neglected; something she must do in just a minute, something about a hammer and boards and nails.

CHAPTER TWELVE

THE AIR GREW COOLER, and the night shadows imperceptibly shifted. There was a diminution in the sky-glow as theatre lights went out downtown, as the crowds reluctantly thinned and started home to bed. The city's breathing quieted. A moon like an unevenly sucked lollypop began to show over the Oakland foothills.

There had been the sound of footsteps in the narrow lane, as the latest home-comers had gone one by one through the dingy paneled doors, leaving the shadows empty once more. In the apartment next to Noel's, the door had closed and water had run, and at last silence had fallen. Much later, if there had been anyone awake to hear, there was a faint rattling and clicking noise in her makeshift kitchen. It stopped; then, subdued and cautious, another sound came: scrape along boards...wait...scrape again, and creaking, and breathing that was kept shallow with a terrible effort.

It may have been the first of those sounds that began to penetrate Noel Bruce's sleep, where she lay flung face downward across her bed. She stirred, and murmured something, and collapsed again. Then all at once she was awake, her head strained backward, all her muscles tense.

She had not imagined those shuffling steps near the head of her bed, that had ceased so abruptly within the past few seconds.

From a mind confused as to time, in a voice still low and husky with sleep, she said, "Chan—"

"Keep still," a quick harsh whisper told her from behind the screen that hid the kitchen door, "or I'll have to kill you. Your bodyguard's not here. If you scream, you'll be dead before anybody can get help."

Noel lay still. Her eyes strained into the dimness that was barely tempered by sickly moonlight. She could see nothing but the outline of her screen; she was unbearably conscious of irrelevant trifles, the tightness of her belt, the rough weave of the bedspread under her cheek, the echoed heartbeat that was like another heart besides her own throbbing away in her ear.

She said in the merest thread of voice, "What do you want?"

"I want you to get out before you remember who I am. I don't want to kill you—God, there's been enough—but maybe you'll have to die. Listen—listen to me, Bruce. Keep quiet. The old man's up there on the roof. He couldn't get into the house but those back stairs go clear up. I said I'd try this door; they think I'm doing the job. I can't hold him much longer. I bribed him with those reefers at first, I'd hand 'em out after he'd done his part, and he got 'em away from me and now he's forgotten about saving his own hide, he'd shoot you as soon as look at you." The savagely controlled breathing grew more audible. "I can't hold him. If you can dodge him, I'll give you a chance."

"Kill—me?" Noel croaked. The words seemed to release a chill air that settled down, down on her through the hot darkness.

"Anybody...You get out, leave town, never come back. Hide somewhere and keep your mouth shut. You've got a chance to live. I'm not going to—" The whisper fell to a broken mutter. "—cold blood—"

She said, with incredible difficulty through a dry throat, "What can I do? I haven't any money, how can I—"

"Somebody'll pick you up. Somebody'll help you. Get out!"

"Let me sit up. I promise you I won't scream." She was raising herself as she spoke, slowly, fearfully, expecting at any second's motion to see the dark shape emerge from behind the screen—or to feel the bullet's impact in her body. Her palms were slippery and wet. She moved them across the bedspread.

The whisperer said, "Sit up, then."

"I don't know who you are." Noel forced the words past the hard knot in her throat. "I never did know. How can I do any harm? I can't leave town, the police don't trust me, they'd hunt me down no matter where I went. I'll stay here and never tell them another word. How can I, when there's nothing more to tell?"

"You're lying. You know I was there in the Plaster Works, you saw me in the office—"

"I didn't see you! It was the man with me who stepped back into the gateway. *He* can't remember how you looked—"

"You didn't see my back?" The whisper had grown harsher; its intensity gave it a note of incredulous panic. "But you told her—"

"Told whom? I never said that. It wouldn't have been true."

"Never mind. You've got to get out of here, now. I've taken too long already, I've put my own head in the noose. Get out, you little fool! The old man'll find some way to get in if you don't hurry. I'm going down these steps outside. You give me five minutes and then you get the hell out yourself, the same way, and hide. Dodge the police and everybody—if you don't want to die."

The whisper seemed still to rustle in her ears for long seconds after she heard the slow withdrawal, the cautious easing of a body into a space behind the kitchen cabinet, the faint scrape of the door which she had not remembered to nail up again.

Now there was silence, except for the thudding of her heart. She tried once to get up, but the floor seemed to fall gently away from her feet. She sat there, staring at the glimmering oblongs of the windows.

"The old man," she whispered to herself. But what old man? Not—surely not Papa Gene? Some people called him old. He drank and pursued women with royal lustiness; had he added another sensation to his list? She knew what reefers were. She had a vague and utterly horrifying idea of their effect. The man behind the screen had said, "I can't hold him." The old man was waiting, up there on the roof.

As if to dispel any possible doubt, there was a faint noise overhead: the smallest of snapping sounds, as if someone had moved on a tarred roof and its surface had sprung back. The silence returned.

Noel was on her feet in the middle of the room with no consciousness of having moved. She had both hands tight over her mouth. She had to get out; and she did not dare to stir.

Get out. *Get out.* "Give me five minutes and then get out the same way—and hide." The same way, down the wooden stairs and into the darkness of the alley, with its smell of dry decay, its emptiness—

But if it were not empty?

That possible way of escape had been made to seem the only one. What was wrong with her using the street door, except that in the lane she might get away or call for help, and in the alley she would be trapped?

It couldn't be that after all the police were guarding the street door?

The thought gave her a little energy, enough to impel her to the bay window. She managed to straighten up and gaze into the tempered darkness of the lane.

No one was in sight. *Dodge the police and everybody, if you want to live…* The roof snapped again, seemingly very close over her head, and she shrank back, looking helplessly from side to side, from the hall door to the high window.

She saw a trap everywhere. Supposing she stayed here, pretending to be dead, pretending that the man who had murmured to her in the darkness had fulfilled his mission? Somebody might come to see; come through the unguarded staircase door, or drop to the balcony from the roof above and step easily across the small gap to her bay window.

Or was "the old man" really on the roof? Its surface might be contracting naturally after the day's heat. Had the whisperer tried to trick her into the corridors? The key to the old lock on her room door had opened the house door as well. How was she to know that the key had not been copied on the day it was stolen, and that death was not waiting for her now, close outside, waiting for her to step from behind her one flimsy barrier? To scream, to turn on the lights, would be to advertise her presence; this way, she might have a few minutes, half an hour, in which to try some way of escape.

Only a block away—if she could get out unobserved—would be safety, lights, communication with the police. This house seemed like an evil maze whose every exit led to danger.

And yet the whole lane slept without motion, except for the slow change of moon shadows, the slight stirring of curtains and of the homely line of washing that someone had forgotten on the roof across the street.

Noel thought painfully, I can't stay here for the rest of the night, doing nothing. I have to try something!

There was one small precaution she could take, it seemed foolish in the face of her terror, and yet it might help. She stepped quietly out of her shoes, and as quietly eased herself across the room to her dressing table. She grasped her hand-mirror, went back to the window and cautiously extended it on its long handle beyond the curtains, tilting it this way and that for a reflection of the roof's edge above. If no one were there, she might just manage to step over to the balcony, to let herself over the edge and, protected by its overhang, climb down the fretwork as Chan had climbed up. They might not think of that.

For a moment the mirror reflected nothing but the dark line of the roof against the lighter sky. She moved it sidewise, and saw something rising across the straight edge: a head, wearing a bulky flat-topped cap.

The image held for the space of two slow breaths. Noel looked at it as if she were paralyzed, dazedly keeping the mirror in position.

There was a sharp crack from overhead, and the mirror shattered in her hand, leaving her flesh shocked and stinging. She let go, and jerked her arm out of range; and from sheer reflex began to scream at the top of her lungs, wordlessly, standing with her hands pressed over her eyes and letting out scream after scream. The senseless noise was so loud in her own ears that she felt vibrations from the roof overhead rather than heard the impact of falling bodies, and then of feet running, scraping, thudding with terrible haste toward the low side parapet.

It was only when these vibrations had penetrated to her mind that her voice was abruptly silenced and she stood listening; and above the other sounds of a household, a neighborhood suddenly aroused, came another shriek in a far-off, inhuman voice...descending...cut off with a dreadful finality.

Knuckles banged against her door. A man said through the paneling, "Noel, are you there? For God's sake, are you safe?"

The hall sounded full of people. She dragged herself to the door and opened it, conscious of dim figures in night clothes, rushing up and down as if there were a fire. She said, "Miles. *Miles*—But I thought you were in jail!"

Grimy, pallid, strained with anxiety, Miles Coree leaned against the door-frame and shouted with irrepressible laughter.

He laughed as if he could not stop, until she grasped his arm and shook it violently. "What happened? How do you come to be here? What was that noise, a few minutes ago—"

"Hush, darling," Miles said, sobering. His breath came hard. She looked toward the telephone, where Miss Ibsen was shouting something incomprehensible about the police. In a minute some words emerged: "Burglars...shots...fell into the alley..."

"I was—watching," Miles Coree said, between panting breaths. "Young Lockett told me he'd been relieved of his job; I—knew you'd told everything you knew and that—supposedly that made you safe, but I—couldn't help being uneasy." He paused and waited for a moment until he could speak more easily.

"I went around hunting for you, after I'd come here about ten and found you weren't at home; must have missed you somehow. Anyway, I stood guard across the street—"

"Miles, did you see anyone going down that side stair that leads to my kitchen?"

"No. There was someone?—Good Lord. I couldn't have seen unless I'd been standing in the alley; those stairs are solid. But a few minutes ago I did see something moving on the roof of this house."

"A head, looking over—"

"Yes. I waited until it went out of sight and then slid across to this side and up those back stairs." His handsome long face grew whiter than before under its Pacific tan. He grasped her by the shoulders. "When I got to the roof I could see the head again, leaning over and looking down at your windows."

"It was by the grace of God I wasn't leaning out my window looking up, just then," said Noel shakily. "I did—stick a mirror out—"

Lieutenant Coree took a quick breath and shook his head. "I thought I could get to the man while his back was turned to me. I was about ten feet away when he—shot. I thought you were looking out. I got his gun, and managed to get him down, and then he got away, and made a dash for the edge of the roof. Probably he meant to try to jump across to that next house, the roof's a little lower than this one—only, he didn't make it."

"He—went down?"

Coree nodded.

"Who was it?"

"The old watchman," he said, and all her thoughts turned upside down and then righted themselves in sudden coherence.

There was the sound of sirens, of authoritative voices, and the low horrified mutter of the crowd as it was pushed back. From the mouth of the alley one of the firm voices said, "Yes, dead. Instantaneous."

Inspector Geraghty, Mr. Kotock and Miles Coree sat in Noel's room and drank coffee while the sun climbed slowly into a warm hazy sky.

Geraghty had come in half an hour before, bearing a curious exhibit. It was an old stiff-topped cap which had once belonged to a chauffeur, with a white handkerchief tied over its crown. At a distance one might have thought it was a naval officer's headgear.

After a few moments something had penetrated Noel's dazed state of shock. She raised her head and sniffed, looking puzzled. "That queer sweetish odor—I've smelled that before, in this room."

"On the day it was searched," Geraghty had said rather than asked. She nodded. "It's on the cap, Miss Bruce. That's marijuana. The old man reeked of it."

Now he was sitting down, relaxing for a brief interlude. He talked as if he were thinking aloud, looking mortally tired but supremely competent.

Geraghty said, "That was my mistake, and a bad one. I felt fairly sure Old Dad was working up for a blackmail racket, but that he might not know anything about the murder itself.

That type doesn't often enter a conspiracy. He'd have been more likely, I thought, to save himself by talking to us; because none of the people involved had enough money to make blackmail profitable enough, if the subject were a murderer. But the reefers—yes; they're more than money to an addict, no other offer could match 'em."

Noel cut in, "Whom did you think he was blackmailing?"

"You," said Mr. Geraghty mildly. She looked at him, stupefied. "Sure, Miss Bruce. It was fairly plain that you'd been in the Plaster Works at some unusual time, under circumstances you didn't want to tell about in full. The old man went away grinning to himself when he heard there'd been a murder discovered there. Seemed to me he figured that was a good chance to put the bite on, and then maybe you tried to stall him, and he got tough with the gun to show you he meant business. You came round to us and asked for protection, but wouldn't say why the men were after you, though I thought you knew well enough."

"I didn't," Noel said faintly.

"In general, you did. Well," Mr. Geraghty remarked in his most melancholy voice, "as I said, it was my mistake. I make plenty of 'em, God forgive me, and I made another tonight in assuming that you'd shut the old man off for good when you told us all you knew. Well, it might have turned out the same if it'd been some of my boys chasing him." He turned an unreadable look on Lieutenant Coree, who sat silently drawing on a cigarette. "A dead man can't tell us who it was that bribed him to take part in this. He can't tell us the other man's name, the one who was behind your screen tonight, Miss Bruce. You know who it was?"

"I—could make a guess. It wouldn't be evidence."

"Kind of handy, Lieutenant, that you turned up on the dot, that way. I suppose you could have gone down those side stairs, and up the service staircase to the roof, and appeared in a quick-change act as the rescuer? You'd make sure that way that your side-kick couldn't ever tell tales."

Fury and fatigue combined to make Noel Bruce forget all her respect for the law. "Oh, don't be such a sap," she said tartly.

Miles Coree looked swiftly round and grinned at her, his hazel eyes bright with love and amused pride. He said, "Don't worry, my dear girl. The inspector and I thrashed the matter out rather thoroughly, last night, and there wasn't any talk of arresting me."

"Then why—"

"I think," Geraghty said, "that Chan Lockett was trying a little shenanigan of his own, and it didn't come off. Never mind it, Miss Bruce. Do you mind telling me your guess as to the other man's identity?"

"I do mind. I think you know already, Mr. Geraghty, from what I told you. I'd rather not put it into words."

"As you like," said the Irishman unconcernedly. She gave an involuntary shiver, and rose to reheat the coffee in the pot. His eyes were on her, grave and paternal. "You know we've got to have some kind of positive identification of that man you saw behind the cement mixer, before we can really put the pressure on."

"I couldn't give you that."

"We may be able to get it just the same, through Lieutenant Coree. It's a long shot, but I'm hoping it'll come off."

She turned and stood by her screen, her dark eyes shadowed, her lips unsteady. "If it's what I guess—"

"Whatever comes out is going to be painful, some way, Miss Bruce. Murder's a painful business."

"I know. That's not what's worrying me. It just seems so impossible; there was no reason, no feeling between him and Verney, nothing to make it—"

"You know," Geraghty said, "I don't believe Chester Verney died because somebody hated him. Seems to me it was something even more primitive than that." He added with seeming irrelevance, "We finally traced Marion Smith. He died on Iwo Jima...But as to your guess, Miss Bruce, if you leave the question of motive aside everything else fits; you've got to admit that. All the puzzles come clear: why Verney died in the

Plaster Works, and had to be concealed there in that particular way; and why the body had to be concealed at all."

Miles Coree glanced at him and frowned as if in dissatisfaction. They drank the rest of the coffee in silence. It was only when Mr. Kotock glanced at his watch and wordlessly picked up his derby hat that Noel voiced her question. "Are you sure you can find him?"

"We've had a man on it since early this morning," Geraghty told her. "As for *him*, he knows he doesn't dare to take a powder. It'd be the smartest thing he could do to go on working as usual, and I think he will. If he's stayed home, we can smoke him out without trouble."

They went out rather slowly, down the stairs into the hazy heat of the morning. In the lane outside stood a familiar figure, large, pink-faced, round and blue of eye. The eyes expressed the utmost reach of longing.

The inspector began a series of those deep-seated grunts that passed for laughter with him. "Okay," he said briefly, and motioned Noel and Miles Coree into the back seat of his car. As they drove off they could see, behind them, Chan Lockett leaping into his own car and following them bumper to tail-light.

A few trucks were bumbling and lurching along the rough street that bordered the Crowder Plaster Works, but the ramshackle building itself was oddly silent. Once Noel and the four men had entered the courtyard, and the gate in the high wooden fence had closed behind them, a Sabbath stillness seemed to hang in the air. It was broken only by the chipping sound of Will Rome's chisel on the limestone of his hooded figure.

He was not in sight at first; the sounds came from behind the statue. Then, apparently halted by the footsteps and the noise of the gate shutting, he came around and stood with one big hand resting on the roughly carved shoulder of the figure, his big head lowered, the sad hound-dog eyes alert and suspicious.

There was a moment when no one moved or said anything. Then Geraghty remarked, "Good morning, Mr. Rome."

"Well?" Rome said in his surliest voice. "What d'you want?"

"Make a little experiment," Geraghty murmured as if absently. He stood for a minute glancing around the yard, with the piles of rubbish forlorn and dismal in the soft autumn light, the small glassed-in office empty in the corner, the scabrous boards of the fence enclosing the scene. A car drove up and stopped outside, but no one got out.

"I'd like you to assist us, Rome," he went on presently. His habitual courtesy had not abated, but a metallic note had come into his voice. "Will you step into the office, please, and put on a workman's white cap that you'll find hanging up there?"

"What the hell for—" Rome began, and stopped. He shrugged. "Anything you say, except that I can't get in the office. The plaster casters aren't here—on strike, maybe."

"They are absent on my orders," said Geraghty. "Kotock—"

Mr. Kotock produced a key and opened the office. Rome looked at Geraghty from under contracted brows, and then shrugged again and moved toward the glassed-in space. They could see his broad back as he lifted a cap from its hook and put it on.

Geraghty raised his voice. "Stand by the telephone, if you please, with your back to us." He turned his head and looked at Miles Coree.

The hazel eyes were intent. "I'm sorry, sir," Miles said, "but it's not the same. The height, the general build, yes; but there's something wrong. That is not what I saw. I can't define the difference."

Inspector Geraghty's face sagged into a mask of amazed disappointment. He said, "That's not what you saw? Hell, man, it's got to be!"

"I'm sorry, sir," Coree repeated steadily. "I could not truthfully say that this is the same man."

Noel dug her hands into the pockets of her light coat. She said in an undertone, "And I didn't see him, on that Wednesday night! If I had—"

There was a deprecating cough from the background. Chan Lockett sidled forward and unfolded a piece of bond paper. He said, "Excuse me, Chief. I—uh—got these out of your wastebasket, kind of for a souvenir. Uh—would you ask him was the back of the workman's head like this?" His large forefinger pointed to the center head on a crumpled drawing which Noel recognized as her own, that two-minute study she had made at the announcement party.

Miles Coree looked at it. His breath caught for a second. He said, "*That's it.* Those shaggy points of hair, below the cap. That was what I saw."

Inspector Geraghty exhaled loudly. "Was that Will Rome, Miss Bruce?"

Noel nodded. She felt her heart thudding loudly, with a painful blend of excitement and shame.

"Nobody," said Geraghty with a repressed sort of fury, "thought of telling me that Rome had had a haircut since September twelfth. God Al—" He checked himself. "Very well, Rome, I guess that does it."

Will Rome came slowly out of the office. His eyes were truculent now, under the shaggy brows. Geraghty said, "We can step inside if you like. I want the answers to some questions."

"Ask 'em here," said Rome uncompromisingly. Once more his hand rested on the stone shoulder, but now his glance sought Noel with veiled rage.

Geraghty saw the look. "Miss Bruce did not give you away," he said grimly, "but we'll have to ask her for corroboration. Did you recognize the voice that spoke to you in your rooms last night, Miss Bruce?"

Noel said, "Whoever it was tried to save me. He could have killed—"

"That is beside the point. I'll ask you to lower your voice to a whisper, Rome."

Rome's mouth twitched. He came a few steps away from his statue, and said in a grating whisper, "I don't know what you're driving at."

"Was that it, Miss Bruce?"

"It was—very similar to that."

"Okay, Rome. You hired the watchman, Old Dad, in the beginning. When you found that you needed an accomplice in your program of terrorization, you took him on and bribed him with reefers. You may as well tell us which of those swing sessions provides 'em. Saves time; we've got the Narcotics Squad checking now and they'll find out soon or late. You use reefers yourself?"

"No," Rome said hoarsely.

"It's not often they'll sell you any to take away, but I guess you got around that. It's no use, you know," said Geraghty somberly. "You were the man who was here on the evening of the twelfth, moistening the cloths over Mrs. Verney's statue. You thought you'd kept out of sight, but you were plenty nervous because Miss Bruce made a sketch of your legs that might have been used for identification. You picked up Old Dad and took the car your Army friend had left for your use, and chased Miss Bruce along the Skyline, trying to catch her alone. I guess Old Dad was to do the dirty work, he wouldn't have been so familiar to her if she'd happened to catch a glimpse of the men who were out to kill her—make it safer for *you*—if you didn't succeed."

Rome's craggy face contracted. He said roughly, "Nobody was out to kill her."

"Just to get those sketches that might incriminate you? And I suppose you figured you were disguised enough with the cervical collar. Okay. You might as well take it from there."

"I wasn't going to kill her. Just throw something over her head and get the sketch pad. I had to—I thought I had to—Well, the hell with it. Yes, I did get the old man to work with me. He took over the keys when I got 'em out of Bruce's bag a few nights later, and went up to her room. He could slide round corners like an Indian when he wanted to. And he couldn't find the sketch book, and we never could get close enough to her to search her pockets. I told him a thin sort of yarn about a divorce case, and he made out to believe me. It was all sort of a cruel game to him. I think he figured that if we did catch her, I'd have more in mind than searching her pockets, but I didn't. I meant to hold him down, it seemed at first as if I could; I struck his arm up when he shot at that woman that wasn't the right one—I'd told him to aim at the sidewalk behind her, and he aimed at her instead. And then I thought I had something on him—"

"While he had something more serious on you, all the time," Geraghty said with deep melancholy in his voice. "No minor shooting would balance that sort of thing, Rome. The old man was here when Verney died, wasn't he?"

The rough head went back. "I—don't know when he died."

"Come off it, Rome," said Geraghty with a sort of weary kindness. At the disarming tone, something happened that no accusation had brought about; the sweat started out on Rome's forehead.

"You see," Geraghty said, "we found your ring, the one you always used to wear on your left hand—I guess, to remind you not to use it."

"That—was the idea," Rome said hoarsely.

"Sure you don't want to go inside for the rest of this?"

"Hell, no. What's it matter who hears it—now?"

"The ring was found where you'd thrown it. Hadn't reminded you soon enough, wasn't that so? And it had made things worse for you; instead of your just knocking Verney out, with your bare fist, the ring acted like brass knuckles. And it's my guess, Rome, that it struck Verney's face *and left a square bruise*, a bruise that left your seal on him after death."

Geraghty waited a moment, watching the beads of sweat as they merged on Will Rome's face. "It's a shame you didn't take it off first, Rome. That seal made it necessary for you to hide the body in a place where it wouldn't be found until decomposition was well advanced, and hide it face down, because the underside of the body would change faster; Mrs. Verney's statue was the only place that answered those requirements. Of course, that choice removed the risk you'd have taken if you tried to move the body to another place; but I guess you knew it'd lead to you soon or late. Too bad you didn't take off that ring. Where were your wits, man?"

"Wits? What 'ud I be using my wits for," Rome burst out, "when it all happened on the spur of the moment, when there wasn't a plan, but it seemed as if my arm was alive by itself, and went up, and I saw him fall—the thing happening all over again—"

"It was a thing that was likely to happen to you, from what I hear," Geraghty said quietly. "No premeditation; you lashed out at him under sudden provocation. It didn't occur to you that you might report the death at once and give your explanation?"

"Report it! You've just given the reason why not." Rome shifted his feet slightly, his eyes on the Irishman's. "Who'd believe I was all but innocent? All right, I'll tell you; I can't be tried twice for the same crime—that first manslaughter trial of mine *was* fixed. The man that died was a son of a bitch, and the witnesses and my lawyer fixed it up so that I got free, and I was guilty of that. I got free, but if it happened again—?"

Geraghty nodded. He said, "It wasn't your left to the jaw that killed him. You learned that at the inquest. What did he do, hit his head as he went down?"

"Hit his head. Yes."

"On what?"

"Corner of a wooden model stand." Rome's voice had cleared, as if he were almost relieved to have the thing in words.

Noel and Miles Coree were standing together, as far back as they could get, against the fence. She was conscious of his comforting grip on her hand, but all her thoughts seemed to be concentrated on the painful breaking down of the man who faced the group. She was looking at Rome, unable to take her gaze from his face, but in the edge of her vision was Inspector Geraghty's back. All at once it took on expression; it straightened, broadened, grew taut as if in sudden triumph.

CHAPTER THIRTEEN

"**O**N THE CORNER of a wooden model stand," said Geraghty reflectively. His voice betrayed nothing. "I'd like you to show me the stand, Rome. Inside."

The heavy figure and the lean one vanished together through the courtyard door into the Works, followed by Kotock. As they went, a pair of big men in plain-clothes tramped through the gate and joined them. The door swung shut and then sprang back a few inches.

Chan Lockett looked sidewise at Miles Coree and Noel. "The guy needs a lawyer," he said disapprovingly.

"I don't know," Miles said. "Seems to me he's doing all right."

"Look, you're not just going to stand here when you could get in?" Chan inquired.

"Mr. Geraghty would have told us if we were needed any more," said Noel in a tired low voice.

"Aw, baby, what's that got to do with it? Come on, folks, what're we waitin' for?"

Miles Coree looked down at her. "It's the last act," he said. "Let's know the true story. You, at least, have a right to it."

She nodded, taking a long breath. She went ahead of the two men, quietly slipping through the small door. The true story, she thought. *Was* this it?

From behind the partition Geraghty's voice came patiently: "Once more, Rome. He fell straight back; was his head turned to the side?"

"No." The answering voice held almost no expression. "I—I thought it was the back of his head that hit. Mistake, I guess."

"Yes. It was the temporal bone that was crushed...Why had you brought your mallet in here?" The question snapped suddenly; there was a brief pause after it, that was broken only by a sound like "Huh?" forced out by surprise. Then Rome said, "*Mallet?* I didn't have it...*God*—you mean you thought I knocked him out first and then—*No!* I never went near him, I never touched him again except to drag his body around after he was dead, to conceal it. I'll swear that. It was manslaughter if you like; it wasn't murder! You think I could deliberately—"

The shaking horror and revulsion in his voice carried a conviction that could not be denied.

Geraghty said mildly, "You knew he was dead, though you didn't go near him. Uh-huh. You didn't examine the head, so you didn't see how much that sharp corner of wood had abraded the skin."

"I—when I was handling him afterward I could— There wasn't any abrasion."

"A fall," the inspector mused as if to himself, "and a glancing blow along the temple that crushed the bone but didn't break the skin. Seem queer to you, Rome?"

There was silence.

"There's one question we haven't touched on. Who was with you, here, on the night Verney died?"

"Nobody."

"You were alone. You knew Chester Verney slightly, you had little feeling toward him one way or another, and yet you got him to meet you here toward dark, on an evening in the middle of his honeymoon, and slugged him, and he died."

There was another silence. In the outer room, dirty and barnlike and still without its workday population, Noel Bruce found herself shaken with a dreadful certainty. She moved closer to Miles Coree, where he leaned unmoving against the edge of a marble casting table. His eyes, and Chan Lockett's, were fixed on the board partition that cut off their view of the sculptors' workroom, and yet was not high enough to muffle sound. The voices, the small noises of motion, came clearly through the dust-laden air.

"Nothing more to say," Rome's voice came at last, gruffly.

"There was someone else here," Geraghty told him without inflection. "No use holding out now. That other person is the only one who can prove that you struck Verney in the heat of anger—that you're telling the truth when you say it wasn't murder."

"I was alone."

"H'm." The inspector's grunt had no laughter in it this time. "Okay, Marshall," he raised his voice. "You and Mrs. Verney can come in."

There was a faint creak as, unseen to the three listeners, the door to the alley was opened. Then Anna Verney's voice came, deep with regret and pain. "Oh, Rome," she said. "Rome, I'm sorry. I tried—"

Geraghty said, "You've heard what we've been saying, Mrs. Verney. It was you, of course?"

"Of course. Rome, you shouldn't have tried to keep my name out of it. I suppose you've talked and talked, and said everything except that. Oh, my poor Rome."

Her lovely voice, rich with compassion and regret, was oddly stirring. The listeners heard someone drawing a hoarse breath; Will Rome spoke immediately afterward. "I'd as soon talk. Maybe it'll keep me from seeing his face looking up at me, like something out of a bad dream you have over and over. Maybe that sentence I didn't get the first time ought to catch up with me. I'll take it."

"You mustn't! It was for me, I can't let you—"

Geraghty said, "If you want to help Mr. Rome, perhaps you'll answer a few questions truthfully, Mrs. Verney."

"I've done so badly at my lying; I'm not used to it," Anna Verney said unsteadily. "But I don't want to talk. I have no one to advise me. If it were for myself—but when there's someone else's life and safety at stake—"

"Call in a lawyer any time you want, Mrs. Verney," said Geraghty. "To save time right now, though, I'll do the talking. I'd like you to know how much of the story we have already. Will you sit down?"

"Thank you," the lovely voice said. Something scraped on the floor, a box or a pail; Noel could see Tannehill settling herself on it, beautiful and serene, investing the makeshift seat with dignity.

"I think we've got the idea of your marriage, well enough," said Geraghty's deep tones, dispassionately. "You would have waited for your fiancé, technically at least; he represented more in the way of money and social position than Verney could ever have offered you, and you're not a woman to stop short of the top. Every step you've taken was upward. You played around, though, thinking it was okay as long as you were discreet. Every man who's described you has talked about your kindness. That's a word that has two meanings at least, in the male vocabulary. It was quite a feat to stay friends with all of them after the affairs were broken off, Mrs. Verney. There aren't many women who could do that, but with your personality I can understand it."

There was a little deprecating murmur. Geraghty went on as if he had not heard it. "You weren't quite discreet enough with Chester Verney, though. You married him in June, by the records, but the child you lost in August was four months along at least."

A sharp creak sounded from behind the partition, as if someone had moved involuntarily on a makeshift seat.

"Uh-huh. We've talked to Mrs. Fritz. Took a little pressure to get it out of her, she only talked at last because she was convinced it was no more than had happened to other women, comparatively innocent; and you were married, after all. I'll hand you something," Geraghty said, "for not having an abortion. Or should I? Could be you were too much afraid of the pain. You took another way out, planning to legitimize the child and then divorce Verney and let him have it. He wanted a child, you thought perhaps that was all he did want. But it wasn't. He wanted a marriage that would stick, and you'd married him with every evidence of good faith. He meant this one to be permanent and he took every way he could think of to insure it. When you broached the subject of divorce, you found out he wouldn't divorce you; he collected enough dirt about you so that his counter-suit would make your name plenty notorious, and you hadn't a chance in the world of marrying Miles Coree."

Noel heard a click of teeth from the man beside her. She risked a side glance long enough to see that his face had gone white.

"That was one thing that spoiled your plans," the inexorable voice went on. "One thing that you couldn't get by being sweet and generous, in advance, and either getting people fond of you or obligating them so they couldn't refuse you. That was one thing. The other was—that Coree's letter had told you he might not be released until the end of the year."

He waited. After a moment Anna Verney's voice said hesitantly, "That's—true, of course; but, Inspector, I don't see—"

"I think you do, Mrs. Verney. You believed you had two months or more in which to find some way out, to keep on getting your own way, that nobody but Verney had ever refused you. You found you didn't. And there wasn't time to sweet-talk your way out of the situation. Probably you'd had the Pruitt business, and the anonymous letters that Verney'd told you about, floating around in the back of your consciousness for some time. Not a bad set-up. And then the last letter came in what looked like your handwriting, and gave you the shock of your life. That piece of spiteful imagination on Hobart's part came near to ruining all your plans; but you had to go on, somehow, because *there wasn't time.*"

"Inspector Geraghty," said Anna quietly, "you're turning this talk of yours into very strange channels. You're implying that *I* thought of killing Chester—that I had a plan. But that wasn't so, how could it have been?"

"Could have been, easily. You didn't hate him, probably. He'd have done well enough if you hadn't had someone better in view, that you couldn't get. Verney was in the way."

Anna said, with a thrill of unsteadiness in her tone, "I loved Coree. He'd never believe that, I suppose, but it was only his being gone so long—and the chance that he'd never come back—I regretted giving way to Chester, long before—"

Noel thought, *She could have got Miles back.* I know she could.

"And to all the other men," Geraghty murmured.

"Whose business is that but mine, Inspector?"

Geraghty gave a quick sigh, in which impatience was manifest. "Very well. You had a right to your lovers by your standards; you figured it wouldn't hurt your chances. But a screaming divorce case would hurt them. Your fiancé might have stood by you, but his family wouldn't have accepted the marriage, and it was that family's place in society you wanted."

"That's not true! But why should I give them pain? I wanted a quiet divorce, a civilized one, and I couldn't— Inspector, Chester Verney was a monster of jealousy, but nobody could have proved it, because he never showed it except when we were alone. He'd be friendly with the man whom he suspected of—absurd things; he'd be smooth and courteous in public, and a devil in private. I had to have a witness to one of his jealous rages, so that I could go to court and—and mini-mize the importance of his own evidence."

Will Rome broke in harshly, "I didn't believe it myself, at first. And then Tannehill asked me to help her with it, to arrange an innocent meeting—everyone knew there'd been nothing between us. I wasn't her lover and nobody'd ever thought—"

"And you'd do anything for her, Rome, because she'd nursed you when you were ill. Yes, I can see that."

"A small enough thing," Rome muttered. "Let him suspect her, let him insist on coming down here with her, and find me as if it were an assignation, see if he'd flare up so that I could testify that he could go half crazy!"

"So that was it," said Geraghty musingly. "He did flare up, and you lost your temper and struck him. Some pretty nasty accusations, I expect."

"He was a swine," Rome said in a harsh voice.

"Uh-huh. Worked in with your plans nicely, Mrs. Verney."

"Inspector, *I had no plans* of that kind. How could I know? I could have died myself, with sheer horror."

"Uh-huh," Geraghty said again, dryly. "That was when you bent over your husband and pretended to discover he was dead. Rome couldn't look any closer...Well, let's go back a moment."

He paused. Chan Lockett said in a barely audible whisper, "She's talkin' an awful lot for someone who wouldn't open her trap without a lawyer." He shook his head. "Maybe thinks that's helpin'."

Noel said nothing. She could not have spoken nor moved.

From behind the partition the voice went on, "You haven't denied much so far, Mrs. Verney. This—let's call it accidental death, or manslaughter, happened earlier than you've led us to believe. Chester Verney didn't call you up on Wednesday night, the man's voice the housekeeper heard was Rome's, and he was telling you he'd been seen here."

Silence.

"It was Sunday night, wasn't it? You had to admit you were here that night because you and Verney parked the car outside while it was still light, and somebody might have noticed it. Somebody did, as it happens, but no one saw you coming out, and the car was there till after dark."

The lovely voice was husky with bewilderment. "Really, *really*, Inspector, I don't know why you should think—"

"The car," said Geraghty patiently. "Your possession of the car was one thing you couldn't avoid. It couldn't be left here that night, you couldn't get rid of it, so you thought you'd drive it home and brazen the business out. It might have worked, except that it worried you, Mrs. Verney. Every time you talked to me you explained how you happened to have that car. The car, the car—over and over. It was Sunday night, all right. Verney died then, and you lied about that and about everything else from then on."

When Anna Verney spoke at last she sounded serene as ever, but pathetically weary. "I knew it was—against the letter of the law. Maybe it seems wrong to you, but can't you see why I had to do it? That dreadful thing happened while Rome was trying to help me. I had to do my best for him, I knew he'd be in a bad spot this second time. How could I let—"

"When did you tell her about the first time, Rome?"

"I didn't—know I had." The answer came in a mumble.

"When you had pneumonia, maybe. At any rate, Mrs. Verney, you knew about his record. Maybe you hoped for something like this—maybe you planned on it when you chose Rome to help you in this innocent little plot?"

Rome burst out suddenly into terrible shouting. "Stop, stop, stop! Shut up, you! Keep your dirty tongue off her affairs! How could she know what'd happen? I killed him! Let me go in for life if I have to, but lay off those hints about *her!* I killed him, didn't I?"

"No, you didn't," said Geraghty almost casually.

The old wooden door, the grimy wooden partition might have been dissolved before the eyes of the three listeners, so vivid was the quality of the silence that followed. They might actually have been able to see the group in the next room: police-like images, motionless and watchful, and Geraghty's impassive face, and the man and the woman who had been partners in a peculiar horror, with that horror now striking them in its full impact.

In the mold-making section morning sunlight came in cloudy bars through the dust of closed windowpanes, and in one clear shaft through an open window. It seemed to Noel Bruce that the very motes in the sun had not stirred since that brief sentence had fallen on the air.

Miles Coree put a hand over his eyes.

Behind the wall Will Rome made a deep, inarticulate sound.

"Make you feel any better, Rome?" said Geraghty, still casually. "It might change a few of your other attitudes, of course. Uh-huh. You didn't go near the body after it fell, but Mrs. Verney did. Maybe that's when you went out for a minute, the way you told me in here a while ago. You saw that Old Dad had come into the courtyard. Was that it?"

"I—I heard him."

"I'd guess that Mrs. Verney said something like, 'Find out how much he knows, or we're sunk.' And you talked to him outside?"

"For—for no more than a minute. I said I had a—a pretty lady in there, and to go away, and I—bribed him a little. He said he'd just come."

"Uh-huh. Mrs. Verney played on that fundamental uncertainty of yours, then and later—later when she convinced you that Miss Bruce was a real danger to your safety. She got you out for a minute, and that was long enough."

"You're crazy, Geraghty," said Rome harshly. "You're stark mad. It's impossible, she couldn't have—there wasn't a weapon that would crush in a skull bone!"

"Sure there was," said the deep voice mildly. There was the sound of feet crossing the floor toward the wall where the clay bins stood. "There were as many weapons as she wanted. Here's one; it's dried a bit even under that damp sacking, but it would still do the work—better if it were moist. One of these heavy balls of clay, Rome, that Paul Watkins used to work on day after day, and toss into a bin when he left; a heavy ball of clay slung in a piece of cloth that was right to hand; a weapon that a one-handed woman could use on an unconscious or groggy victim—who was lying down."

"That's a lie; you can't prove it," Rome said in a shaking voice.

"Maybe not. We'll have a try at it. Just remember, Rome, that Mrs. Verney let you think, for all these days, that it was your blow that killed her husband, when it could not have been—because of the lack of abrasion and the position of the fracture. She would have fixed up an abrasion, too, I've no doubt; but there wasn't time. You came back."

Noel said on a mere thread of breath, "Let's get out of here, I can't stand any more. If only we hadn't stayed. It was herself she was talking about when she said she didn't dare tell what she knew—oh, Miles, Miles, she made me think it was you!" She took a step toward the door, feeling as if she were breaking away from a dreadful compulsion. "Miles, please come—quickly, before—"

"Yes, dear," Coree said softly. "We'll go." They began to move as quietly as they could toward the courtyard; Chan Lockett stayed where he was. Coree had a blind look of pain in his eyes. "She never would have believed that it was over, that I couldn't have—It wasn't me that she wanted," he murmured. "It was some fairy tale she'd built up about my family and my uncle's money. I knew that before I sailed, but—"

His hand was on the doorknob when the door in the partition opened, and Anna Verney came out, with a plainclothes man grasping her arm. She looked bewildered and incredulous; her lovely star-sapphire eyes were wide, and she looked up into the officer's face and shook her head. Anyone could read that gesture: "You're making a terrible mistake..."

She saw Miles Coree and Noel and stopped dead.

"You heard what they were saying?" she said to them appealingly. "Both of you must know it isn't true. Why, Bruce, you know me! You could tell them—"

Noel looked at the woman who had been her friend, whom she had admired and trusted, and who had tried to buy in advance the loyalty which she was now demanding. There were some things that could not be paid for by outward sweetness and generosity; things that cost too much.

She said, "Tannehill, I'm sorry. I'm so sorry."

Someone propelled Will Rome through the doorway; he jerked violently to one side to avoid brushing Anna Verney's sleeve. He came to a standstill a few feet away, facing Anna but gesturing backward at Noel. "I'd have had her blood on my hands, too," he said in a husky monotone, "if I hadn't gone soft. You—telling me in every way but the actual words that I'd never be safe so long as she was alive! Saying she had to be got away where nobody'd ever find her—and I thought—I thought—"

Anna Verney shook her head helplessly again, and looked about the barnlike room as if searching for one person who had not lost his senses.

"So that was why they kept on, afterward," Noel breathed. "Tannehill, why on earth did you hate me?"

"Why, Bruce honey," Anna said, "I never *hated* you!"

"She didn't have to hate 'em," said Rome, still in that dead level voice. "They just got in her way. Verney died—and then she saw how it was with Bruce and this fellow, and she knew so long as Bruce was around it would all have been wasted."

Miles Coree spoke in an almost inaudible murmur. "And it was wasted anyway." There was infinite compassion in his eyes.

Anna looked full at him. She had heard the words, but it seemed as if their full meaning did not reach her for several seconds. Then she made a stifled sound, wrenched her arm from the momentarily relaxed hold of the detective, and darted for the far side of the room. Marshall was after her with a cat's leap, but before he could reach her she had swung up onto the table underneath the open window, poising to hurl herself through. The big man reached the table, his arm stretched high and grasped her ankle; for an instant the two stayed in equilibrium, the gold head straining away, outlined against the morning light, the black-clad arms outstretched; then she slid down slowly, swaying, trying to regain her balance.

"That's done it," Chan Lockett said in a conversational tone. "Tryin' to make a break for it, when—*look out!*" He started forward futilely; there was a crash of glass and a concerted shout from the other men, and Miles Coree swung Noel around and hid her face against his shoulder.

But before her eyes were shut she had seen Anna Verney pitch sideways, losing her balance from the pull on her ankle, and strike her head on the cheap glass of the next window—the window that was closed. She had seen the glass give way in a jagged, long-rayed star.

"I guess she'll live," said Inspector Geraghty. He stood in the sunlight of the courtyard, hands in his pockets, his face graven with those deep lines of fatigue and distaste that made him look so much older than his fifty-five years. "No, Miss Bruce, there's nothing you and the lieutenant can do for her. I wouldn't try, if I were you. You don't owe her a thing, any more."

He turned his head and jerked it in a wordless summons. His assistant went to the gate, looked out and nodded.

"I'll be going," said Geraghty. "I'm grateful to you young people for your help." He sighed heavily. "I hate to admit it, Miss Bruce; you did everything wrong, but those antics of yours proved a couple of things we might not have been able to get otherwise. That ring, for instance. Gene Fenmer probably would have returned it to Rome when he found it, in his pocket, and we'd never have known just when it was discovered here. And I got Gene to talk a little after you'd thought up that crack about the beard. He knew her. He'd half suspected, and tried to give us hints all along—but no more than hints. She'd been 'kind' to him, too." He gave one of his mournful sighs. "Well, goodbye," he said, and the gate shut behind him.

They heard his car drive away down the rough street. They looked at each other and at Chan Lockett, who like themselves seemed bound to this spot in complete inertia.

"Chan," Noel said, "what on earth possessed you to tell me Lieutenant Coree was in the clink?"

"Just—just an idea I had," Lockett said. His round face reddened. "I thought maybe—considering you and the widow and how you both felt—maybe somebody'd out with the truth to save him." He sighed. "And when she didn't, I guessed she was savin' her own skin. I was worried about you, baby, and I did the wrong thing. I stuck around and watched *her* last night."

"So you really knew after all, in spite of the wild-goose chases." Noel got up, with weary slowness, from the ledge of Rome's statue. "And I never thought to ask how you got on with the ex-nurse. Which of us did she pick out as the forger's wife?"

Chan said with suspicious vagueness, "Well, none of 'em, exactly. She couldn't put her finger on one, see, and say yes, that was the wife. And she kept sayin' it was so long ago—"

"Was there one that might have been her patient?"

"Well, yes, you might say—it was the nearest, anyhow. But Sarah's only twenty-five *now*," he burst out as if reassuring himself. "And I don't see how—"

"Never you mind, Chan. It was mean of me to include that sketch, I might have known what would happen to you." She drew a painful breath. "I feel as if we shouldn't be laughing."

"You laugh when you can," Miles Coree said quietly. "Geraghty was right, you don't owe Anna anything. And there's a chance; she still hadn't admitted a thing in words when she— tried her break. I doubt that she ever will."

"Surely nobody can convict her," Noel murmured. "Not of first-degree murder." She hunched her shoulders, shivering. "She looks so candid and serene, and she's so beautiful."

Chan Lockett started to walk away. Over his shoulder he said, "Don't blow your top, baby, but she won't be beautiful any more. No matter what happens, she won't be beautiful. Well," he turned the corner of the gate and his words floated back to them, "so long, baby. So long, bud."

Miles Coree put his arm around Noel. They moved slowly toward the gate in the dingy wooden fence, leaving behind them the courtyard empty in the morning sun; empty except for the unfinished statue by Will Rome, holding its own secret life behind the scarcely indicated features, under the cowled head.

"So this was our fifth meeting," he said. "Not without its awkward moments, was it?"

She looked up at him and smiled. "I suppose we can always try again. Do you feel like risking a sixth, and a seventh, and—"

"How high can you count?" he said, and stopped just inside the gate.